THE ALEXANDRIA CODE
An Isabella Carter Adventure

MIKEL B. CLASSEN

Modern History Press

Ann Arbor, MI

ISBN 978-1-61599-783-1 paperback
ISBN 978-1-61599-784-8 hardcover
ISBN 978-1-61599-785-5 eBook

Published by
Modern History Press   www.ModernHistoryPress.com
5145 Pontiac Trail   info@ModernHistoryPress.com
Ann Arbor, MI   tollfree 888-761-6268
fax 734-663-6861

Distributed by Ingram (USA/CAN/AU), Bertram's Books (UK/EU)

To all of the great action heroes I've read and loved over the years searching for lost cities, treasures, and villains while defying all odds to defeat evil wherever it may be found. I throw this humble offering into the world of adventure, thrills, and suspense as homage to those writers I've loved all my life.

Also by Mikel B. Classen

Faces, Places, and Days Gone By - Volume 1: A Pictorial History of Michigan's Upper Peninsula

True Tales: The Forgotten History of Michigan's Upper Peninsula

Points North: Discover Hidden Campgrounds, Natural Wonders, and Waterways of the Upper Peninsula

Lake Superior Tales: Stories of Humor and Adventure in Michigan's Upper Peninsula, 2nd Edition

As Editor -- U.P. Reader Seris: Bringing Upper Michigan Literature to the World

≈ 1 ≈

The dark alley dripped with foreboding. The bricks of the building were slick and shined with the wetness from the Lake Superior mist. Dark, black puddles appeared as pits in the pavement meant to be avoided at all costs. There had been death here that much was sure. These old waterfront alleyways had been places of dark deeds for 250 years.

Isabella Carter had known death before, she recognized its mark. This was where she had been told to meet the seller. She knew now that it was a setup. She had been lured back here to the Sault where she grew up in a large cabin on Whitefish Bay. But for what purpose? Why bring her back all the way to the Soo? It made no sense. Isabella turned around and started to retrace her steps back to the street. Enough was enough. This alley wasn't for her. Now she was acutely aware of the feel of the gun that she carried inside her coat.

The mist stuck to her shoulder length black hair. It had a natural curl to it that now was going crazy with the mist. Her dark brown eyes scoured the old alley for the danger she was certain was out there. She had made many enemies over the years and lived her life wary and always aware of her surroundings.

Whoever had lured her here had been clever. They knew which buttons to push. The possibility of restoring a lost antique from the black market into the hands of academia had been too much to resist. Sault Ste. Marie was on the Canadian border which made it an easy entry point for contraband. She knew this town and it had been a hotbed for smugglers throughout most of its history. She thought of the bait that had brought her here, a jade statue of the Mayan goddess Ixchel. It would have enhanced University of Michigan's archaeological studies tremendously not to mention their museum, but now she knew she'd been duped. She had shut off her phone, but had left the GPS on. That way she hoped someone would be able to locate her body after this was all over.

Two men stepped out in front of her. Isabella's hand instinctively reached inside of her coat. Her legs tensed as she prepared to evade an attacker.

One of the men spoke, his words seemed muffled by the thickness of the air. "Dr. Carter?"

She didn't answer hoping that ignoring them would make them go away. It didn't work. The two moved to block her way. Years of experience told her that their next move would be to pull their guns. She beat them to it. Her practiced hand held the .45 automatic steady, deadly.

"Where's the statue?" she asked, suspecting, no, certain that there had never been one.

"No statue, Dr. Carter, Just a ride."

"Surprise," she muttered. "But no thanks."

One of the men moved towards her and the metallic click of her taking off the gun's safety stopped him short. She tried to get a feel of what they were thinking, their motivations, their mission. Isabella could only sense confusion. She wasn't meekly following their gameplan and it had them uncertain. "Good," she thought, at least she had them off balance.

The overpowering feel of death in the alley clouded her mind. It had been notorious during the prohibition. Executions had been carried out here in the past by bootlegger gangsters. Though it was rare these days, an occasional body would still be found, murdered. Probably by these two men, she thought, why else would they have called her here?

"We need you to come for a ride with us. Lazarus Fane wants to see you."

"Well if you thought that would put me at ease, you're dead wrong. The only thing I'm going to do with Fane is put a bullet between his eyes," she retorted. So that was it. This was Fane's doing. She should have known, should have guessed. The two enemies, over the years, had come to know each other too well. If she remembered correctly, Fane controlled a shoreline warehouse in the Sault. No doubt a front for illegal imports.

Lazarus Fane was the kind of person she fought to rid the world of, a black market antiquities dealer, no, looter. They were the bane of her profession, the blight of discovery, her lifelong crusade.

When Isabella had discovered the lost Mayan city of Itchen Balam, Fane had tried to take over her dig and discovery. He then had her close friend and Head Archaeologist on the project murdered. Fane had made it personal. The two of them had a long history. She had sought her retribution more than once, each time certain that she had rid the world of him. Fane simply wouldn't die. But, she still had hope. Someday, she'd finish the job.

"Mister Fane wants to talk to you. Our job is to bring you. We can carry you, as easily as not."

Isabella smiled at them, cold and hard.

"Now, now, that kind of behavior will get you nowhere with this one. She can put you both down and that would be embarrassing," came a voice from behind the men.

Isabella stiffened at the sound of Lazarus Fane's voice. Years of their war came flashing through her memory. He was ruthless, cold-blooded, evil, and she had been forced to become all of those things fighting him. She hated him for that. She could see his face now, pale and drawn, the poor lighting reflected off the scar that ran down the side of his face, the scar she'd given him. She smiled a little at the sight. The memory was sweet. Her free hand clenched as if she once again held the machete she'd tried to take his head off with.

"Dr. Carter, I have not brought you here to kill you, I've brought you here for privacy. This alley has a reputation, a reputation for death, one that I encourage, so it is avoided by everyone. Not even bums and junkies dare venture here. The only ones that visit here, don't leave, so you can consider yourself lucky. You get to do what others have failed at, leave here alive. Funny thought, that, letting you go alive. Besides, I have something for you that I'm sure will pique your interest. Your help will be invaluable," Fane continued, his pale blue eyes were but slits as he stared at her with intensity.

"My help? That's not likely to happen."

Fane nudged one of his men and ordered "Give it to her."

One of the men slowly reached into his pocket. Isabella still had her gun poised. He drew something out. Isabella's finger tightened. He held something small in his hand. It wasn't a weapon. Isabella's finger relaxed a bit.

"Take it, please." Fane still stood behind his men. "This is something I believe could change history as we know it."

"What is it?" she asked.

"That's what I want you to find out. Take it with you, back to NYU and look it over carefully. Study it. Closely."

Isabella was on loan to New York University from U of M for the past year. She was working with them helping identify Central American artifacts and teaching a graduate class.

Isabella held out her free hand and the man dropped something into it. She looked at it. Shining, even in the gloom of the alley, was a quartz crystal. "OK, it's a crystal. What's so special about it?"

"That's what I want you to discover. Believe me, there is something to discover. I just don't want to taint your findings by too much information."

"Why shouldn't I shoot you where you stand? Rid myself of a lot of trouble." It was a long awaited pleasure she was having a hard time not fulfilling. "That river over there could carry your body into the lower Great Lakes and they would never find you."

"Because, when you come to some conclusion about that crystal, you're going to want to know where the rest are. You know how to contact me." He turned and was gone leaving behind his two shields. When Fane was safely away, they too then turned and left the alley.

Isabella Carter looked at the crystal in her hand. Even in the low light she could see its details. "What was the big deal?" she thought. It was the typical six-faceted clear quartz about three inches long and about ¾ of an inch thick. The only thing she saw unusual was that the crystal hadn't been broken at the base, it was smooth and flat as if it had been cut or ground flat by some jeweler making it ready for a setting. This wasn't Fane's usual fare. Outwardly this didn't relate to black market antiquities. Had he stolen this from some idol somewhere? Fane was insistent that there was something more to it, something deeper, and knowing him, something darker.

She returned to her car and drove to the airport at Kinchloe. She was lucky. There was a plane she could grab back to Detroit and then catch a flight to New York. Because it was Fane she was more than tempted to throw the thing away, but it was because it was Fane that she didn't. He wouldn't have given it to her if there was nothing there. He wouldn't have risked his life for something as mundane as an everyday quartz crystal. There was something special about this crystal that he wanted confirmed. As much as it galled her, for the moment she was working with him. Thwarting him would have to wait until later.

When she got back to her office at NYU, Isabella put the crystal in a locked drawer in her desk. None of the students were around this time of night and this looked like a job for her graduate class. They could cover more ground quicker and get this over with as soon as possible.

The classroom was littered with tablets, statues and artifacts from all over the world. Isabella's reputation had always been in her knowledge and discoveries of the Maya in Central America. The Maya were her true passion but she studied and taught all aspects of archaeology. Professor Carter lectured and taught across the world having worked dig sites in a dozen countries. She personally viewed all ancient civilizations fitting together in one neat package. The problem was that there were too many pieces missing for neat, let alone a package.

It was something that she diligently tried to pass on to her grad students. All five of them were filing in behind her. She let them settle down for a minute and then began. She held up the crystal between thumb and forefinger for them to see.

"I have a project for all of you. There's something hidden about this crystal. I'm making it your task to find out what it is. Sometimes, in our field the smallest items may hold the greatest secrets. Subject this to every test possible. Assume that there is something to discover, it's up to you to find the secret. Of course your grades will reflect your participation in this. Any questions?"

Jeff Barnes, spoke up. He had long brown hair, clean shaven with sharp intelligent blue eyes. "No hints as to where this came from and how it was discovered?" Jeff was the head of the class. He took over when Isabella couldn't be there. He was on the fast track to his own Phd. He was smart, ethical and Isabella had a lot of confidence in him.

"None."

"So what you're saying is that you have no idea either and you want us to figure it out for you." He grinned at her knowing she would take the joke.

"That about sums it up. This one is a bit personal. I don't want to participate in the research, but I have to know what's so special about this crystal. This is a private project. I don't want a word of this to go beyond this group. Let's brainstorm it first. What are the uses of quartz crystals?"

"Quartz has always been seen from an ancient perspective as a conduit for power," said Jeff as he rolled it over in his finger and then held it to the light. "It is used in jewelry and particularly amulets and talismans. I'm guessing that's why the sawed off bottom. It's meant for a setting of some kind."

One of the other students spoke up, Sandra Gonzales, "Quartz is used for everything, today. It's in our computers, CD players, cell phones. Nearly everything is based on quartz technology. The ancients weren't wrong in their beliefs that quartz was a power stone. It has conductivity properties that they seemed to instinctively be aware of. I always felt that maybe some of the ancients knew a lot more than we give them credit for." Sandra was from Mexico and was studying to do Central American archaeology and be able to study the past of her heritage. She had the traditional dark hair, brown eyes and brown complexion.

"Of course that brings us too our ever popular crystal skull discussion," began Bob Peters. He wore glasses and liked to delve into fringe theories of X-files types of subjects. He was also a programming genius that wanted to apply those skills to archaeology and deciphering languages through technology. "Skulls made entirely from quartz, flawlessly created so that they are near impossible to make, even with today's technology and tools. They are believed to be endowed with supernatural power. No one knows definitively when or where these were made so they remain a complete mystery."

Alicia Case, another student who had been occupying her time texting lifted her head up long enough to comment, "What about crystal balls? They're believed to foretell the future."

"Those are usually glass, not quartz," Jeff reminded her.

"Seems to me the common denominator in all this is power. Electronic power, psychic power, magic power, computing power, quartz is even used in watches so time is involved. The ancients viewed it as a source of power and we see it as a source for technology. We've even learned to grow artificial quartz in methods similar to those of cultured pearls. After the quartz shortage of the 80's, steps were taken to make sure that it didn't happen again so now we even have laboratory artificial quartz," Karen Arntsen added. She was from the mid-west, but it was obvious her ancestors were Scandinavian. Blonde hair, blue eyes and skin that rarely looked like it has seen sunlight. There was a definite snow queen appeal to her.

"Well," it was Isabella this time, "This has to have some antiquities connection. The source of the crystal determines that. It also has to do with multiples, my source also mentioned that there were more of them."

Jeff spoke up. "Maybe we should take a closer look. Let's start looking at it on a micro level. Maybe it's in the shape or structure of the crystal, possibly the molecular makeup. Maybe there's some scoring or etching somewhere, but it feels perfectly smooth to me."

The students took the crystal to the electron microscope computer lab. First they studied its surface. Over and over they scoured. It was a quartz crystal.

The next phase was to look deep inside of it, right down to the layerings that make up the interior itself. As a crystal grows, it does so slowly, building flat levels of quartz similar to the floors in a high rise building. Each one of these layers is a cleavage point where the stone can be broken. The microscope focused in on those. A computer next to the machine transferred the image to a monitor. The students surrounded the monitor and watched. The layerings were acutely evident at this magnification. Still it was a quartz crystal.

"What if we were to scan it and have the computer take a close-up, build a 3-D image. That would take us right inside of it, right to its heart." Sandra suggested. "Then we can enlarge it, move it around to any angle and examine its smallest details."

The crystal was moved to the laser scanner. The red light flashed up and down the crystal's length while the computer built a model of the crystal. The digital enhanced image began to fill in, take on detail, that old familiar structure of a quartz crystal.

They began to magnify and enlarge it, look into the interior structure. Lines began to appear. They seemed to be in layers. They magnified more. The lines were definite. They flowed in an organized pattern running parallel up and down as well as across. They were not random. The patterns corresponded to the layers of quartz. Each layer had more of the lines. They enlarged it more and focused in on the lines. They were everywhere, thousands of them. They looked similar to Sanskrit, micro sized lines of what looked like language!

Sandra was first to speak up. "Is that writing?"

"Well, it definitely looks like something imprinted on there. This can't be old," concluded Jeff.

"I think it's laser etched," suggested Bob. "This has to be modern. This must be some kind of new technology that's etching on crystals. It's like a crystal version of a thumb-drive. The problem is the language. It's not like any formatting language I've seen." We need detailed printouts of every layer that has the etching. I can't believe they're antique. This has to be some new tech that we've never seen."

"Of course we've never seen it or we'd recognize it," Sandra's sarcasm made them all turn. "Let's think about this, I agree it's probably something new, but what if it isn't? What if it's old like Professor Carter said? It changes everything just by its existence. "

"It can't be, the technology it would take to create this couldn't have existed. It has to be modern. Somebody better go get Dr. Carter," said Jeff.

Alicia left and ran to get Isabella. "We've found something," she said as she burst into the teacher's office.

It didn't take long. They came into the lab, Isabella showing some anxiety. The students showed her what they found. She studied the printouts. "You're sure about this?"

"We're not sure about anything," replied Jeff, "You see what we see, inscribing on the interior of the crystal."

She looked at the printouts. They were there, lines that appeared in the shape of symbols. Many were repeated while others were rarer. For all purposes it looked like some form of language. "Do we have an order that these appear in?" she asked.

"The printouts are in order but we're not sure about anything beyond that. Being layered like this, the text could run in any direction. We're going to need some form of reference. First for the direction of the text and then for what each character represents. Is this an alphabet? Is this a type of hieroglyph? Or is this maybe some type of new computer formatting. Essentially we need the key to the coding. The only thing that could do something this small is laser tech," commented Bob.

"Tear it apart. See if you can make anything out of this." Isabella gathered the stack of printouts. "I'm going to work on these in my office and see if I can find something in here. I have a call to make."

She detested doing it, but she knew she was going to have to talk to Lazarus Fane. Certainly this was what he had wanted her to find, but why? This had nothing to do with antiquities. This was likely some new technological direction electronics was going, formatting crystals for data storage. It obviously wasn't a binary coding, it was more complicated than that. The big question was: Why would Fane pass off new technology to her and then ask her to find it? It made no sense. Fane always made sense. Fane was up to something, she was sure of that much. That he was trying to involve her, there was no doubt. Was he setting her up? Was there some way he was arranging for her to take a fall for some black market scheme he had going? Did he think he'd finally come up with a way to destroy her reputation and her career?

She went into her office and called the number for Fane Imports Inc. The company was a front that appeared legitimate on the surface, but in truth it was one of the largest black market distributors of art and antiques in the world. Fane had a battery of accountants and lawyers doctoring the books so that prosecution was impossible. She was put through to Fane immediately.

"Well, what did you find?"

She went off on him. "What kind of game are you playing? You give me a crystal that has some kind of coding imbedded in it. What's the idea of all of this. New technology isn't my field. As sleazy as you are it's never been yours either. What do I care if there's more? Why did you bother me with this? Secret meetings. Alleys. I knew I should have shot you when I had the chance."

He interrupted her tirade. "So you did find the information buried inside of the crystal?"

"Yes," she confirmed.

"I'm assuming it's too early for you to have an idea what any of it says."

"Near as I can tell, it's some kind of new computer formatting using crystals as data storage."

"It's not new."

"That's impossible, it has to be new. There's no evidence that anything like this has ever existed. You're doing this to set me up for something."

"Alexandria," was all he said.

"What about Alexandria?"

"That's where it was found."

"Found, what do you mean found."

"It was found in Alexandria, Egypt. I'm sure you know about the recent project there where the Egyptian Ministry of Antiquities has been excavating and sifting through the rubble of old Alexandria in the bay. The rubble that was created when the earthquake toppled the Library, the lighthouse, and Cleopatra's palace, are strewn across the bottom of the bay. The Egyptians have this idea that they can clean the seaweed and silt off the statues and remnants and create a kind of tourist attraction with an underwater monorail for sightseeing. In the process of removing some of the silt, some crystals were found. Of course I had some of my own people slipped into the project, thinking we might be able to come away with a few items of interest."

"You mean steal a few items, don't you?"

"Now now, we were getting along just fine. Let me continue. One of my men discovered that several quartz crystals had been found during the silt removal of the Library of Alexandria. The Egyptians didn't think much of some common crystals found on the floor of the bay. They were looking for more traditional Cleopatra era treasures. My man came away with one, the one I gave you and brought it to me. I had to ask myself the question, why would there be dozens of crystals at the library? That was when I decided to have them examined, inside and out, right down to their molecular structure if I had too. That was when I found what you found, the embedding."

"I'm not sure you haven't been played. My students assure me that this could only have been done by micro-fine laser impression. It has to be modern."

"You let your students have this? How much do they know?" she could hear the irritation in his voice. "I had hoped you would do the research yourself, keep this between us. I see I was wrong."

What had she done? A dread filled her. She had put her entire graduate class in danger. In her effort to keep her hands clean, she'd only made matters worse. Fane was ruthless. He would have no qualms about causing them to have…accidents.

She back-pedaled. "They're not involved."

"You're lying to me, but that's alright. I'll leave them alone on one condition. You help me. You have an uncanny ability to decipher language unlike anyone else. I want to know what's on these crystals and where they come from, though I already have my suspicions."

"Damn," she thought, she'd given him the leverage he needed over her. She mentally berated herself for walking into it. "That's why you gave it to me in the first place, you can't do this without me. Stay away from my students and I will initiate my own research. Do you have the other crystals?"

"No, the Egyptian Ministry still has them. An academic like yourself might be able to persuade them to part with them as they are unsure whether they are simply a part of the seabed or Egyptian treasure or artifacts. Either way they aren't viewed as any great discovery."

"Another reason you need me, the ministry won't take your calls."

"My reputation precedes me."

"I have no doubt of that. I still don't think you're playing me straight, that this is some kind of hoax, some kind of weird trap you've concocted. Just remember, if something happens to one of my students, there'll be no place on earth you can hide."

"And I remind you, if you cross me with this find, well, you already know well what I'll do."

"Those aren't wounds I'd open if I were you. I'm still weighing whether killing you isn't the better option."

"You've tried. It hasn't worked. Listen we both win with this. You get possibly the greatest discovery in the history of mankind."

"And you get?"

"The information. I get exclusive access to all of the information in those crystals."

It all made sense to her now. If these crystals were truly old, they had to have been founded on some technology that would at least have been equal or more advanced than mankind currently achieved. There might be histories, images, or ...schematics! If genuine, she still had her doubts, the information could be worth trillions, especially on a corporate level. The implications and applications of it would effect every corner of the world. Cultural, theological, archaeological, historical, technological, the impact would be staggering.

She played dumb "What information?"

It didn't work. "You know as well as I do the implications of this. If I control the discovery, I control the profits."

"I'll get back with you." She hung up and went back down to the lab. "Lock this place down. Has anybody said anything about this project?"

She looked at the faces of her students. Jeff spoke up, "We've been hanging here. We've been discussing the encryptions."

Sandra Gonzales spoke up. "I really think this could be related to a type of cuneiform. It has that look to it."

Bob leaned into the group and pointed at a couple of images on the monitor. "You see that area there. Those two marks facing each other, they look a little like parenthesis, and separated by several of the other symbols. It looks like a type of code, formatting language. Like XML. It must be something experimental. Let me guess, this was an experiment from another grad group."

The rest of the group just looked at him. He'd struck a nerve. Just for a moment they all considered it until Isabella laughed at them. "No that's not what's going on here. Tighten up. We may actually have something here. My source tells me these were found as part of an archaeological dig. We're very possibly looking at something that should not exist."

"Bob," she continued. "Is it possible for you to write a program that will correlate, how many different symbols there are, how many of each, indexing their location throughout the crystal, and what appear to be repeat phrases?"

"It would take a while but I think I can. It should be fairly basic. It's essentially combining database and object mapping programs."

"Do it, please."

"On it."

"Now I want to proceed on this with complete confidentiality. If this is what it is supposed to be, the discovery is too big to leave this room. We dare not be wrong about this. First we have to analyze every aspect of this thing. We need a chemical analysis of the outside and carbon dating. Keep in mind you have to act like these tests are routine. Don't show any urgency or impatience. I don't even want a whisper of rumor. I want all information downloaded to portable drives and each drive will be handed into me and then checked back out. I will know where each one is at all times. Nothing is to be left on the university's computers." She handed out five drives. One to Bob. One to Jeff. One to Sandra. One to Alicia and one to Karen. She then produced her personal drive and handed it to Bob. "Download all of that imaging onto this. I need to be able to study it in my office."

She waited for it and then walked back to her office. She had only one thing on her mind. Coffee, she needed coffee.

⁊ 2 ⁊

One Year Earlier

The Bimini Road had always held a fascination for him. He'd read everything he could find that speculated on its origin. It only seemed right that one of history's greatest mysteries should be in the heart of the Bermuda Triangle. The diver always felt the idea of an undersea road beginning nowhere and ending nowhere as, well, humorous. He'd always wanted to scuba dive it, explore it. It was one of those things on his list.

Aiden McKenzie swam amongst the coral and schools of fluorescent fish. The underwater beauty of the Caribbean never failed to inspire a sense of awe. He never tired of it. Laid out before him on the sea floor were massive coral covered square blocks of stone. They were set out in a pattern that really did look like an underwater roadway. He thought he could feel the reputed energy that was supposed to emanate from it. "That was new age crap," he told himself. He didn't buy into that. Maybe his oxygen mix was a little off. The underwater growth around him swayed to the movement of the water and rays from the sun danced on the bottom. A flash from the sand and coral distracted him from the sight-seeing.

He swam over to it as it winked at him from the barnacles and fan coral. There was something lying on the seabed that looked like it had once been square before layers of sea life distorted it.

Aiden pulled out his dive knife and poked at it. Things hid in the coral, poisonous things. Nothing seemed to be hiding so he grabbed the box shaped cluster of coral. Sand and debris trailed behind the thing as he pulled it free from the bottom. He looked it over and he saw something through a small crevasse. It flashed at him. It looked crystalline. Jewels? Had he found a small bit of treasure? The region was famous for its sunken ships and lost Spanish galleons. Maybe, just maybe, this was a lost remnant.

He swam to the surface to his launch. He pulled himself over the gunwales and then rolled into the boat. He laid his mask on the seat next to him and slipped off his fins. He picked up his prize and began prying it open with his knife. There was snapping and cracking as the crust of shells broke under the prying of the blade. As it broke open he could see the inside was man-made, had been a box at one time. The treasure he'd discovered was a box full of crystals. He scratched the glass of his diving mask to see if they were diamonds. They weren't, just Quartz. Still, it was Bimini, he had a souvenir, a coral incrusted box of crystals. At least it was easier than trying to lift one of the giant Bimini Road rocks. He snorted to himself as he thought of it. "Yea right."

He was happy. He'd seen the road, and he had his prize. It was something. It was better than a kick in the teeth, which he couldn't guarantee wouldn't happen right after he got back into shore and had half a dozen shots of Scotch. He looked at them closer. The crystals were about three inches long and about ¾ of an inch thick. They were smooth and flat at the base, like they were ready for a jewelry mount or some kind of setting. They probably washed over the side of some passing ship. They would look good in his bungalow.

He started up his motor and headed back to shore and Alice Town. He wouldn't be able to stay in the Caribbean much longer. The work had died and he would have to move on. There was always somewhere he could go to make money on his diving skills. Besides, his reputation as a brawler was beginning to make him unwelcome. There was very little McKenzie liked better than a scrap.

He pulled into the harbor and up to the dock. He jumped out and tied up the launch. North Bimini was incredible this time of year. "No place better," he thought, "except in hurricane season." The dive and his modest find had made him feel like the day had been truly memorable. "Scotch," that's what he needed to complete the perfect day.

He headed up the beach to the End of the World Saloon. Unlike so many things in Bimini that were being built up for the influx of tourists, the End of the World still retained its roadhouse style and charm. It was Aiden's kind of place. He opened the screen door and walked in. The bartender looked up. He was black with short cropped hair. "No, you're not coming back in here."

"But I like it here. Besides, he started it."

"I don't care who started it. It's not like this is the first time."

"Come, on, I won't bother anybody. There's nobody in here to fight with anyway. Come on, just a couple of Scotches and I'll move on."

"Alright, against my better judgment. Mac, I wish you'd switch to rum. That scotch addles your brain, man. It makes you weird. Rum, lays you back, makes you not care what the hell's going on. It'll change your life."

"Glenlivet's," was all Aiden replied as he bellied up, placing his souvenir on the bar next to him.

"I know, but hey, I'm a bartender, I'm supposed to be giving advice." He grinned with lots of teeth showing.

Aiden grinned back at him. "Thanks." He raised his shot in a mock toast to the bartender. "Here's to bartenders, someone you can never truly live without. God's gift to lazy drunks."

He threw back the Glenlivet's and ordered another. Another patron came through the door and approached the bar. "Mind if I join you?"

"No, don't mind the company a bit."

The bartender asked the man's pleasure. "Rum."

"See, I told ya," the bartender pointed at McKenzie. "Watch him," he told the newcomer. "He gets grumpy."

"He seems perfectly fine to me. Hi, I'm Eldon James." The man stuck out his hand for the customary shake. He was impeccably dressed and left no doubt as to his personal gross national product. Everything he wore was white, hat, pants, shoes, socks, jacket, all white.

MacKenzie stayed with custom and shook it. "Aiden McKenzie, nice to meet ya."

The two drank together, sipping their liquors through conversations. Aiden told him of his day of diving off the Bimini Road. "It sounds like something I should do," Eldon commented. He'd listened intently to McKenzie's story as men drinking will.

Aiden reached over and moved the coral decorated box and showed it to Eldon. "My prize for the day. Here," he reached in and pulled out one of the crystals. "I think they were going to be part of some decoration or jewelry. See how the bottom is flat and even. It had to be cut and polished."

Eldon rolled it around in his fingers. It was a fine specimen of a quartz. Clear and unflawed. "May I see the box you found?" As he looked at it, Eldon couldn't tell much other than it had been on the sea bottom for a long time.

"Sure," McKenzie said and passed the box to Eldon.

He looked at it closely and opened it. Eldon took note of how the crystals were laid out inside, wrapped in old fabric, none touching the other, tiny pieces of now decaying wood separating them. "You say this was laying amongst the rocks of the Bimini Road?"

"Yea it was how I ended my dive. You don't often find much out there, just fish and coral. I've been diving a lot of years, but this is the first time I've found something like this. It's not much, but I'm happy with it." He threw back some more scotch.

Eldon looked thoughtful for a moment and then spoke, "Better than a kick in the ass." Eldon smiled and set Aiden's prize back on the bar. The man in white continued to look at it, study it.

"That very thought occurred to me earlier." Aiden laughed , Eldon joined him.

"Well, I've got to get back to my place. My days are numbered here. I'm going to have to move on soon," concluded McKenzie. He stuck out his hand, "Been nice meeting you Eldon. Keep that crystal. Maybe it'll bring you good luck." He laughed again. "I've got more." MacKenzie raised the box for emphasis.

"Thanks," said Eldon. "I hope we meet again sometime." He then took out a white handkerchief and carefully wrapped the crystal with it.

MacKenzie went out in the twilight. He'd blown most of the afternoon and a large portion of his pay drinking with Eldon. It didn't matter. That's what he liked about the islands, little mattered and no one cared what you were about. Hurricane season was a couple of months off, good time to move. Besides, you know you've worn out your welcome when even your bartender doesn't want you around.

≈ 3 ≈

Alexandria, Egypt, Present Day

Isabella Carter stood in front of the airline terminal in the staggering heat. This wasn't like New York and it certainly wasn't like the Upper Peninsula. The Egyptian sun blazed down causing a brightness that her eyes struggled to get used to. "Dr. Carter? I'm Hasan from the Ministry of Antiquities. This way to the car." Shielding her eyes, she moved towards one of the vehicles that were parked in front of the terminal. Her bags were put in the trunk and she climbed into the back. Hasan drove.

"I trust your flight was good." He began.

"Just fine," she replied.

"What brings you to our country Dr.?"

"Book research. I'm looking into the various and traditional uses of crystals within ancient societies. It's something a little different for me, something a little more mundane."

"We never know where the mundane will take us," smiled Hasan. The ride was short and uneventful, with meaningless talk exchanged between the two.

Hasan pulled up in front of one of Alexandria's busiest hotels. "Your room is all ready for you, just check in at the desk. Your meeting with Mr. Hawas is tomorrow at 9 am. I will be around to pick you up. Until then, enjoy your stay. "

The door was opened and she stepped out into the Egyptian heat, but here a breeze off the bay mingled with it. She looked up. "Great," she thought. "A Radisson. Of all the historic great places in town that just scream Egypt, I get the Radisson." She went inside. It was a traditional chain hotel lobby, patterned wallpaper, broken by mediocre Egyptian art knockoffs. She went to the desk clerk who smiled. "Dr. Isabella Carter," she announced. The clerk looked at her computer and smiled again. "Room 218." She then handed her a key card and a printout to sign. She did it and then went up to her room.

She sat her luggage down and walked over to one of the windows. Alexandria. The bay glittered with the afternoon sun. Modern buildings poked their tops out contrasting with the old timeless structures that dated back to an older more mythical Egypt.

Alexandria was one of the cradles of civilization. With the library, it had been a place of enlightenment and scholarship. With the ancient lighthouse, it had been a beacon to all that sailed the Mediterranean. The lighthouse had been one of the seven ancient wonders. Cleopatra had made her palace here. Her and Antony, Julius Caesar, the city reeked with its own antiquity. Alexander the Great had founded the city on the principal of a place of enlightenment where scholars and philosophers could come to exchange ideas. He had envisioned a gathering place that would lead the world by its example. Like the lighthouse, the city itself would be a beacon to humanity. It would be a message to the Gods that their children were growing up.

Her thoughts were interrupted with the hotel phone ringing. She didn't answer it. She knew who it was. Let the desk take a message. She wouldn't have anything to say to Fane until the next day anyway. She'd given her students three days break while she was in Alexandria. There wouldn't be a way to police the information from Egypt. Besides, if she succeeded in bringing back the other crystals, they would have more work than they could handle. It was better for them to have a break now.

A knock came from her door. "Who is it?" she called out. "Abdul," was her answer. She quickly went to the door and opened it. In stepped a middle-aged Egyptian wearing white pants and a thin white shirt.

"Good to see you again, Dr. Carter," he bowed slightly to her. She and Abdul had worked together before when she was in Egypt. She'd called him and asked for a meeting, though she knew as soon as he would have known of her coming, he'd be by her side.

"I'm glad to see you again too. It's been too long since we've worked together." He grinned at her. "What can I do for you."

"I need information," she said. "I know you will keep anything in confidence between us. There's no one here I trust more." He smiled slightly at this. "There have been some things brought up from the bottom of the bay. I need to know any rumors, outside of the official channels. Has anything been found that's unusual, causing more of a stir than normal. Possibly in the form of a box or device, I want to know anything. I don't care how inconsequential it seems." She knew it was a long-shot but maybe along with the crystals being misinterpreted maybe a device that read them might have surfaced too. "This might seem a bit odd but I'm not exactly sure what I'm looking for."

"Not coming from you. I will start right now." He said and turned to go. Then he looked back at her and grinned. His teeth were brown and one eye seemed to wander off in its own direction. "Welcome back. It was too quiet. You always have trouble behind you. I missed it."

The door closed behind him and she relaxed. Abdul's eyes and ears were her safety net during her stay. He knew Egypt better than anyone and particularly Alexandria.

She went out on the small hotel patio that overlooked the city and sat on a white wicker chair. She loved these types of chair, they were more comfortable than they looked. She eased back in it and relaxed. She smiled to herself. Abdul, she was glad he was here. Her mind wandered back.

* * *

She'd met Abdul in Cairo. Isabella had been sent there as an emissary from U of M. The university was sponsoring two digs in the Valley of the Kings, south of the city. Isabella's job was simply as an observer and liaison, be on-site, and then document progress reports for the university's records. Upon her arrival, she'd been assigned an assistant, it was Abdul.

The two digs were promising and both had found tombs, though the chances of them being undisturbed was near zero. Virtually every tomb ever uncovered had suffered the fate of looters. There was no reason these should be different. Pot shards, pieces of broken walls that once were adorned with murals, all needed to be catalogued and inventoried as they came out of the digs. These were her duties since she wasn't actively involved with the, sifting and sorting on the digs. Abdul was ever at her side.

Hers was a tedious and routine job until the discovery was made. The head archaeologist, Prof. Arnold from Syracuse, had come to her and asked her to join him inside the tomb he was excavating. "Please Dr. Carter, I'd like your opinion on this as well as a documented witness to what we've just found." She nodded and followed him into the depths of the burial chamber. Not much had been left behind by looters except broken scraps of pots that were once to have accompanied the dead.

Broken on the floor was the mummy, also the product of the rough treatment dealt out by the tomb robbers. It always sickened her when she saw burial chambers vandalized even though it was what she had expected.

But where Prof. Arnold pointed was the unexpected. A large chunk of the richly painted mortar that made up the burial chamber walls had fallen away. Behind it glittered gold! She felt a rush of thrill run through her. She could see in the lamp's illumination that there were small hieroglyphs imprinted into the gold.

The piece had fallen out from the section of the wall that met the ceiling. If the gold ran level to the chamber floor, it would be seven-feet long. How wide it was they could only guess. The muralled wall would have to come down, carefully so that the mural would not be destroyed in the process. It would take days.

That was when some of the workers seemed to become sick. Abdul brought the news to Isabella. "Some of the men have fallen ill. They claim it is from the dust in the tomb."

"How many?" she asked.

"At least twelve."

"That's over half the men working, the new men will outnumber the remainder," a look of shock came across her face.

"Yes, Prof. Arnold has gone to hire more to replace them."

Isabella looked at Abdul hard. "I don't like this. This can't be coincidence. Those men have been working in those conditions right along. One or two, I might believe, but this many, all at once? I'm not buying it."

"I think you are right and I took the liberty of having two of my sons placed on the crew," agreed Abdul. "They will be our eyes and ears."

Isabella grinned. "Good work Abdul." The two sat and spoke quietly. "It's apparent that none of this has aroused Prof. Arnold's suspicions. He's replacing the excavators, which means he's doing exactly what someone would predict he would do. He's preoccupied with his discovery and isn't seeing danger growing around him. I'm expecting the worst."

"I'm going to need a weapon," she continued. "If things go bad, get yourself and your sons out of here."

"We won't do that," he said. "This is our country, our heritage. This is our responsibility. Besides, why do you get to have all of the fun?"

Isabella grinned at him. "Don't say I didn't warn you." Then she reiterated, "We're going to need weapons."

Abdul nodded, "I can take care of that."

The next day Abdul brought her a pair of Walther PPKs. They were light and small, easy to carry and easy to conceal. Isabella was used to a heavier gun, but in this situation, she saw the appeal.

After close to a week, the wall had been painstakingly removed. A large rectangle of gold had been revealed six foot high and about five feet wide. Hieroglyphs decorated every inch of the gold. Normally, the hieroglyphs found in a tomb are writings from the Book of the Dead. Not on the gold tablet. The hieroglyphs spoke of things never read by modern scholars. The value of the great gold tablet was now incalculable.

The Egyptian Government and the Ministry of Antiques were informed. The tablet would have to be moved out of the tomb and brought back to Cairo. The government kept the find under an informational blackout. They wanted to get it back to Cairo with as little attention as possible.

There had been no incidents, there had been no hint that there might be a bigger plan at work. Isabella began to think they might breathe a little easier. Abdul spoiled it all. "One of my sons overheard some of the workers getting instructions. Somehow, the drivers of the government truck that will pick up the artifact, are plants."

"To get someone in there, this would have to be well financed. Since the Egyptians haven't announced the discovery publically, if it were to come up missing, officially it doesn't exist. The bribes had to go to the top levels. Here's what's going to happen as I see it. They will try to get in and out without any disturbance. So, here's my plan...."

A truck had been brought to pick up the treasure from the tomb. It was accompanied by an escort. Though they were armed, there were no overt signs of any heavy arms. Prof. Anderson informed Isabella that the government felt that if they were too heavily armed that would attract more attention than the seemingly innocent truck caravan.

The heavy gold panel was slowly and carefully removed from the tomb. The size and weight made it cumbersome to maneuver. It was wrapped in thick padding to prevent any accidental damage. Isabella stood outside the tomb at its entrance waiting for the artifact. Her eyes were alert and she watched everything. The Walther PPKs were tucked in a very cozy place.

Abdul had positioned himself near the truck that would carry the golden discovery. He was waiting for when the artifact would make its appearance. Everyone's attention would be diverted then. No one would see him.

Isabella turned her attention back to the tomb entrance. She could see them coming out now. Using rollers and ropes they pulled it up, ever upward. Even with modern technology, they still had to do it like the ancients had, rollers and ropes. Everything moved slowly, carefully, it was almost agonizing to watch the process.

When it was out of the tomb it was maneuvered to the truck. Isabella was next to it the entire way as was Prof. Anderson. They preceded it into the truck guiding its placement. The weight displaced the truck's suspension considerably.

Isabella studied the men and their faces. They were calm at ease. And why not? Everything was going like clockwork. They suspected nothing. It was what she had hoped for. Her plan had counted on it.

There was constant chattering and milling of the workers as the day's work was complete. The back of the truck was closed and locked. The escort was set and ready. They were ready to drive away.

Isabella made her gamble. She went to the passenger side of the truck and banged on the door. "I'm supposed to ride along with it." She yelled at the passenger, one of the phony guards. He looked over at the driver. Isabella continued banging and yelling. She was creating a scene, one that might upset everything they'd achieved. The truck was almost out of there, she saw the fake guards look at each other. She kept up the racket until the door was flung open. The passenger guard reached and pulled her inside placing her between them. She'd done it. She was in.

Then she started chattering, about archaeology and about the dig and how great it was to be out of New York and Egypt was too hot and how did they stand it and so on and so on. They were away from the dig site and heading towards Cairo.

Isabella continued with her chattering. The look on the guard's faces was one of torture. She knew she had them. While her incessant blathering went on she stretched, her hands hitting the cab of the truck. The driver and guard paid no attention.

Abdul's face was in the window. He'd carefully hid in the gap between the cab and the cargo trailer. The window was down and he smiled. Isabella pushed as hard as she could against the unsuspecting guard while Abdul released the door. The guard flopped out the door as Abdul grabbed him and pulled using the momentum Isabella had provided.

As Abdul was finishing the job she started, Isabella pulled both guns and held them against the driver. The truck jumped a little as the rear tire ran over something while Abdul climbed into the now vacant passenger seat. Abdul looked into the side mirror and saw their rear escort hit the guard they'd tossed out.

No more secrecy, no more surprise, it was up to them now. They had the truck, they had the artifact, now, they just couldn't let anyone stop them.

Isabella didn't speak Arabic well. She had Abdul tell the driver to speed up. In front of them was another escort. The truck ran up on them faster and contacted their rear bumper. The men inside turned and saw the grill of the truck as it pushed them again. The driver clung to the wheel to maintain a precarious control. One of the men managed to grab a gun and fired at the truck window. The glass was tempered and slanted. The bullet ricocheted.

Abdul leaned out the window and fired one of the handguns he carried. He hit one of the men in the shoulder. Another returned Abdul's fire and then, one shot pierced the glass. It hit the driver in the head. He died instantly. Isabella let her guns drop to the seat and grabbed the wheel. She shouted "Get the door," to Abdul.

He crawled over, reached across her and the dead driver, then released the latch on the door. The two shoved him out of the door and Isabella climbed behind the wheel. "That's better, I didn't like his driving anyway," she muttered as her foot hit the accelerator.

They sped up again and continued ramming the car in front. Abdul shouted, "Keep the speed up, don't let off. He leaned out the window and got a bead on a tire. In the car ahead, one of the men took aim at Abdul. Isabella floored the gas. The man's shot went awry but Abdul's didn't.

The blown tire made the car spin as the driver lost control. Isabella never let up and the truck pushed past and kept going as the car went sideways and then rolled. As they went past, they saw men with broken bodies flying out into the sand and rock.

Isabella poured it on. There was no one in front of them but the rear escort was still in pursuit. A couple of shots flew by the truck but they had little effect. "They are going to have to get alongside to do any damage," shouted Abdul.

"I know, we're well shielded from the rear," she agreed. They were getting close to Cairo now and time was running out. If the escort of looters were going to regain their prize, they would have to make their move soon. They did.

Isabella felt the truck jerk hard as one of the dual rear tires took a bullet. She struggled with the wheel to keep the truck on the road. The rear of the vehicle swerved and swayed. It made it difficult for the pursuers to hit with another shot.

Cairo was just ahead. Isabella prayed to whatever god was listening that the road ahead was clear and not full of the usual pedestrians. "That's them," said Abdul. He pointed to four vehicles waiting ahead, two bore the markings of the Cairo Police. He grinned, "We're here." The vehicles pulled in front and behind them cutting off the escort of thieves. The sight of the police inspired them to take new a new tact and flee. The vehicle entered Cairo with a different armed escort. "It's good we could count on your sons to be trustworthy. Having a couple on the police force is handy."

"I raised them right," said Abdul wearing the proud father smile. They surrounded the truck on all sides as they made their way to the Cairo Museum where a group of expert handlers were waiting for the truck and artifact to arrive. "Once it was there, it should be safe," thought Isabella.

They moved through the city with smooth precision. Two of Abdul's sons had taken the outside lane, in effect, creating a blockade around the truck.

She had the wounded truck under control and as she maneuvered the streets to the museum there were no more surprises. The sons of Abdul had driven off the last of the looters and now they were where any more attempts would gather too much attention, it would be doomed to failure. As long as the operation had been discreet, it could have succeeded.

The truck limped to the museum without mishap. It had been a good day. She and Abdul had won and they were unharmed. The golden panel was turned over to the museum undamaged. Isabella went public with the story which got a lot of attention.

Because of her and Abdul, an internal investigation took place that cleaned Egypt's house thoroughly. A new minister of Antiquities was named and now they are once again recovering and restoring their heritage properly and ethically.

The memory made her grin as she lounged in the veranda chair. It was one of her favorites.

* * *

Hasan was prompt picking Isabella up the next morning. The only thing she carried was a small backpack or daypack that was a permanent fixture of hers when she travelled. She carried water, camera, a notebook and a paperback copy of the Woman Lit by Fireflies by Jim Harrison. Often she'd have a gun inside but not this time. This trip she'd left it home, too many visits to government offices were required and she didn't have that kind of time.

They drove to the old white building where the Alexandria offices of the Ministry of Antiquities was housed. Hasan showed her up a stair and into the office of Mr. Hawas. He rose to greet her, a smile on his face. "Welcome Dr. Carter." His English was excellent, but there was still the hint of accent behind his speech. "What can we do for you?" he asked. This was the kind of visitor he enjoyed, an academic, highly respected, and needing his help. Hawas was a smart man and fostered every connection within the archaeological world he could make. He was also not afraid to use those connections. It was one of the reasons why Egyptian archaeology had made so many advances over the last few years. He was the man that had made it all work. He'd restored respectability to the Ministry.

"I'm here to talk about your Alexandria Bay project. I've been working on a new book. Something a bit different for me, I'm researching crystals and their use in ancient societies. I had heard that you had found some among the ruins in the bay. Where did you find them? Cleopatra's palace?"

"Well, you know how rumors are," smiled Hawas, showing a rare moment of humor, "but in this case it happens to be true."

"No, they were found among the ruins of the Library," he continued. "Our theory is they were used for decoration, probably during the reign of the Ptolemys. Of course you know that Cleopatra was the last of that descendancy. We know that Rome had bled the riches of Egypt taking most of what they could find back to Rome leaving behind little of Egypt's splendor. Essentially they picked up anything of value and ran away with it." He smiled at her. "We are theorizing that to retain some semblance of former Egyptian decorum, the quartz was used because of its low value and abundance. It wouldn't have been something Rome would have coveted."

Hawas called Hasan in. "Could you retrieve the crystal artifacts from the bay project?" Hasan nodded and disappeared out the door. It appeared her interest had been anticipated somewhat. Her conversation with Hasan in the car ride from the airport may have been slightly more than simply small talk.

Hawas continued, "We're not considering them much of a find at all. They seem to be representative of the decline of Cleopatra's rule and the death of Egypt's wealth. They should make an interesting chapter for your book. This is the first time we've ever seen quartz put to this kind of use in ancient Egypt. We think that they may have been part of door or window hangings. When the sun would shine through them, the prism effect would have been quite nice."

Hasan re-entered carrying a tray. He set it down on Hawas' desk. "Thank-you. That'll be all." Hasan dutifully turned and exited.

Hawas picked up one of the crystals. "You see the bottoms of these? They are cut flat, all of them exactly the same way. They had to have been set into something. That's why we are looking in this direction. They were like, what do you call them, hmm, suncatchers, that's it. Just because we have our modern day fads doesn't mean the ancients didn't too." He laughed. "Sometimes I think that we forget in our search through the past that people have been people right along and we focus on the facts and academic aspects of the past in our search for the profound, sometimes overlooking that some of these things we find had very little significance other than daily entertainment. Often with the past, simple was the most attainable for the general population. They're still important because they complete the picture like all artifacts, but beyond that, they change little about how we view the ancients. "

"Do you mind if I look at these closer?" Isabella asked.

"Not at all. Please feel free."

She picked one up and examined it. It appeared to be exactly the same as the Fane crystal. He'd been right. They were here. Now, to the next step.

"This will make an interesting chapter in my book. The ancients substituting quartz as a surrogate in their decoration for the loss of richer gems through foreign occupation, it's just the kind of things I've been looking for. It's something different from the current mystical, new age perspective." Isabella couldn't help but think about what was really buried within these crystals, the great secrets they might hold. She could see there were close to thirty of them.

"I don't suppose it would be possible for me to take these back to the states with me to further my research?" She knew she was treading on thin ice here.

Hawas raised an eyebrow at the request. "Normally I wouldn't even consider such a request. But you're something of a hero to our country and to me personally. A few years back when you exposed that black market smuggling operation, you did an invaluable service to this country. The amount of our past heritage that we were losing through corruption and payoffs was incalculable. Thanks to you Egypt's heritage now remains in Egypt. I think this country owes you a favor. I'll have these packed up for you."

"Thank-you so very much. This is a great help. Also would it be possible to speak to the man that actually located these. I'd like to get a first-hand account about the positioning of the crystals on the bottom, the discoverer's impressions of the find."

"That shouldn't be a problem either." He looked at his paperwork accompanying the tray. "It was found by one of our divers named Aiden McKenzie."

"Does he speak English?"

"Actually I think he's an American."

"Well, that will make it easier," she thought. She stood up, thanked Hawas and shook his hand.

"You are welcome here anytime, Dr. Carter, I'll look forward to seeing your book," the tone in his voice was genuine.

Hasan escorted her from the building and back to the car. "I've been informed you wish to speak with one of our divers."

"Yes, a Mister Aiden McKenzie." Hasan nodded and they quickly drove to the bay. One of the piers that reached out in the water was flourishing with activity. The car pulled up and they could see that something was being pulled out of the water by a crane. As the two approached, one of the workmen stopped them. He spoke to Hasan in Arabic. "He doesn't want us to get any closer while they are trying to raise the block out of the water."

"What are they pulling up?" she asked. "

"It's a stone panel from Cleopatra's palace. It is one of the more spectacular remains of the palace and it is completely intact. There are hieroglyphs on it and carved reliefs. We have to be very careful with it though. Removing it from its seawater environment will cause it to decay. We will submerge it in a tank of brine until we can get it cleaned up. Then we return it to where it was found and place it back in its original position."

The huge monolith shaped piece of stone swung in the air, streams of seawater soaking the men and the pier below. Padded cables surrounded the mammoth artifact. It dwarfed the men steadying it and giving directions to the crane operator. He moved it slowly, carefully taking the care it deserved. A tank of salt water was waiting for the panel.

Isabella pictured it before the earthquake. Long, distant years ago it had been part of a building which had seen the splendor of Egypt mixed with the might of Rome. How many slaves had it taken to cut and carve it? Julius Caesar and Cleopatra had both gazed up at it, undoubtedly remarking at its message and beauty. Or had they not noticed it at all, jaded with the endless splendor of Egypt, Rome and Babylon. For them would it have been as insignificant as a strip of wallpaper might be to someone now? The precious piece of Cleopatra's palace came to a rest gently.

Hasan pointed to a man walking towards them carrying diving gear and still dressed in a wetsuit. "That's him. That's Aiden McKenzie."

She moved to intercept McKenzie. He was walking quickly, in a hurry to get his day done. That was one thing about diving professionally, the days were short. Diving underwater once a day was usually the limit. To dive more, increased the chance of nitrogen bubbles in the bloodstream, an ailment commonly called the "Bends."

He saw Isabella move in front of him and it annoyed him a bit. He didn't want to have to stick around.

"Mr. McKenzie?" she asked.

"Listen, I'm wet and tired and I don't have time now, no matter what it is," he tried to derail any distractions that might delay his end of the day routine.

Isabella could sense his agitation. She'd always had a strong intuition about other people's feelings but when she had returned from Central America it had increased considerably. Isabella now bordered on psychic. She tried harder to get an insight. Something was on his mind...scotch?

She responded. "I understand. Why don't you get some dry things on, we'll go somewhere and get some food and I'll buy a couple of drinks. Besides I could use some of that strong Egyptian coffee. What do you say?"

He wanted to tell her to go take a flying...but he changed his mind. She was good looking, and she had said, she'd buy. "You're buying the drinks?" he asked. "Usually it's the other way around and all I end up with is less money." He grinned, he was getting into a better mood.

"Well at least this time you won't end up with less money."

She turned to Hasan, "I'll get a cab back to my hotel. I'm sure you have duties." He nodded and left. There was a small café on the waterfront they went to. It was open air and a red and white striped canopy sheltered the patrons from the intensity of the Egyptian sunshine. They found seats and a waiter came over. "Coffee," she ordered. "Glenlivet's," was his.

She introduced herself. "I'm Dr. Isabella Carter."

"So do I call you Izzy?"

"Not more than once," she thought, but didn't say it. "Dr. Carter is just fine," then she continued. "I want to talk to you about some of the items you found out here in the bay."

"Ok, but it hasn't been much. Mostly we've been sucking out silt from the ruins. I'm afraid there isn't much to tell."

"I'm interested in the crystals you brought up."

His eyes raised at this. She could feel he was being cautious and she was unsure why. "Why would you be interested in them? They're just a bunch of crystals aren't they?" He put emphasis on the "aren't they" like it held special meaning.

She gave him her rehearsed story about the book she was working on and he listened, politely. "I want to know they're positioning in the seabed and any details you can remember about when you found them. Were they next to anything? What else was in the sand with them?"

"Listen Doc, that's a lot of questions. They were on the bottom like someone had tossed a handful of them there. You got a pen?"

She took a pen out of her pack and handed it to him and he began scribbling on one of the café napkins. He drew a crude sketch of the seabed and then laid the crystals as single lines on the drawing. "As well as I can remember they were like this." He handed her the sketch.

She looked it over. She studied it in silence for a minute. Then, shook her head. "You're right, not much to tell here."

She motioned the waiter to get him a refill. "Thanks Doc. What's the big deal with these?"

"Like I said, just research."

"I'm not buying it."

Isabella frowned and asked, "Why not? It's the truth."

McKenzie cocked his head and gave her a smirk. "I don't believe that someone like you came all the way over here just to look at some crystals."

"There were interviews to do. Like the one I'm trying to do now."

"Sorry, Doc you could have phoned that one in. You could have gotten pictures emailed. I could have done this drawing in Photoshop. You could have used Zoom."

"I needed to get out of the office." She remarked, a bit sourly. "What makes you think I'm not telling the truth."

"First off, my nose, it's very good at smelling manure. Right now it's deep enough at this table, I'm thinking I need boots. Two, I picked those crystals up off from the bay for a reason, their flat bottoms. They were unusual. They were taken to the Ministry and then you show up asking questions. Coincidence? I think not. You see, I've seen crystals like this before." He'd slowly leaned over the table as he brought his commentary to an end. Then, he sat back and watched her face.

Isabella was shocked. She tried not to show it, but she failed. She hadn't expected this revelation especially from a Joe workman. He was sharp, not the typical blue collar mentality. This was supposed to be simple and routine. He had beat her at her own game.

"You've seen crystals like this before?"

"Yeah, about a year ago. I was diving the Bimini road..." he proceeded to tell her how he found his Bimini souvenir.

Isabella was trying to wrap her head around it. Bimini, Alexandria, they were half a world apart. The implications were staggering. It was one thing for them to be found in the cradle of civilization, but the Caribbean had been largely uninhabited except for a few tribes of Arawak Indians. "Where's this box now?" she asked.

"Back at my room," said McKenzie.

"Would you take me there?"

"This is my day. First, she buys me drinks, now she wants to go to my place."

Isabella scowled at him. He grinned back at her.

"I'm only in it for the crystals," she told him.

"Come on, I'm in great shape, a bit athletic and when you come to your senses, you can dump me. I'm easy to get rid of." McKenzie grinned big.

"Crystals," she reminded him.

"OK, but I'll take a rain check for when you change your mind." He stood up. "My place is this way."

They walked through a region of the city that was at war with itself. Old Alexandria versus new Alexandria waged a battle over progress. New modern buildings were placed next to hovels that could have been there during the reign of Cleopatra. Like most cities it was a battle that the old was losing. There was sadness in that, a feeling of the loss of something priceless that permeated the very air, the extinction of something great.

It was into one of the older buildings that Aiden led her. He looked back and reassured her, "Cheaper living here." He needn't have tried. Her guard was up. Isabella's feelings were telling her, something had been disturbed.

The smell of tobacco and hashish scented the hall. They climbed the stair, McKenzie leading the way. She was acutely aware of the absence of her gun. It made her feel uneasy, something she actively tried to keep to a minimum. She often carried one abroad and had an international registration to use one. Because of the possibility of looters and thieves, archaeologists sometimes found them a necessary tool for their excavations.

McKenzie reached his door and saw that it was ajar. He motioned her back. She pressed as flat against the wall as her pack would allow her. He pushed his door open. No sound except the hinges. He poked his head around and peered inside. The place was a mess. He stepped inside. His clothes, drawers, furniture was tossed everywhere.

"I've been robbed?" he spoke to himself. Then a little louder, "It's clear, nobody here," then quieter, under his breath, "anymore."

Isabella came into the room. "Well somebody did a pretty thorough job. Forget to pay your bar tab somewhere?"

"Why would somebody try to rob me? Anyone who knows me knows that robbing me isn't worth the prison time. Hell, it's not even worth doing to kill a slow afternoon."

There was something very wrong in all of this and Isabella could feel it. The room was permeated with the energy of the ransacking. "We were lucky we just missed them."

"How do you know? You a psychic, Doc?"

"Some. Enough that it's gotten me out of some scrapes."

"Then what do you think they were looking for? 'Cause I'm baffled."

Her first thought was Lazarus Fane, that he'd somehow found out about McKenzie's crystals, but how? It just didn't sit right. "Where's your crystals?" she asked. She had a hunch.

"Right to business, huh Doc?" He went over to an air vent. The cover came off easily. Inside was his coral encrusted box. He handed it to her. She looked inside. It was empty. "Ok, so where's the crystals?"

His face fell. "What do you mean?" He took the box. It was obvious he was baffled. He shook his head. "I thought they'd be safe there. I hid them after I found the ones in the bay thinking there might be something to them. I guess I was right, first you, now this."

"I hate to tell you this but that would have been the first place I looked. It's an old, overused trick. Every movie I've seen, they hide the money in the air vent and nobody finds it. Unfortunately it only works in Hollywood."

He looked a little embarrassed. He'd seen it in a movie.

"They probably found the crystals first. The place was messed up as a distraction. It was meant to look like a robbery, one without purpose. They even put the box back so it would be a while until you reported it or started looking. They knew exactly what they wanted."

Something moved behind them in the door. Instinctively she spun to fend off an attack but it was Abdul standing there. He was grinning at her. "How'd you find me?" she asked.

McKenzie had watched as she had side-stepped and prepared herself. "Wow, Doc, you got some moves."

She ignored him and Abdul responded, "You didn't think I was going to let you wander the city alone did you? Then I'd miss out on all the excitement." He was holding a package. He continued, "I saw which building you were going to. So, I went to the back of it to check the rear entrance. I know how you seem to walk into trouble. I saw a man running out so I had one of my sons follow him."

Isabella smiled. They still had a chance to recover McKenzie's crystals. "As always, you did well. I knew I could count on you Abdul." He smiled at the compliment. "Is that for me?" she continued pointing at his package.

He handed it to her. Inside was a gun. Again she smiled, pulled back the chamber sleeve and cocked a bullet into it. She hefted the weight of it, smooth, balanced. Abdul knew a good gun when he found one. "Just what I was missing," she let out a long sigh.

McKenzie watched her with more than a little fascination. "Shouldn't I be the one with the gun?"

"No!" they both answered in unison.

"Hey I'm the one that got robbed here. It seems to me I'm the one in danger."

"They got what they were looking for. You're not important anymore." Isabella responded.

"You really know how to build up a guy's ego don't you."

"Listen you're out of this now. You can go back to your job, your shots of scotch and have quiet afternoons on the bay."

"Out of what? You still haven't told me anything of what this is about. They're my crystals, I found them, I want them back."

"And you're not going to know what this is about either. I can't talk about it."

"Well, then I guess you're stuck with me until you do."

Abdul listened to the two of them with a quiet smirk. Yes, it was good to have Dr. Carter back. There was a ringing in Abdul's khazaki. He reached in and pulled out his cellphone. "Let's go. My son has followed the man to the market.

Isabella took the gun and stuffed it in her pack. She felt much better.

"What about me?" protested McKenzie. "Where's mine?"

"Sorry," said Abdul. "I didn't know we were going to have company."

The market bustled with activity. People moved everywhere, a milling mass of humanity. Local Egyptians mixed with the tourists looking for trinkets and treats of all kinds. Most were selling while the others bought or haggled. Mixes of foods, cloth and trinkets, many of which were replicas of Egypt's past, were sold from every advantage. It was a disorganized chaos that was part of the city's culture.

Abdul moved through the milling humanity like it wasn't there. McKenzie and Isabella stuck close behind, but the constant jostling made McKenzie short tempered. Occasionally, a vendor would grab his sleeve, "Buy for the lady, buy for the lady." He'd pull his arm away and keep trying to not lose his companions in the crowd.

He saw Abdul ahead, stopped, talking to someone. Isabella was listening to the conversation when he caught up. Abdul pointed to a small open café. My son says he went in there. He's sitting at the table with the man dressed all in white. McKenzie stared at the café. He could see several men in white. White was the predominant color in Egypt. Then he caught on to the meaning. He was referring to a man that wasn't Egyptian, man to him was foreigner.

Of course Isabella knew immediately Abdul's meaning. There was an immaculately dressed foreigner, very white, not just his clothes but his complexion, very northern European or American talking to a pock-faced Arab. She thought from this distance there might even be a touch of Albinism there. She pointed him out to McKenzie. He stiffened.

"I think I know that man. What was his name. It was something odd, Elwood, no that's a Blues Brother; Elroy, no; Eldon, yea Eldon, that's it. It was back on Bimini. We had some drinks together. End of the World Saloon. He seemed like an upright guy."

"Well it appears he's started to stoop a bit. You seem to spend a lot of time in saloons. I suppose you told him about your crystals."

He looked chagrinned. "I gave him one, sort of a souvenir for a good day drinking. At least we didn't end up in a fight."

She gave him a sideways look.

"Hey you like guns, I like a tussle. Where's the harm. My way's less jail time."

"Well we need to get those crystals back," she said.

"Hey, they're mine. Shouldn't I be the one saying that. But, yea, we need to get those crystals back." He knew it sounded weak when he said it. "And why do we need to get those crystals back other than the fact that they were mine to begin with and stolen from me?"

"Not now. We need to move quickly, before he spots us and we lose him in this crowd. Dressed like that, he's not going to stand out. Let's move."

She went to the café. With her pack she looked like any other tourist. The man didn't pay any attention to her as she sat at a table next to him. He wasn't watching as she sat her pack down, unzipped it and reached her hand in. He was sipping some coffee while the pock-faced man chattered at him in Arabic.

Abdul and his son had moved closer and stood at the front of the café. It was McKenzie's turn. She could see him approaching from the market, having waited for the rest to get in their positions. She saw Eldon look up from his coffee and spot Aiden. She jumped into the seat next to him and pulled her gun. The move was doomed to failure.

McKenzie saw him look up. He picked up his pace. He saw Isabella slide in next to Eldon as Eldon jumped up. In one motion he sent the table flying into the air in McKenzie's direction. Isabella toppled backwards from the unexpected move. McKenzie threw his arms out in front of him and altered the table's course. Shocked patrons yelled and began to scramble, they were like panicked livestock.

Isabella rolled backward as Eldon slipped past her. She was angry. "Well, that went wrong," she muttered under her breath. This had not gone at all how she had foreseen it.

McKenzie kept coming, following after Eldon James. As he passed Isabella the pock-faced man threw himself into Aiden careening him into some of the scattering patrons. He lost his balance and went down. His assailant didn't even slow down. He looked up and saw Abdul and his son had disappeared. "If they're smart, they're avoiding arrest," he muttered.

Isabella saw Abdul and his son slip into the crowd behind the disappearing Eldon James. She discreetly slipped her gun into her pack. All of the attention was on McKenzie. She looked like one of the patron casualties of the disturbance.

McKenzie had gotten up and was backing out of the café in the wake of unintelligible patrons scolding him and shaking their fingers at him. He got the gist. He didn't even have to be drinking to get thrown out of a place.

Isabella grabbed him. "Let's go. Abdul's on him." McKenzie followed her leaving more shouting behind him. Isabella skirted the crowd and the café coming out in the rear. She couldn't see Abdul anywhere.

"Did you see which way he went?" She looked around anxiously.

"No I was too busy getting chewed out by the locals," he replied.

They walked back out into the market place. It had gone back to its daily chaos of selling. The café incident was forgotten in favor of daily routine.

"Let's go back to my hotel. I'm sure Abdul will try to contact me there. What did you say that guy's name was? Eldon? Eldon what?"

He scratched his head. "Eldon, Eldon James I think it was. I only met him the one time."

"I need to get some answers," she had a look he didn't want to be the recipient of.

They left the market place and hailed a cab. A short ride and they were stepping out in front of the Radisson. As Isabella went past the front desk, the clerk that had checked her in the day before called her. "Dr. Carter, there are some messages here for you." She walked over and took the stack of message notes and started thumbing through them. Fane, Fane, Fane, Fane, Hawas. She looked at that one.

"I enjoyed our meeting very much. The artifacts have been packed and shipped to your offices in New York. If there's anything else I can ever do for you just ask." It was signed Dr. Hawas, Ministry of Antiquities.

At least that package was safe, for now. She'd have to beat it back to New York to be sure it was delivered to her personally. Knowing there were other parties interested could put the shipment in jeopardy. She'd lost once today. She didn't like to lose.

Another message was from Bob, her graduate student. "The program is finished." Was all it read. It was enough. They could start dissecting the crystal's writing as soon as she returned.

McKenzie had stood waiting impatiently as she read the messages. "Good news Doc?"

"Well, not bad news anyway."

She then led him up to her room and closed the door behind them. She set her pack on a chair "Let's talk," she said. "First, did this Eldon James give you any indication who he was and what he did?"

"Not really. We were just drinking and I seemed to be doing most of the talking. As I recall, he just sat and listened. Sometimes that's better in a bar, just sitting and listening. I had showed him one of my crystals and he seemed quite interested in it, though he really didn't say much. So when it was time for me to go I let him keep it. I didn't think those crystals were any big deal then. What's going on here Doc? Why is my place ransacked and the crystals stolen? I think I deserve to know."

"Let's get something to eat," she said changing the subject. "I'll call room service and order us some food. How's that?"

"Sounds fine, but it doesn't answer the question and I'm not going anywhere until I know what this is about. And I like my steaks rare. " He settled back into the only couch in the room.

Isabella put in the order and then spoke to McKenzie. "I really can't tell you what's behind this." She smiled. "If I did I'd have to kill you."

McKenzie wasn't sure if she was joking. She did have a thing for firearms. But still, he wasn't about to let it go. "Then you're stuck with me until I know. I want my crystals back. They represent a very important moment in my life. They've got sentimental value."

She rolled her eyes. "I have to make a call."

~4~

Lazarus Fane was sitting in his office when the phone rang. Fane leaned forward as his secretary paged him. "Dr.Carter on the line sir." It was about damn time, he thought. "Where the hell have you been?" There were never any formalities with Fane. "Have you got them?" He expected everything to be done right now. That's what he paid people for. Or, as in Carter's case, threatened them. The answer he got was "They're on their way." He relaxed a little. His scar took on an involuntary twitch at the sound of her voice. He needed her now, but someday he'd succeed in killing that bitch!

He stood up and paced his elaborate office while he talked. The walls and shelves were decorated with archaeological discoveries from around the world. Dozens of lost cultures were represented: Greeks, Romans, Incas, Mayans, Chinese, Sumerian, Egyptian. Fane was a collector. Why should they go to a museum when they could belong to him? What he didn't want he sold on the black market to other private collectors. He'd made a fortune looting tombs and temples, desecrating holy shrines, and stealing relics from the hands of museums. This was his passion, his blood, his life. Fane was the most determined kind of collector, he was obsessed and he had the money to afford his obsession. It was those short-sighted academics like Carter that made acquiring his passion so difficult.

Isabella continued on the other end of the line. "I've run into some difficulties here and I need some information."

"I thought you said they were on their way?"

"I did, but there are others."

"Others? What do you mean?"

"I've found someone here that has some other crystals identical to the ones from the bay."

"Get them at all costs. You know what's at stake here."

"Well that's the problem, they were stolen. Someone else is in on this. There's a man here, name's McKenzie, he found some of these crystals about a year ago at Bimini. When we went to get them, they had been stolen. Know anything about that? Got anyone here working for you freelance?"

"No. I have people there, but the only one active currently is you." Fane could hear knocking in the background. Isabella said to someone, "It's room service, get that would you?" Then she said back into the phone, "Know anybody by the name of Eldon James?"

Before he could answer, there was a crash. Then he heard the sounds of muffled gunshots. "Carter!" he yelled into the phone. "Carter!" There was no answer. The phone had gone dead.

Eldon James, that was the last name he had expected to hear.

* * *

Isabella was on the phone when room service arrived. The porter rolled in the customary cart. McKenzie had let him in and saw the man pull the gun from under the tray. He jumped to the left as the first bullet whizzed past him. He hit the man with a right cross as the second one went off.

Isabella leaped from the phone as the second bullet narrowly missed her and hit the phone. Plastic pieces flew as she grabbed her pack on her way behind the bed. The third shot was hers and it hit the porter in the knee. He went down and struggled to get up. McKenzie hit him hard. He stayed down.

McKenzie grinned, "It's never a dull moment with you, is it Doc."

"Funny, I was just thinking the same thing about you," she replied.

"Well dinner's probably ruined," McKenzie looked at the scattered silver food servers.

"And we can't even call room service to complain. He shot the phone." She held up what was left of the murdered instrument.

"Well that makes me cranky." McKenzie looked at the would be assassin who was slowly coming around. "This ought to wake him up." He put his foot on the wounded knee and applied pressure. The man moaned in pain. "What was the meaning of this? Who put you up to it?" The assassin began talking in Arabic. McKenzie shook his head. "I never was able to pick up on that lingo."

Now there were noises coming from the hall. Hotel security was coming in response to the shots. Two men in suits came through the open door. "What happened here?" said one who appeared to be in charge. His English was adequate, but poor.

Isabella had hidden her own gun under the mattress. She assumed Abdul had purchased it illegally. She kicked the assassin's gun across the floor towards the Security man. "He tried to kill us," she replied. "Fortunately he missed. He's not getting a tip though."

The man on the floor was moaning in pain. There was enough blood that cleaning the mess would be a challenge for the house-keeping staff. "The police coming. They going have questions."

Isabella knew that was coming. Someone was desperate to have done this where it would draw this much attention. Fortunately the assassin had underestimated the job and had done it poorly. They both should be dead. McKenzie had saved her life. It was an unsettling thought.

Next the police showed up with medics. A detective, spoke with the security man who left after the conversation. He introduced himself to Isabella and McKenzie. "I'm Inspector Amir. Could you tell me what happened here?"

"Sure," said McKenzie, "My steak was overdone."

The inspector wasn't amused and looked at Isabella. "Maybe you could be a bit more helpful?"

She introduced herself and related what had happened with the attack but ended with, "But I have no idea why. As soon as he came through the door, he started shooting. I wasn't able to ask him what his issues were. Maybe you'll have better luck with that."

The wounded man was being loaded onto a stretcher. The inspector ordered one of his men to put a guard on him until he could question him thoroughly. He then looked at McKenzie and Isabella. "Please don't leave the country, right now. We may still have some questions after we've interrogated the suspect."

The inspector turned and left taking the police, the medics and the would-be killer with him. They got here too fast," grumbled McKenzie. "I wanted to squeeze him for some information."

"His screams wouldn't have left a very good impression on the hotel staff." Isabella looked around the room. "I think we're going to need a different room. The phone doesn't work in this one."

The pair went to the lobby for a room change when Abdul came in. He motioned for Isabella to come talk with him. "Dr. Carter. I was able to follow him. He went to his hotel. It's the Alexandria." She smiled. There might still be hope of catching him yet. She yelled at McKenzie. It was easier to bring him than argue with him about whether he was coming along. He was a pain in the ass, but he had just saved hers.

They got a cab and drove to the Alexandria Hotel. It stood in all of its antique splendor, an old hotel with a long tradition, a rich history. "Listen, McKenzie, I have an idea. He doesn't know me. I think all of these attacks have been aimed at you. I want to see if I can get to him first. If he sees you, he's just going to panic. Give me a few minutes then follow me in." McKenzie tried to protest, but she wouldn't hear it. She pointed at him. "My way this time." She took her pack and got out of the cab.

She entered the spacious lobby. There was a beautiful fountain in the center. The ceiling was high and open with decorated whitewash plaster. It was the epitome of Egyptian architecture. She went up to the desk and smiled. "Hi, I'm looking for a Mr. Eldon James. Could you tell me if he's in?"

The clerk looked at her computer screen. "You just missed him. He's checked out."

"Did he leave any forwarding?"

The clerk looked again. "None."

"Do you have his home address?"

"I'm sorry but we can't give that out." The money that Isabella had placed on the counter convinced her to scribble something on a note and hand it to Isabella.

"Thank-you." Isabella smiled and left. She looked at the address, it said New York. And she was forbidden to leave.

* * *

Back at the hotel, Isabella Carter was angry. "He sent that lame assassin on purpose. He knew that even if he failed, we'd be tied up here in Egypt long enough that he'd be able to make a getaway."

McKenzie and Abdul sat looking at her while she stormed around the room. Everything had been one frustration after another, near misses every one. At least she still had one clue, one trail to follow.

She was running out of time and she knew it. Hawas' shipment would be there soon and she needed to be the one to receive it. The crystals were too hot now. She could have Fane intercept them, but that seemed like an incredibly stupid thing to do. She still had hopes that she would be able to somehow keep the crystals away from him without getting her students killed. As long as Fane thought he had the upper hand, everyone was safe. But if James had somehow found out about the shipment, the Alexandria discovery, then danger was being delivered along with that package.

How much did he know? How much could he know? How well connected was he? What was his interest in this? And the big question, did he know about the embedding? It almost seemed reasonable that he did. This was serious overkill for some quartz crystals.

There was no telling how much this Eldon James actually knew, but it stood to reason that he knew as much as Isabella. But, he only had information about McKenzie's crystals. His being in Alexandria was only because McKenzie was here too. He seemed ignorant of the Egyptian find. She hoped that hadn't changed.

She wanted to meet him face to face, find out what his game was and why he was so willing to do anything to acquire them. Was he like Fane? Ruthless, underhanded, a killer selling to the highest bidder and just as importantly did this mean the beginning of a war that she was caught in the middle of? It was beginning to look that way. He'd already proven he wasn't afraid of bloodshed. The situation seemed to be spiraling out of control quickly and she couldn't let that happen.

She plopped in a chair. McKenzie decided to dare a conversation with her. "Do you think you might like to tell me what's behind this now?"

Isabella, looked at him and was about to say something when there was a knock at the door. McKenzie let out an audible sigh and

Abdul opened the door. It was Inspector Amir. "So what have you found out?" Isabella didn't wait for courteous amenities.

"The suspect confirmed your story. That he was hired to kill Mr. McKenzie here. He'd been hired right after his place was robbed." McKenzie looked a little dumb. "Yes Mr. McKenzie I know about that, even though you didn't report it. He followed you and saw you and Dr. Carter come into the hotel. It was just the opportunity that he was waiting for when you ordered room service. He knocked the real room service employee out and took his place. We found him tied in a janitor's closet."

"Any idea who the man was that hired him?" McKenzie asked "Do we know anything about him? Why he wants me dead?"

"The suspect was quite forthcoming about who he was. He said he was an Arab, a pock-faced man. He handed him a lot of money and pointed you out. Apparently, the only reason he targeted Dr. Carter here is because she was with you and would be a witness. He hadn't counted on her being a better shot, which brings me to another point of interest. Dr. Carter. It seems you have no gun registered to the Government." Isabella knew she was caught.

"Dr. Carter, I would like whatever illegal firearms you might be carrying. They are not permitted in this country as I'm sure you know. Currently you are on very friendly terms with this country, I would hate to see that change over a small incident like this."

"I suppose you wouldn't believe he shot himself in the knee?" Isabella said hopefully.

"The bullet didn't match," responded Amir.

"A small incident. Someone tries to kill me and he calls it a small incident," mumbled McKenzie.

Isabella went to her pack and retrieved the gun. She handed it to the inspector. "You wouldn't like to tell me where you got this would you," he asked.

"Just someone on the street," she replied. She would have gone to jail before giving up Abdul.

Inspector Amir continued, "As for why someone wanted you dead, Mr. McKenzie. Though I don't know for sure my suspicion is your sense of humor was the likely cause. Personally I can see someone wanting to shoot you. Good day to all of you." He turned to go and then "You are all free to leave the country, we won't be requiring anything else from you other than an address where we can send the bill for the damage to the hotel room."

"Give it to McKenzie," said Isabella. "It was him they were trying to kill."

"Mr. McKenzie, unfortunately, because of this incident, the government is revoking your work permit. We would like you to leave the country."

"What I'm losing my job over this? Great. First I get kicked out of bars, then I get kicked out of countries. What's left?"

Inspector Amir left and Isabella was on the phone immediately making a plane reservation. "The very next flight going out."

"Better make that two, Doc," McKenzie said to her. "Apparently I can't stay here."

"I'm going to New York. You wouldn't like it there."

"I told you Doc, until I know what's behind this, you're stuck with me."

She didn't have time to argue. "Make that two tickets," she said.

* * *

Lazarus Fane hadn't wasted any time when the phone went dead. The name Eldon James was not unfamiliar to him. Actually it was very familiar and he knew this meant trouble, big trouble. Fane immediately called Alexandria. He had connections there, all of them illegitimate. Within twenty minutes Fane had men looking for Eldon. He had offered a large sum to anyone that could get near him. Lazarus Fane knew that wouldn't be easy.

If Eldon had some crystals and knew their secret, what he would do to get them all wouldn't be pretty. Eldon gaining control of the crystals simply was not in the plans and that was something that Fane had to stop.

The next thing he had to do was contact Carter. He had to find out what had happened. This initiated another series of calls. It wasn't long and he had pieced together most of the story of the shooting at the hotel including the information that Carter was alive and unharmed. He sat down. He was through pacing for the moment.

He lit up a cigar and sat back to think. Carter had said "they were on their way." That must mean they were shipped somehow. He hated the idea that she might have entrusted them to some incompetent parcel service. Then again, she might not have had any choice. Where would she have sent them, certainly not to him, so that left her office at NYU or her apartment in Greenwich. That would be easy enough to cover.

If Eldon knew about them, then there would be no doubt he'd be trying to intercept them. Carter would be trying to get back and beat the shipment, but with this delay in Egypt, she was likely not to make it. That meant the smartest choice would be to intercept them himself and then give them over to Carter as needed for analysis, possibly only letting her have them one at a time. It would slow down the analysis, but in the end, it might make more sense. This was a better idea anyway, call it Isabella/Eldon insurance. This gave Carter less of a chance to double-cross him too. He knew if there was any way for her to do it, she would. Once her usefulness was over, he'd personally execute her. There were so few pleasures left in life, one must savor them when they come around.

He got back on the phone. When he was done he had men watching both places. If parcel delivery men showed up, his men would be there to grab it. He had another ace in the hole as well, the plant. The grad student that was in Carter's class would send him back reports on the progress of the research. If any of the research took a direction he didn't like, he'd know about it right away.

He sat back, drew deep on his cigar. Lazarus was confident, relaxed. He had his options covered. That was how he had survived so long in this business. You never take your eye off the game. He smiled to himself. He thought about how many ways there were to kill Isabella Carter.

≈ 5 ≈

The plane landed at Kennedy airport twelve hours after they took off, eight hours flight, four hours waiting for landing clearance. The cold New York chill hit McKenzie right away as they got into a cab. "I told you, you should have gone somewhere else," commented Isabella.

"I'll live." He replied.

"I need to go to my apartment first and then to my office," she told him and then, "Where are you planning on staying?"

He looked at her, "On your couch until I know what's behind all of this. Besides, all my money is tied up in Egypt. It will take a little time to get that straightened out."

"Don't you have any credit cards?"

"Maxed."

"I'm telling you, you should have just chalked it all up to a bad day, went back to Bimini or something."

"Is there scotch back at your apartment, maybe some food?"

"I have American cheese and a loaf of bread. There's a two-course meal for you. No scotch."

They got out in front of Isabella's apartment building. She punched in her security code number and the lock buzzed open. She walked in and then went to her mail box. It was one within several rows of small aluminum doors. Another tenant was trying to get his box open and not having much luck. Isabella grabbed the handful of papers and envelopes and went to the elevator. It wasn't long arriving.

As the elevator door closed, she looked at McKenzie and remarked, "That man doesn't belong here. He's not a tenant. The building is being watched."

McKenzie replied, "So how do you want to work this Doc?"

"Right now I just want to get inside my apartment. The rest we can figure out from there."

"OK, I'm right behind you."

The elevator door opened and Isabella looked down the hall of apartment doors. It looked empty so she motioned him forward. She went straight to her door, got the lock open and they were inside.

Her apartment was not how McKenzie had pictured it. He figured Spartan, clean, organized. However, there was clutter everywhere. File folders, archaeology magazines, thumb drives and portable hard drives covered the computer desk. There were artifacts, and parchments, all things she was studying and researching. The next thing he noticed, lying on an end-table was a book titled It's a Good Day to Die by Jim Harrison.

"Now I see how you recognized my room being ransacked. Looks like it happened here too."

"You can always go to a hotel."

McKenzie saw a newspaper article hanging on the wall, framed in a silver metal frame. The article was matted proving its importance to her:

> A previously unknown Mayan city was discovered last week by University of Michigan post graduate, Isabella Carter. Her historic discovery is the culmination of years of cooperative research by her, University of Michigan and the Museum of Natural History. It is still too early to tell what discoveries and cultural information will be revealed in the excavation of the lost city named Itchen Balam, but speculation is that it should be considerable and it is anticipated to shed new light on the Mayan culture.
>
> The city of Itchen Balam's existence had been told about through ancient writings of the Mayans, but many scholars had come to the conclusion that it was irrevocably lost or didn't exist at all. Carter's discovery puts all of the arguments to rest and as the city is revealed, there will undoubtedly be more arguments to come as the artifacts and writing finds the hands of scholars.
>
> Initial reports say the city is comparable in size to Chichen Itza, another important Mayan city that has been estimated to house 50,000 Mayans.

"This will add a large piece into the Mayan puzzle," said Isabella Carter.

Isabella Carter is also notable for being the great great-grand niece of the famed Howard Carter who in 1907 discovered the undisturbed tomb of Tutankhaman, the richest find in the history of Egyptian archaeology. Her parents were John and Annabelle Carter, noted antiquities and relic experts. They are presumed dead in a plane crash in Central America 15 years ago."

McKenzie was impressed. "So you discovered a lost Mayan City. That must have been quite a feather in your cap."

She looked at him a little distant. "Actually it was the greatest thing and the worst thing that ever happened to me. I lost some good people there. Not just colleagues, but friends."

He could see that it still gnawed at her. Then he saw what she was doing. She was loading a 45 automatic. She saw him watching. "Over the years I've learned that you never know when you might need one of these. The way things are going right now, the odds are pretty good this is going to come in handy. Do you want one?

"What, do you have your own arsenal?"

"Well, let's put it this way, if someone broke in here, they'd be Swiss cheese before they got through the door."

"Do you always shoot first and ask questions later?"

She grinned, as she slipped it into her police style under arm holster. "It's New York, you can never have too much personal security." Then with a serious tone, "Listen McKenzie. We could be in some serious trouble here. This might get very deadly very quickly. You have no idea what's at stake here."

That was it. McKenzie had had enough. He'd been patient long enough. It was time for her to spill. "Why don't you enlighten me. I'm sick of being in the dark here. I think you owe me an explanation and I'm tired of waiting for it."

He was right, she thought. He'd been through enough that he deserved to know the truth. His ass was on the line here too. As far as she knew, Eldon James would continue to try to kill him just to insure that he never told of the crystal's secret whether he knew it or not. And if Fane discovered he was involved, McKenzie would likely end up as a corpse in the Sault Ste. Marie alley where she had met Fane. "Those crystals have information on them."

"What? How can they?"

"As to the what, it is some kind of writing that is embedded inside of them. As to the how, we're not sure. I can show you, but we don't have time right now. I have to get to my office. There's a package coming and someone will try to intercept it. I promise to let you in on everything. I'm beginning to think I might need your help and since you're refusing to leave, screw it, you're in. Here." She handed him a 38 revolver. "Sorry I don't have a holster for it.

He took it and looked it over. "You know, I never knew archaeology was so dangerous." McKenzie stuck the gun in his pants.

"Usually it isn't," she said as she headed for the door. "I've kind of made it that way."

She poked her head into the hallway. A couple of tenants were moving around but there was no sign of the man she had seen downstairs. They went down to the lobby. Exiting the elevator they saw he was still there. He didn't try to follow as they went out the door.

"He's waiting for the package," she told McKenzie.

"What package."

"A package with the crystals you found in Alexandria."

As they made the street they hailed a cab. It was rush hour and getting near NYU took some time. It made Isabella impatient, frustrated.

Finally they made it. She bailed out of the cab with McKenzie on her heels. She wasted no time getting to her office. There was no package and no outward signs that it was being watched. She was relieved. But then, where was it? It should be due.

She got out her key and went into her office. There was a pile of notes and letters on her floor. One stood out. It was a slip for registered certified mail for a package from Egypt. She looked at the clock. Too late the post office windows were closed for the day. She swore.

McKenzie looked at her. It wasn't something she did often. "What's the matter?"

"It's at the post office and we're too late to get there."

"Well then, maybe you can show me a little more of what this is about."

Isabella looked at him and nodded. "Close the door and lock it." A book titled True North laid on the keyboard so she hastily moved it and then she booted up her computer and unlocked her desk. She pulled out one of the thumb-drives and plugged it in. It wasn't long and McKenzie was seeing for the first time the information on the crystal she had been given. For once he was speechless.

Isabella began. "We don't know what it says but it is old. We don't know who produced it but certainly we can guess. I've always had a theory and this could prove everything I've believed. Plato in his writings about Atlantis talks about a very advanced civilization. He writes about flying machines and vehicles that travelled under the sea. He even talks about a power that they had harnessed that was based on crystals and gems, gems being simply crystals of another type. Ruby, emerald, very similar to quartz. We know today that all lasers are based on focused light through ruby crystals. Even diamonds are basically quartz only they were subject to geological pressures far greater than those of quartz and were transformed to carbon. A Diamond is a very high quality quartzite. So if we consider the writings of Plato and then those of James Churchward..." McKenzie's face had gone blank.

"He was an explorer, archaeologist that investigated and wrote extensively about another lost continent called Lemuria or Mu. His writings also spoke of an advanced civilization that had wonders of technology similar to those described by Plato. So, of course the hypothesis then becomes that these crystals had to come from either one of them or at least some civilization like those described by Churchward and Plato. I've always believed that this is not the first time that man has risen on this planet to a technological level such as ours. I think we are in a second or even third rise of mankind. Plato claims that Atlantis was destroyed through some natural catastrophe. Maybe Lemuria was destroyed at the same time by the same natural disaster. Both civilizations seemed to be thriving at nearly the same time, if you believe in that. I do, but if I were to say those things to my colleagues, I'd be laughed out of my position here. I'd lose all credibility and essentially I'd be out of a job. These crystals may prove my theory. They were found in the ruins of the library of Alexandria. That means that they were probably in use at the library in some form. The Greeks would have had access to this information. Now the next question becomes. How did they read it? There had to be some kind of machinery or technology that read these crystals for the ancients.

"Well if that was the case, why haven't we found any of these readers or technology?" asked McKenzie, thinking he was seeing a hole in her theory. Personally, he was willing to chalk it all up to extraterrestrial aliens.

"Well, I think it was one of two things. Either the devices were made of some type of material that has decomposed over the centuries or we have found them and classified them as an unknown artifact. That was one of the reasons I was quizzing you on what you saw on the ocean bed where you found the crystals. I thought maybe there might be some debris that didn't quite fit in with the ruins. In reality I have no idea what I would be looking for and probably wouldn't recognize it even if I had seen it."

"What makes you so sure this isn't some kind of hoax? After all, you've only actually looked at one crystal."

"Well, if it is some kind of hoax, obviously I'm not the only one taken in by it."

"That's what makes a good hoax," he commented.

"Good point. Well, maybe you can help me determine that. How deep was the silt where you found the ones in Alexandria?"

"A couple of feet anyway," he answered.

"How long do you think it would have taken for that amount of silt to accumulate?"

"Well, certainly it would have been years, but I'm no expert. I just dive and I know, with currents and water movement, things can get covered up pretty quickly. They can get uncovered the same way. So I say that proves very little. Someone could have thrown those in there a few years back. We've had laser technology for quite some time now, several decades. I know, I got a CD player when I was young. As I recall there were even these things called laserdiscs at one point. They were huge, like old vinyl records. They didn't catch on so they quit making them. Now everything is based on laser technology. These could have been faked. Who knows, there might be someone out there just waiting for the announcement so they can have a big laugh."

She had to concede he had some points. Having him along might be good for her. She really wanted to believe these were real. A skeptic can be important. They were a balance. She smiled at him. It was the first time she didn't see him as a nuisance.

"But," she said, "Even on the possibility that they're not faked, genuine, then we have to try to bring the information to light. It's what my job is. But also, we certainly know some parties are convinced of the authenticity. Convinced enough to kill anyone to get those artifacts. So, real or faked, we need to solve the riddle of what these things are and what they say."

Suddenly, she heard some movement beyond the door into the hall. She put her finger to her mouth and a quiet "shh." Footsteps approached the door and stopped. A note slid through the mail slot and floated to the floor. Then they turned and went back the way they came. McKenzie bent over and picked it up, then handed it to her.

It read: I know about your research. Expect to hear from me, Eldon James.

She handed it to McKenzie. He eyed it for a moment and sighed, "I guess he's figured out your end. He won't be just trying to kill me anymore. Seems you made the list too. "

Isabella looked grim. "This may be worse than you think. There's someone else involved too. His name is Lazarus Fane. We go way back, further than even I knew at the start. It was years later, but you read the newspaper about how my parents were in a plane crash? He caused it. I found out when he came to the dig where I discovered Itchen Balam the lost Mayan city. He tried to take over the dig. I'd found a crystal skull..."

McKenzie interrupted her, "A real crystal skull, one of THE crystal skulls?"

"Yes. I'd found it inside one of the ruins and Fane thought that if I'd found the skull, I'd found a treasure room, so he wanted me to tell where it was hidden. Let's just say that things got ugly and things got messy, very messy.

"Over the years I've tried to kill him in the times our paths have crossed. Every time it seems I fail. The son of a bitch won't die. So anyway, Fane is the one that contacted me about the crystal. I have to decipher the language on them or my students will start turning up in the morgue. I can't let that happen."

"Have you asked them about that?" commented McKenzie. "Shouldn't it be up to them whether or not they want to take the risk. You never know, you might have a lot more help in this than you think. It seems to me you've spent a lot of your life trying to do things by yourself. You're shielding everyone around you when maybe you don't need to. Maybe that's why this guy isn't dead yet. You let those around you distract you from the goals you need to be focusing on. The world is a dangerous place, we all face it every day. Maybe you don't need to go it alone and begin to trust those around you and those that care about you. I don't believe for a minute that your students won't get your back. Actually I bet some of them would jump at the opportunity to get their teacher's bacon out of the frying pan. It could get them extra credit."

She smiled at the speech. He'd made her feel better for the moment. It was what she needed. She was going to have to go back to her apartment and worry through the long night waiting for morning when she could go pick up the package.

McKenzie said one more thing, "By the way, where's the crystal skull?"

Isabella replied quietly, "In a safe place." She looked at the note they'd just received. Well, it appears Mr. James will be seeking us out. She pulled the note she'd gotten in Alexandria out of her pack. She handed it to McKenzie, "We have an address. Maybe we should beat him to it."

"Somehow I don't think it's going to be that easy," remarked McKenzie.

"Should we go see? We have to kill some time until tomorrow anyway."

He nodded.

* * *

The address was an office building in Manhattan. It was evening and there weren't many people around. They walked through the empty lobby to the elevator. The building appeared to have been built in the 1920's. It had the art deco look of that era.

The office was on the 12th floor, suite 1240. The pair stepped out of the elevator warily. Neither had any idea what they'd find. As far as they knew, James could be some kind of mob boss with an army of gunmen at his disposal. A brass sign on the wall pointed the directions of the suite numbers.

"Well," said McKenzie, "That seems easy."

"That's what worries me," replied Isabella.

They both went to the door, hands on their guns. Suite 1240, it was unlocked. There was a sign on the door. It read "Please Enter." They went in cautiously, ready to react at the slightest indication of danger. There was none.

The office was spacious, but empty except for a computer monitor that sat on a steel cart with rollers. It was logged into a video chat to another computer. The image of a man, who spun around in his chair and faced his screen, was on the monitor. Eldon James said "Hello. I've been expecting you."

McKenzie looked at Isabella bewildered and confused. Isabella replied. "I received your note. I thought maybe I'd save you some trouble."

He smiled into the webcam. "The only trouble I foresee is what you will do with those crystals when you get them."

Now, she was confused. "Why would research into their origin and content be trouble? It's what is done with discoveries of this kind."

"Not discoveries of this kind." He put a strong emphasis on "This" to prove some point he hadn't reached yet. "Discoveries of this kind weren't meant to be shared with the world." Again, the "This" emphasis.

"I don't see how you can possibly stop it." Isabella was baiting him into letting her in on his motives.

"I have my ways and beware, if you or Mr. McKenzie come between me in this, I will push you aside." His emphasis was on "Will" this time.

"The project has already started, you can't stop it."

"That is where you would be in error Dr. Carter. I can and will stop it, by any means necessary." The ominous tone in his voice brought with it implications she didn't want to have to think about. "I know about the Alexandria discovery. I know Dr. Hawas shipped a package containing the crystals to you. I will obtain them. I prefer you stay out of the way and in the process have nothing happen to you or Mr. McKenzie, but if you insist on continuing to get in my way, I'll have no choice but to remove you as I would any obstacle. The choice is yours. I will be in touch"

The webcam went dark. The conversation was over. There would be no reply. She turned to McKenzie. "I think you're right. It's time to bring the students in on this. They need to know where things stand."

"I want my crystals back. He stole my crystals," muttered McKenzie.

≈ 6 ≈

Lazarus Fane was shouting, "What do you mean they're dead?"

"Just what I said, sir. They were both found in a trash bin shot in the back of the head," repeated the man who was now in fear of his life for having brought Lazarus such distressing news. Frequently, when the boss got mad, the messenger was killed.

"Damn," Fane spit out. He was up and fuming, pacing back and forth. It was a habit of his when he was agitated. "Both of the men I had watching for the package, dead. What caliber of bullets?"

"They were .44 Mags sir. I dug them out myself. I knew you'd want to know. These were professional hits," said the lackey. He still had blood and bits stuck to his shirt from the project of retrieving the causes of death.

"Well, dispose of the bodies, your efficiency saved your life." He looked at his frightened employee.

The man forced a smile, "Thank you, sir."

That left Carter out. She had a .45. There was only one other conclusion, Eldon. He was now seemingly aware of his connection to the crystals and Carter. But how had he found out? Carter would have never told him. The whole project was in jeopardy now. There was another player in the game, one he knew to be as cunning and clever as he.

Fane knew Carter had left Egypt, but she hadn't contacted him since her return. This didn't bode well either. This made him angrier. Fane wasn't in control. Things were happening around him that he hadn't counted on. He didn't like that. It needed to be fixed and first on the list was Eldon. Carter he'd be able to find. She was predictable, wouldn't leave the research until she knew what was buried inside those crystals. Besides, he still had an ace up his sleeve with her. That put Eldon at the top of the list.

He walked over to a folder he had been studying. "Contact Cicero Smith." He took a picture out of the folder and handed it to the gore spattered man. "Tell him I want him to find and take this man out. He goes by the name of Eldon James. He has my permission to gather and hire as many men as he thinks he needs to do the job. I just want it done!" He slammed his fist on his desk for emphasis, his voice had reached an angry shout. The picture was of Eldon James and Lazarus Fane together!

The man's brow pinched as if there was a question coming, but all he said was "Yes sir, right away sir." He then prudently left satisfied he still had his life.

With the two men dead, it told Fane everything. Eldon had to have known about the shipment from Egypt to have his own men in position to kill Fane's. Since Eldon had given his men orders to kill any others watching the boxes, that meant he was aware or at least suspected Lazarus' involvement. The discovery of the now dead men would have confirmed Fane's involvement simply by their presence. All of Eldon's suspicions would now be confirmed.

Eldon had cost him control of the crystals. Eldon may very well possess the crystals if he was able to intercept the package or even waylay Carter. This was a particularly unsettling thought. No, he would have left Isabella alone, she was too high profile, her death would set off too many alarms.

Fane was muttering as he left."If he wants a war, I'll give him a war. We could have done so well together. Now it comes to this. Well, I won't disappoint you."

* * *

Isabella was up early the next morning making some calls. McKenzie had slept on her couch. Truthfully she was happy he did. With everything going on, having the extra person there made her feel a bit more secure. She had been able to sleep. She might not have if she were alone.

McKenzie had slept with the gun under his pillow. If someone was going to bust through the door he wasn't about to make it easy for them. He hadn't slept well. He was dozing in and out when Isabella started making her calls. He sat up on the couch.

She pointed to the coffee pot where the newly born, morning, nectar of the gods was waiting. "OK, I want seven. Thanks," she said into the phone, then hung it up.

McKenzie barely heard as he rummaged in the cupboard to find a cup and then blindly began to fill it. His brain felt like fudge and there was as little as possible happening inside of it.

"It's a new dawn. We've got things to do this morning," she said to him.

He opened one eye and looked at her sideways.

She was way too awake for him to deal with right away. "Do I have time to actually drink this," he pointed at the cup. "And maybe get a shower?"

"Yes to both," she answered. "You're going to need them."

"That sounded a little ominous," he thought.

He let the comment go and fifteen minutes later he felt immeasurably better. The coffee and shower had changed his perspective on the morning which he had been wishing would simply go away. "OK, what's on the agenda for today?"

"First we have to get the package from the post office to the university. That's not going to be easy. Are you ready? I'm going to need your help with this."

He nodded. He was as ready as he'd ever be.

They got a cab and rode to the post office that was holding the package. There were several in New York but the postal slip she'd gotten in the mail at the university told her which one to go to. Like most buildings in New York it was older, spacious and bustling with people. It reflected inspirations of the art deco period of the time of its construction.

"Stick close. I need you to keep watch for me."

"Not a problem," he grinned. "Do we know who we're looking for?"

"That's the best part, haven't got a clue. If they seem interested, it's a good guess it's them." Then, she got in line for one of the windows.

McKenzie watched everyone and everything, especially her. The crowd milled in a constant movement. James' men could be anywhere, anyone. They could emerge undercover of the crowd from any direction with little difficulty. Aiden knew Isabella was putting a lot of faith in him, trusting him. That hadn't happened often his life. He appreciated it now, he wouldn't let her down.

The woman in the window handed Isabella a package. She discreetly put it in her pack. The package had been visible for only a moment, but that might have been enough. A glimpse would be all James' men would need to identify it. She came back to McKenzie. "Got it," she confirmed and the pair headed for the door, their eyes scanning the post office.

McKenzie was behind her, the pack between them. He watched the crowd closely and saw when the four men began to follow them. He grinned to himself. Now, things were getting interesting. Hell, he'd had worse odds in a bar fight. He whispered to Isabella, "Four behind us." She nodded but kept going, never missing a step, showing no signs of hesitation.

It was what she had hoped wouldn't happen, but knew better. The key now was to stay in the open, stay public, make it difficult for them to make any moves without attracting attention or other people getting in the way. It was a plan, she reassured herself. They were being stalked, but they weren't trapped. The instincts she had learned in the Central American jungle began to come back to her. She was wary and alert. Her eyes scanned everything taking in details most would overlook, seeking possibilities where there seemed to be none.

She could tell McKenzie was too. His breathing was steady, regular. His pace was marked, even, yet quick. It was good. They might succeed at this yet. McKenzie was proving to be a good ally to have.

Suddenly, she spotted her chance. It was moving down the street coming towards them. Its pace was perfect. "Get ready," she told McKenzie.

"I'm with ya."

Without another thought, Isabella bolted out into the street with McKenzie right behind her.

A cab was moving by slowly as traffic bunched up briefly, it was already picking up speed as Isabella, followed by McKenzie opened the rear door and threw themselves in. The cab continued to gain speed and they could see the four men run into the street as they pulled away. There wasn't a chance of catching them. The surprised cab driver turned and started to protest, "Hey, I'm off duty."

Isabella replied, "Not anymore," and flipped what looked like a police badge at him. "Take me to NYU. Hurry."

"OK, OK, I guess I can take one more fare," the cabbie relented.

McKenzie was caught between amazed and baffled. He was just getting used to the gun-toting professor idea, but then she has another surprise in her arsenal. He whispered "Where? What? You're not a cop."

She smiled and whispered back, "It's amazing what you can find on the internet."

"This is something you use so often, you have to plan ahead?"

"Hey, never underestimate the power of something that looks official."

It wasn't long and they entered Greenwich and then the University. Isabella paid the cabbie and the pair got out.

"You can bet those four goons back there called ahead. We're not out of this yet," said Isabella.

"I figured that. I'm watching."

NYU was bustling with students coming and going from classes. Isabella and McKenzie went directly to the lab and avoided her office. Someone would have it staked out for sure and would think she'd take the package there. The thing she needed to do now was to be as unpredictable as possible. Her next move, she hoped, would be just that.

Her grad class was waiting for her at the lab. As she and McKenzie came through she closed and locked the door. The students were staring curiously at the newcomer, McKenzie.

"I need all of you to listen." She began. "This project is becoming very hot, very fast. I know of two other parties that are aware of the crystal embedding and they are dangerous. They want it and are willing to do anything to get their hands on it and our research." There was surprise mixed with uncertainty on some of the grad's faces. Jeff Barnes interrupted. "I thought this was supposed to be a secret. We were the only ones to know."

"When I left here, I thought that too. I was wrong. Everything was all under control and then things managed to degenerate very quickly. " Isabella explained a condensed version of the incidents of the last three days and confessed to her attempting to uncover the secret for Fane in exchange for their safety. "So here's what I plan to do. We're leaving."

The students looked around at each other struck dumbfounded. There were several choruses of "What?" and "huh?" This news had confused them thoroughly. "Right now?"

Jeff and Bob seemed to be the only ones unruffled by the revelation. "Where to?"

"You'll know when we get there. Right now, we're leaving straight from here. Grab your laptops, your notepads, anything else we have or any of you think we need to complete this project."

"But professor, it's the lab we need. We can't solve this without the deep probe microscopes. We need the digital mapping systems, I don't see how to finish this without them," declared Jeff. Bob nodded behind him.

"There will be equipment like we have here, where we're going," assured Isabella.

"How long do we have to pack?" asked Sandy.

"No packing. I also want all of your cellphones," she directed. "There is no argument about this and no negotiations."

Isabella looked around at everyone, she had all of their attention except one.

Alicia Case's eyes looked up from her phone, looked sheepish, shrugged and muttered, "Sorry" under her breath. She'd been texting since they walked in.

"A perfect illustration of my reasoning. I don't want to be tracked through these," Isabella continued. "It's risky enough letting you take the laptops. No Facebook, no Twittering, none of it. We have to be extremely careful if we want to get through this. Are we clear? We are dropping off the face of the earth until we discover what's inside these stones."

"No phoning home telling the family? Nothing?" Karen Arntsen asked.

"No, we can't leave a trail. Anything you need, we will buy on the road or once we get there. Listen, I know you didn't ask for this. It all started as you doing a favor for me. But, as professionals in any field there may come a moment when something comes across your desk that may change things, change things so much that they might subject you to ridicule, controversy, or even danger. As researchers in any field, we can't be strangers to taking chances, asking the questions and looking for the answers that may change the world. It's who we are, it's what we do."

"Sometimes there are going to be those that don't want us to make those discoveries. They will try to threaten and intimidate us, but we can't let them, because what we do is important, meaningful. And sometimes, just sometimes it can make a difference in how the world lives. We can be proud of that." Isabella finished.

For a moment McKenzie realized he had just gotten to know the real Isabella Carter. He was impressed. He had heard worse pep talks in locker rooms.

Isabella's students had gathered around her and started handing in their cells and other similar gadgets. "Also," she continued, "No credit cards. I have all of our expenses taken care of. Let's get ready, we have to go. There are men out searching for us now. Keep your eyes open as we go. Our adversaries may try to stop us. McKenzie, I need you to watch our backs. You've been doing a good job of that so far, might as well keep it up. Are you in?"

"Why not, it's been interesting so far. Besides, I'm getting used to all of this crazy stuff you archaeologists do. Who knew?" Then he looked at Isabella, "I told you they'd back your play."

"I only hope it's the right move." For the first time, McKenzie saw some uncertainty in her expression. So, she was fallible after all. Strangely, he was happy to see it. She really was like everyone else. She buried it well, but it was in there. Something had happened, she had mentioned it back at the apartment. Someday he'd find the time to find out. Now wasn't it.

* * *

Cicero Smith looked at the man he had kneeling in front of him. Smith's gun was pointed at his head. "I need to know how to find Eldon James," he repeated.

"I don't know. I've never seen him. We just get our orders and follow them," answered the man.

"How do you get your orders?" Smith's patience was running thin. This was taking too long and he needed answers. The space between the buildings was deserted, but who knew how long that would last.

Whether it was a moment of misplaced loyalty or simple stupidity, the man answered, "I can't tell you that."

Cicero's silenced gun whispered. The bullet went through the man's right calf. He began to talk. Cicero smiled. That usually worked.

"The information usually comes through the Third Avenue Bar. All of us wait around until someone contacts us. We're paid ahead of time and we go take care of whatever the assignment is. We never see James."

The gun whispered again. The police would have difficulty identifying the face. It would be a closed casket funeral.

Cicero caught a cab to the Third Avenue Bar. If this was the way James was communicating, then he didn't think he'd have to wait around long. There was too much going on, a courier wouldn't be long in coming.

When he went inside he noticed a group of men surrounding a table near the back. They were smoking and had a card game going. None of them seemed to be drinking or drunk. They weren't loud enough. Cicero had an experienced eye for these things. He knew how to size up people quickly. It was his job. It was how he stayed alive and not attract attention from the law.

Smith took a seat at the bar near the door. These men weren't who he was looking for. He wanted the courier. "Whiskey and soda," he ordered.

The bartender smiled, "It's about time somebody ordered something that would pay the bills."

"Why is that?" asked Smith, "This is a bar isn't it? There's never a shortage of people crying in their beer."

"It's supposed to be," the bartender answered, "But you see that crew over there. They sit in here day in and day out. They come and they go, they play cards, have the occasional soda and take off when someone comes in and gives them a message. They buy nothing and certainly not enough to contribute to the overhead on this joint."

The door opened and a man came in. He walked straight to the table of men.

"Watch," said the bartender. "That's the guy there. Some of them will get up and leave." He was wrong. They all got up and left.

Smith paid for his drink with a twenty and followed them out. They weren't paying any attention to him. The group went one way, the courier went another. He followed the courier.

He didn't have much difficulty, the man seemed quite at ease winding his way in and out of the pedestrians crowding the street. The courier seemed to be completely unaware of his presence. This will be easy thought Smith. No one had told the courier that delivering messages could be a dangerous job. He chuckled to himself, class was in session.

Suddenly the man disappeared into a building. Smith wasn't far behind. He went to an elevator and pushed the "Up" button. Cicero made a decision and walked up next to the man. The elevator arrived and he stepped in right along with the courier. The courier pushed the 18th floor and spoke to him, "What floor?"

Cicero smiled, "The same." The man scowled a bit, but said nothing more as the elevator headed up with the Muzak version of *Yellow Submarine* playing. "Catchy tune," Cicero thought as he hummed along.

The elevator stopped and opened its doors on 18. The courier stepped out and went down the hall. Smith pretended to look at the plaque that showed directions to the various suite numbers. He watched sideways as the man entered a room. Harrison moved quickly down the hall to the door where the courier disappeared. A sign next to the door proclaimed "New York Message Service."

Smith was angry, then, he decided what he'd do. Tonight after they closed, he'd pay a visit. There had to be records of messages sent. They had to get paid somehow. There had to be clues in there. He went back to the elevator. "Later," he thought.

* * *

Eldon James was preparing for the inevitable. He knew Lazarus was aware of his involvement now. By now he would have found the bodies of the men Lazarus had watching for the package from

Alexandria. There would be retaliation. There would be war between the two.

It would have been disastrous for the crystals to have fallen into Lazarus' hands. God only knew what he would do with them. One thing was certain, that he would have sold anything of value to the highest bidder. Lazarus was a man without conscience, he didn't question motives. He simply cashed the checks.

He shook at the thought of it, obliteration of life as we knew it. The secrets couldn't be revealed. With the evils he'd have found, he would have unleashed the darkness upon the world once more. The world couldn't take it. It needed to move on, mature, evolve. We couldn't go back to the stone age, only to start over again. We had to finally get it right.

He knew Lazarus would be searching for him by now. He would have most of his men out hunting, but Eldon had been careful. He'd spent a lot of energy and money to cover his tracks. He'd developed an infrastructure that would shield him well. He had no illusions about what Lazarus would do when he found him. He knew full well that this would lead to a war between them. There would be blood, lots of it.

Right now he had to get those crystals from Dr Carter and McKenzie. They'd left NYU with a group of students. From the descriptions, it was her entire graduate class. She was on the move. If he could get the crystals away from her, then she would be out of it. He didn't think she had solved the riddle of their meaning yet. Then he could concentrate on Lazarus. He'd dispatched the Third Avenue men, but they were going to have to be quick to pick up Isabella's trail. This was something he hadn't counted on and he was sure that was why she did it. She had been clever. He liked that. She had been a thorn in the side of Lazarus for years. It had afforded him endless amusement.

He would be willing to let her go if she would just let it go. But Dr. Carter's reputation said she wouldn't. And McKenzie too, he was only a bystander. He knew that when he had the drink with him, he was just a working Joe. He had had no idea what he had found. What were the amazing odds, billions-to-one, him being the one to uncover the ones in Alexandria. Well, chalk another one up for the annals of the odd, strange and curious.

The crystal had made Eldon suspicious, he had had a hunch. It was found on the Bimini Road itself, so he had taken it to be researched. It was done privately at a research lab in Austria. After days of tests, they had found the embedding. When Eldon saw the strange language of the crystals for the first time he knew their power, their evil. The possibilities stretched out before him and he knew he had to find the rest of the crystals at all costs. He made sure no trace of the research and researchers remained. They were valued men but, what was on the crystals was more important than a couple of lives.

His search for McKenzie hadn't been easy. He'd moved on from Bimini and had left no information behind as to his future destination. Eldon had pegged him for a vagabond, drifting to wherever there might be work. Then moving on when the work or his welcome dried up. Finally he had stumbled across him in Alexandria, diving for the government, desilting the ruins of the Library.

The door to his office buzzed. "Open" he said and the voice activated lock released. The door swung open and in walked his best operative, Jason Hand.

"Our man inside of Lazarus Fane's office says that he has re-employed Cicero Smith. There is an order to stop or kill you at all costs. He said Mr. Fane was unclear on whether it was stop or kill," Hand said matter of factly.

"He probably didn't care which," Eldon replied. He walked over to his burgundy wood desk. It stood out against his overwhelming white. "Smith will try to infiltrate our ranks somehow. He's smart and we shouldn't underestimate him." He seemed small in the spacious room. "Lazarus is taking this personally. If I outsmart him, he won't be able to live with it. Somewhere along the way, only one of us is going to walk away from this one."

"The men have been dispatched for Dr. Carter, but they are having difficulty tailing them. It appears Carter, McKenzie and the students have left NYU in a group. Most of our men are on their way to La Guardia and Kennedy airport to watch the terminals.

The others are at Grand Central. If they try to leave they'll pick them up."

"Make sure they don't lose them. Bonuses for success. Failure doesn't profit so well."

"I'll pass that along," Hand turned to leave.

"Also, I want a list of Carter's students. We might be able to find them through a trace on their cells. Lock into any internet social sites they might be a part of as well. You should be able to get that information right from Google."

His thoughts drifted back to Lazarus. If only they had gotten along, hadn't betrayed him, things would have been so different. Together they could have been the most powerful men in the world. They just never could agree and then, the competition. One had to be better than the other at all costs. When Lazarus had left him to a fate worse than death, a Singapore prison, he knew how far things had gone. They hated each other, they wanted to kill each other. Now it looked as if that might be exactly what happened. Family was supposed to treat each other better, weren't they?

Asia, Asia, the name stuck in his head, it burned there like a hot iron. Eldon's memories came back, they washed over him like a wave taking him into the places he'd tried to bury, where the memories dwelled, where the horror lived. Asia, Asia, god he hated that place.

It had been Lazarus' doing, he'd set him up to take the fall. It had been Lazarus' doing that Eldon had to rot in Singapore, brutalized by his captors. He'd always held a jealousy towards Eldon. Eldon was the privileged one, the smart one, the one that the pair's father had always favored.

Thomas Barclay Fane had been a patriot, decorated for his services during the World War II. They were services that required feats that no one else seemed capable. Thomas Fane operated an underground, a very specialized underground, art, in all of its myriad and forms.

The Nazis were looting and stealing all of the art treasures of Europe. Museums, private collections, and storage vaults all saw the ravages of the Nazi lust for treasure. Nothing was safe.

As the lootings began, countries would smuggle out as many of the collection pieces as they could. That was where Fane came in. His network provided a route for the art to be shipped to Britain and then the States. Countless works of art were saved the ravages of the Nazi burnings by Fane. When the war ended, he was a hero to most of Europe.

He had profited well from his endeavors. He'd become a rich man. He was no longer smuggling art to save it, but now he was using his resources to recover what remained, return what was lost to its rightful owners for which he was paid handsomely.

It allowed him to retain an impressive estate at Cape Cod. Now married, he'd fathered two sons, Eldon and Lazarus. In his father's eyes, Eldon showed the most promise, though Lazarus was the eldest. Thomas Fane made it well known that both sons would work in the family business, but Eldon would one day take the reins when his father deemed him ready.

This was no secret and Lazarus resented it. Using his father's connections, he was able to establish his own, dark, shadow network, that, instead of recovering and preserving the art of the world, he distributed it to the black market of private collectors and dealers. It was the one thing his father would abhor. It was the one thing that would make Lazarus rich.

Eldon had risen alongside his father learning attentively and questioning things until he was satisfied at his own understanding. His knowledge and education was varied. He was careful and meticulous. Eldon analyzed and studied people and their responses to all things. He became a student of behavior and human nature. Eldon became able to predict what a person would do in almost any situation. It was invaluable in business.

Thomas Fane sent for Eldon. He directed him to sit down in the leather seat across from his large King Louis desk. "I need you to go to Singapore with Lazarus," his father began. "He's bringing a shipment of Buddhist sculptures back here to the States. Their government is counting on us handling the transportation and transfer and for some reason they've requested you."

Eldon's right eyebrow raised at this. "Why would they request me?"

"I don't know, but I want you to go. There have been rumors that your brother has got his own agenda, one that could bring down everything we've worked for, our reputation, our credibility."

"Exactly what do you think he's going to do?" asked Eldon.

"I'm not sure. I've heard from sources that he's up to something, but there are no details. I could be wrong, I hope I'm wrong. If you're there, I know our interests are protected."

"I'll do what I can. Lazarus tends to be independent, he's capable of many things. He resents me and is envious of our relationship. Being the eldest, my place should've fallen to him."

"It was never about birthright. It was about ability and who was best for the business. Lazarus is always working for Lazarus, it is never about the good of the whole."

Eldon grinned, "He doesn't play well with others."

"Watch him and watch your back."

Two days later, Eldon and Lazarus were on a plane bound for Singapore. It was a tense flight, Lazarus speaking little to the brother he despised. Eldon finally broke through, "Lazarus, I've got to know what plans you've set up. I can't represent the company, if I don't know what arrangements are set up."

"I could have handled things fine on my own. I didn't need you as a watchdog," snarled Lazarus.

"I'm sure you could have. But I'm a part of it now, we might as well make the best of it."

"We'll make the best of it all right."

Eldon wasn't sure what Lazarus meant by the remark, but he knew there was meaning in its statement. He would have to be wary. "About the arrangements…"

"Alright, Eldon, when we get there we will be met by the government representatives in charge of the transfer. We then take it to the docks to be loaded and sail home. Simple as that. There's no reason for you to come other than father either doesn't trust me or thinks I'm a complete incompetent. Neither prospect gives much of an opinion about me."

"I'm sorry, Lazarus, I'm just following a request by Father. He asked me to come along. I did what he asked. We're working for the same thing here. Let's get through this like brothers should."

"When we get there, just follow my lead. I know who we're supposed to talk to and who we need to avoid. There are factions in Singapore that aren't happy about this exchange. They don't think the Buddhas should leave. So, there could be problems."

"Do we get an escort, police, military?"

"Police. Military aren't involved. There will be a small escort."

"Will it be enough?"

"We get what we get."

Eldon contemplated the situation Lazarus had laid out. It could be dicey, but more likely routine. It depended on the nature of the dissenters. The Singapore justice system presented a strong deterrent from any crime. Someone would have to be serious before even attempting something like this and if they did attempt it, he could rest assured it was well thought out. They would have to be confident of success. This thought bothered Eldon.

"Lazarus, if someone were to make an attempt, would we be able to stop it?" he asked.

"We will know that after we are there and see how things are set up. It's not like we're alone. We have our own employees too. We have about 30 men at our disposal. Hopefully the numbers will make someone think twice."

A few hours later they were disembarking. They were met by an employee of Fane Ltd. who drove them to a hotel. Lazarus and Eldon were told the exchange would happen the next day.

Lazarus met Eldon in the morning and told him preparations were all ready. They were driven to a building that claimed to be the Singapore Museum. A man that was dressed in a guard's uniform met them. "Eldon Fane?" he asked.

Eldon put his hand out and shook the guard's. "At your service," he smiled.

"Can I see some identification?"

Eldon brought out his passport and company ID. Lazarus did the same. The guard seemed satisfied and led them inside. As they passed through, they saw the displays of artifacts and relics of the Malay region's past. Eldon and Lazarus both looked around, taking in the treasures of the South Seas.

The guard led them into the back of the building. There were four crates waiting for their trip abroad. "Can we get the truck around to this side of the building?"

"It's on its way."

"Guard can we get this door opened?" They went past the crates and unlocked the door that stood behind them.

Lazarus had a hand radio. "Bring the truck around to the back, they're waiting."

"On our way," a voice answered.

They stepped out into the light and watched the drive. The truck wasn't long in coming. Lazarus waved it into position so that the truck was backed to the door. The back was opened and two men got out. They wore Fane Ltd. shirts. So far, Eldon had seen no police. It was the first sign that something was wrong.

The men had the crates loaded quickly. The guard asked Eldon to sign the transfer papers, which he did. Lazarus motioned for Eldon. "You ride in the truck with the statues. That should make father happy."

Eldon nodded and climbed in.

"I'll meet you out front," shouted Lazarus. "Oh here, take my radio. I'll have one in the car, so we can still talk. We'll escort you to the ship." He handed it in to Eldon through the window.

Eldon took it. The truck began to move with a quick grind of the gears from the driver. In the mirror, Eldon saw Lazarus re-enter the museum with the guard.

They reached the street and pulled alongside Lazarus' car. There was no sign of any police. Now Eldon was worried. Either any danger to the transfer wasn't taken seriously or something wasn't right. His instincts favored the something wasn't right conclusion.

He lifted the radio and spoke. "What's the deal Lazarus?"

"Everything's fine. Going off without a hitch," Lazarus came back.

"I don't see any police."

"Just because you can't see them, doesn't mean they aren't there. Start to roll. We'll pull in behind you," directed Lazarus.

The driver pulled out and began to wind through Singapore's crowded streets. They made a couple of turns that Eldon was sure went away from the waterfront.

The driver smiled, "It's better if we avoid the crowds."

They took a couple of more turns, each one heading away from the Fane ship that was to take the statues. "Lazarus," he shouted. "What are you doing? We're going the wrong way."

"No, we're going in the right direction to suit my purposes."

"What do you mean."

"Well, keep in mind you had to sign for the shipment. Everything I've done over here, I've done in your name. This entire operation was run by you, my name is nowhere."

Eldon felt slightly queasy. He had an inkling of Lazarus' plan. "You can't do it," he said into the radio.

"Too late, I already have. The police are on their way to arrest the man who stole the national treasures."

"You'll destroy everything."

"Only you and Father. Fortunately I have other prospects."

"Lazarus, don't go through with this."

"Why not, Fane Ltd will fall. I move into the space that it's vacated while Father is preoccupied with trying to get you home from a Singapore prison vacation. Let him get you out of this one. I'm not seeing a down side."

Eldon looked in his rearview mirror, Lazarus was gone. He turned and looked at the driver. He pulled over to the shoulder of the road. A police car had come up behind them. The truck stopped. The officers got out and came towards them with their guns drawn.

The driver slowly got out with his hands in the air. Another police car came down the road from the other direction. Eldon raised his hands and slowly got out.

The police came towards them cautiously. They grabbed him and put him in handcuffs. The officers dragged him to the car and threw him inside. The rest was a blur.

They booked him and put him in a cell. Whenever an officer would walk by, he'd ask to make a telephone call. He was ignored.

Two days later his father arrived. Thomas Fane looked tired, the ordeal having already left its mark. Eldon was brought to a block room so the two could talk.

Thomas spoke first. "Son, I'm doing everything I can. Singapore has a very rigid legal system that is going to take some time to negotiate."

"Lazarus set me up," Eldon hissed, his anger venting.

"I know. Unfortunately, he did an excellent job of it. He left behind a paper trail that is going to be hard to discredit. I've got lawyers working on it. If this were any other part of the world, I would have some clout we could use, but again, Lazarus planned well."

"How long do you think it will be before I can get out of here?" Eldon asked.

"I truly don't know son. This could be a long process."

As it turned out it was a very long process. Then came the trial, which turned out to be a mere formality. The judges listened to his lawyers and then pronounced him guilty.

Eldon was moved from the holding cells to the prison proper. The cells were anything but clean, with insects and rats for no extra charge. Any behavior perceived as requiring discipline was punished by bamboo floggings. One of the popular beatings was to tie the feet to a bar and then beat the bottoms until they were well swollen. The crawl back to the cell was long and seemingly insurmountable.

His father continued to visit him each time with the same news, "I'm doing everything I can." Each time his father looked more aged and beaten down by his efforts.

Eventually Eldon shut himself off to his surroundings, the occasional beatings were now things that marked a break in the monotony. He'd given a couple of the rats that had become regular guests names, there was Lazarus One and Lazarus Two. He'd had time to think, to plan and now that was what he held onto. One day there would be a reckoning.

Eldon was evolving. Everything he was, had gone through a metamorphosis. There would never be anything anyone could do to him that would be worse. He had learned patience too. The endless waiting for a result from an uncertain future, but knowing inside, sometime, somehow, there would be an end. He began to overcome the Singapore prison. He sat straighter, he walked without limps, even the crack of the bamboo no longer held the sting it once did.

All the while, Thomas Fane's determination never wavered. He'd dedicated himself to the task of getting Eldon released and he never wavered in his efforts. His health had been failing, but he wasn't going to die before his son was free and back in his own country. He'd vowed that.

He'd been pressing the American Ambassador hard. The Ambassador in turn had been pressing the Singapore government to release Eldon on the assurance he'd never return to the country. It could even be done quietly so that Singapore wouldn't lose credibility in the press. The Ambassador wanted Thomas Fane off his back. He'd had five years of Fane on his back. Singapore was supposed to have been a quiet assignment.

The government of Singapore saw no reason why they should set such a high profile individual, who committed such a high profile crime, free for no real reason other than the American's wanted them too. There was no benefit. They were inclined to ignore the Ambassador's requests.

Finally an opportunity turned up in the Ambassador's lap. Singapore imported a large portion of its products to the United States. The trade contract was coming up for renewal. The Ambassador decided to attach Eldon to the negotiations of the contract renewal. Singapore needed the U.S. more than the U.S. needed Singapore. It was the match he'd been waiting for.

It worked. Eldon was freed. He stood tall and straight when he met his father. His father smiled, "Let's go home."

The ordeal over, Thomas Fane was never the same. His strength and health had been sacrificed for Eldon. Eldon quickly discovered that his father's holdings had been severely bled. Fane Ltd. was destroyed, its credibility successfully brought down by Lazarus' setup. Eldon would have to restart his life and rebuild what once was. Somehow, he didn't mind. It seemed…appropriate.

Within two months Thomas Fane was dead. Eldon stood at his father's grave, stoic, composed. He had everything that was left in the Fane estate. As he watched the lowering of his father's coffin, Eldon buried the Fane name with him. Lazarus had seen to the tainting of the name. Eldon Fane would be seen forever as the criminal he'd left back in Singapore. That simply would not due. He would now be Eldon James. He was a new man with a new life bound for a new destiny. He turned and left the grave, never to return.

Yes, Asia, how he hated Asia.

≈ 7 ≈

McKenzie was in the rear cab. Isabella was in the front. He was watching the weaving cars constantly shifting in and out and between to see if they were being followed. So far it didn't seem as if they were. He had a hard time believing it was a clean getaway. Things just didn't go that smooth.

Isabella, the grad students, followed by McKenzie had left the NYU lab together and went straight to the street. Their eyes never stopped searching, always wary for any one that might pose a threat. It wasn't an easy task on the busy, bustling campus.

They were able to hail two cabs. Bob and Jeff went with Isabella in the lead and McKenzie had gotten the girls, Sandra, Karen and Alicia. There had been no sign of a tail, but he didn't believe they weren't there. James' men had been too diligent up until now to chuck it all without a whimper.

That was when he spotted it. The vehicle was several cars back, but it seemed to be sticking with them. They took several turns and were heading in the general direction of New Jersey. The car was still with them. McKenzie was certain enough to call it. Better to take as few chances as possible. He watched the lead car with Isabella in it. He leaned forward and told the taxi driver to flash his lights at the cab in front of them. It was the signal he and Isabella had decided on if he spotted trouble.

The front cab flashed its brakes signaling that Isabella had gotten the signal. Now came the fun. The front cab started to pick up speed. McKenzie leaned over to the driver. "There's a hundred dollar tip waiting for you if you keep up with that cab. We need to stay together so make sure we do."

The driver nodded, "Not a problem," and the cab stayed behind the other like there was an umbilical cord between them. McKenzie watched behind and lost sight of the car he'd suspected. They were entering the bridge that would take them from Manhattan to New Jersey. So far, their escape had gone relatively smoothly.

McKenzie had no idea what Isabella was planning or where they were going. It was something she had concocted all herself. Maybe, he thought, if they could get the students out of the way somewhere safe and working on solving the riddle of the crystal language, then Isabella and he could focus on getting Fane and James off their backs. He never liked to run. He always met things head on. He understood why they were doing this, but he didn't like it. He didn't think the Doc did either. She seemed like a kick them in the head, ask questions later kind of girl. He smiled. He kind of liked that.

* * *

Lazarus Fane had about had it. Nothing was going his way. If Carter knew she'd be laughing right now. God, he wished he could kill her. One of his men was talking to him. "They've left. We haven't heard from our insider since Carter entered the lab, but they were seen leaving as a group. Tracking the phone that we were in contact with shows its location is still NYU."

"Was anyone smart enough to follow?" Fane said the words through gritted teeth.

"Two of our men had a car and were in pursuit of them, but they report that they think they were spotted and have lost the pair of cabs. They are still in pursuit in the direction they were going, but they no longer have visual. At last report, they were headed for Jersey."

"Jersey? What the hell's in Jersey," spouted Fane.

"Nothing I want to see, sir."

"Is there any report from Smith?"

"Yes, he reported that he is delayed in his investigations until business hours have ended. He says he will be moving forward then, but he reports he is on a trail. He requests two men to meet him for this evening."

"Send them, now."

At least that was something. He always could count on Smith. They'd worked together for many years. Once he was on the trail, nothing could pull him off. He was like a good bloodhound and he had never let Fane down. When things got too difficult for regular measures, Smith was the one that got things done.

The phone on the desk buzzed. "Call for you sir." He picked it up.

"Hello big brother," it was Eldon. "It seems we are once again at odds."

"What do you want?" said Lazarus. It was just what he needed right now, more aggravation.

"You to go away, but Santa just refuses to bring me that for Christmas. I suppose you wouldn't be willing to drop off the face of the earth?"

"Did you call just to annoy me or is there possibly some point you're going to reach before I grow much older?"

"It's been a long time. I thought maybe you might like to reminisce. But since you insist, I will get right to it. This is a warning. You only get one. Keep away from Dr. Carter and her research and there won't be a repeat of my warning. You have five minutes before the bomb explodes. Remember, brother, there doesn't need to be a second one..."

Fane didn't hear the rest. He ran out of his office yelling for his people to follow. As soon as the word "bomb" was out of his mouth, everyone moved. Papers flew and chairs were upset. The word bomb in New York got immediate results.

He and his employees were in the street when it went off. He stood and watched as his office became an orange-red ball of flame. Then the shock and sound surrounded them leaving their ears ringing and the surrounding street littered with parts of his office. There was nothing left. He looked down and saw pieces of some of the treasures of his artifact collection. He shook with anger. The waste, the loss of such priceless works of art and mastery, his collection. His collection was gone. It was senseless destruction of a lifetime of acquisitions, of an incredible fortune invested, the one thing in the world Lazarus held truly dear. Lazarus Fane did something he hadn't done in recent memory, he wept.

* * *

Eldon James Fane knew what he had done when he had the bomb planted. His brother had retained the same offices for many years and had made the name Fane infamous the world over. More than Eldon's past ever had, particularly with organizations like

Interpol. The problem was, when it came to Lazarus, there was never any proof. He'd become a name implied but never connected.

The war had started now. Lazarus would stop at nothing to get to him. He knew full well what he had done, what he had started. There was no turning back. He had a small window of opportunity. His brother would be in disarray briefly. He had to move now. He called in Hand.

Jason Hand came promptly. Eldon knew he would, he was loyal to a fault. There was nothing he wouldn't do for his boss which was what Eldon was counting on. Hand wasn't going to like his new orders.

"I need you to personally find Isabella Carter and bring her to me with the crystals," ordered Eldon. "It's time she and I talked in person. If we lose any more time, she will have solved the secret and then there will be nothing we can do to stop the progression that will follow."

"That will leave you unprotected. I can't leave now. After tonight you're going to need me," came the protest Eldon had expected.

"We have some time. Lazarus will go to the warehouse in Michigan now. This will force the move. Have the warehouse wired before he can get there. Once it's tied in here, Lazarus surprising me will be a feat indeed. I need you worse on this assignment. I need someone I can trust to not only carry it out, but won't stop until it's done right. We've bought some time while Lazarus recovers his organization, but Cicero Smith is still a problem. I have men getting ready for him. I really need you on this. It'll get you out of the office. Look at it as 'field work.'"

Hand nodded "I respectfully disagree, but I'll do my best. I'll check credit cards first."

"She won't be using her real name. Look for something with an association to Jim Harrison. She has a passion for him and I think any aliases will reflect some Harrison reference. I'm sure she is going somewhere where she can be undisturbed while she puts all of this together. Normally I would expect her to go back to her home on Whitefish Bay in Michigan, but that's too predictable. My brother and I have put her between the proverbial rock and a hard place. If she holds true to her past history, if Dr. Carter regroups she won't be on the defensive. Remember, she shot the man I'd hired in Alexandria to shoot McKenzie."

He slid a file across his desk. "I suggest you read this, Jason. It's the Carter file. You might be surprised."

He picked it up. "Alright, I'll get right on it. I'll contact you the second I have something."

Eldon smiled, "I knew you would."

Jason left leaving Eldon alone. He paced. It would all be in the timing. If he was even a little off, he would fail and failure wasn't an option. The unpredictability of Carter was the problem. She was an unknown variable. The more he'd learned about her, the more he realized she was a human anomaly. Most people follow the path of least resistance. Carter didn't follow paths, she made them and then knew how to cover them up. She had two flaws, Jim Harrison and she was a good person. Because she was good, she could be threatened, even forced to relent with the right leverage.

* * *

The cabs stopped at Union Station in New Jersey, not far from the bridge to Manhattan. They all piled out quickly. "I think we lost our tail," McKenzie said before anyone else spoke. He continued to look around scanning the moving traffic nearby.

"We're going to have to get to the train as quick as we can. I already have our tickets waiting," said Isabella. She led them into the terminal and she went straight for the ticket window.

"Can I help you?" The clerk at the window was young, but courteous.

"Yes, seven tickets reserved for Dalva Wolf."

"Right here," he said. "Prepaid. All set," and handed them to her back through the window. "Train leaves in ten minutes."

She thanked him and went back to the group. Everyone was there...except Alicia. "Where is Alicia?" she asked, a frantic tone had entered her voice.

Sandra spoke up, "She was just with me. I don't know what happened?" The rest looked around. The crowd milled but there was no sign of Alicia.

McKenzie had already left. The first place he looked was the restroom. She wasn't there though the yells of two indisposed women made his search brief. Then he spied Alicia's feet poking out from under a phone stand. The old relic was still in operation. He snuck up on her as she spoke into the phone. "What do you mean you can't connect me. Mr. Lazarus Fane, Fane Imports. I insist you put me through." McKenzie's finger on the disconnect tongue startled her. Her eyes grew wide as the realization came over her that he'd heard.

"Did you really think we wouldn't notice your absence? You do realize that this means you'll probably not pass the class." McKenzie ushered her back into the terminal.

"It's about time, we only have a couple of minutes left," began Isabella, then she saw the look on McKenzie's face.

"It appears, Mr. Fane had someone working for him all the time. I caught her trying to make a call to him. Fortunately she didn't get through."

Shock, then anger crossed Isabella's face. "Why would you do that to me? Your classmates?"

"It was easy," she answered, a self-assured look on her face. "Money. Fane offered me a lifestyle, one I'd never be able to get any other way. All I had to do was play the good student and keep a watch on you. Easy job, easy money."

"Until now," said Isabella. "Let's go. The train's going to pull out."

"What about me?" cried Alicia

Isabella didn't answer but McKenzie did. "Call Fane. Ask him."

The rest boarded the train leaving the traitor standing in the station. They found seats facing each other and sat close as a group. McKenzie spoke to Isabella, "I guess it was a good thing keeping everybody in the dark about where we were going. You're smart Doc, I'll give you that. This whole thing would be a bust right now."

"Well it does explain why she had the lowest grade in the class. It was all that texting, she was reporting to him all the time, right in front of us. How could I have been so blind."

"It happens. Sometimes we overlook what's right in front of us. Hey Doc, I gotta ask you, what's with all of the Harrison stuff?"

"My father gave me Harrison's writing just before he died in the crash. I devoured them, I loved them. Some of his stories like *Sundog, Woman Lit by Fireflys, Legends of the Fall, Dalva*, all inspired me to reach out, be myself, stand up and follow my soul. His stories that included Native Americans made me want to study Archaeology. It also didn't hurt that it ran in our family. But, when my parents were killed, the books my father gave me became more than just stories. They were a part of him too, one of the only parts of him I had left. It's strange that a writer so obsessed with death gives me comfort over their death." She turned and looked out the window.

They felt the train move and they were on their way. Where? No one knew except Isabella, but the train was heading south. They'd made it out of New York in one piece. They had the crystals and they were one less informant. All in all, they'd done alright.

⸗ 8 ⸗

The two men Cicero Smith had ordered from Fane showed up at dusk. They carried with them the news of the bombing. Smith was silent for a moment and then spoke. "Then that makes what we're going to do tonight that much more important. The boss is going to want results. If we don't get them we better be packing for a horizontal vacation six-feet under. He won't take it well."

The newcomers nodded, understanding full well the import of failure. From here on out lives were on the line, theirs. They went inside the building where the New York Message Service was located. A short elevator ride later and they were outside the door. The after business hours hall was empty and quiet.

All three men pulled out linen gloves. Cicero picked the lock with the ease of a professional. In seconds they were in. He ordered one of the men to listen and watch at the door in case security decided to pay a visit. He looked around.

The inside of the office was small, but efficient. He went straight into the dispatch office. There were several sets of file cabinets. He opened one and instructed the other man to dig into the other. "We're looking for anything that remotely references the name Eldon James or Mr. Fane. We have to locate some clue to James' whereabouts. Show me everything, No clue is too small."

The man next to him grunted and nodded his comprehension.

They began their search. File after file was searched. They were coming up blank. It was frustrating Smith. There had to be a record somewhere of the messages being sent to Third Avenue. He moved away from the files and looked at the dispatcher's desk. There was a computer monitor sitting there. He moved the mouse. The screen popped on. What luck, they hadn't shut it down. He was in. No passwords. He couldn't believe his luck.

He sat in the dispatcher's chair and put in Eldon James' name for a file search. The hourglass icon appeared for a few seconds and then it stopped. "One File Found" appeared on the screen. Harrison clicked on it. A list of messages that had been dispatched came up, the last of which was an order for men to watch the airports and Grand Central Station for Dr. Carter. At least he was on the right track.

He found a charge for the message and clicked on it. The billing account came up. Bingo. There wasn't an address, but there was a card number it was charged through. Usually they were encrypted, but whoever the dispatcher was had kept the full number on record. Again, he couldn't believe his luck. It wasn't much, but it could be traced. There were ways to get all card activity, amounts spent, where, when. This was something.

"Boss," the man behind him spoke. I think I have something. It was a file marked "E. James." He handed it to Smith who opened it and perused its contents. Mostly it was hand written copies of messages to be delivered to various individuals. They were dated from a few years back, apparently before they kept everything in computer records. There were no addresses, no clues… except that they were all signed by the same man, a Jason Hand. Cicero looked up from the paperwork.

He went back to the computer and typed the name Jason Hand into the account search. It came up. Again there was a credit card number, fully displayed and an address! If Hand was connected to Eldon James somehow, this could be the break they were looking for. Now they had two clues to follow. The break-in had been worth it. He took the file and shoved it in his coat. He went back to the computer and made sure that it was back on the screen where he had found it.

He got up and told the men to get set to leave. The man at the door opened it a crack. The hall was empty. So far, so good. The three exited and the door latched behind them. They beat it to the elevator and then out into the lobby below. As they walked past the security guard he spoke. "Have a nice night."

Cicero muttered, "You too," and they kept on going out the door.

Once on the street, Smith pulled out his cell and made a call. "I think we've got something." The voice on the other end was sharp, impatient. Smith had rarely heard this before from Fane, but when he had, Hell had followed close behind.

He hailed a cab and he got in. He dismissed the other two men. They weren't needed any more. He went to the place Fane had told him they were meeting. It was the offices they had used back in the "old days," before they had taken the business up town. This was down along the waterfront, an old warehouse. They were back to their roots. It took him back to the days when they were more violent, taking what they wanted and leaving behind a bloody trail. Back then, they were tomb robbers, thieves of the worst ilk. Smith missed those days. He liked being ruthless. He enjoyed hearing the protests of a doomed man. He reveled in seeing them beg for their lives. Now, that was a good time.

He went into the old steel and brick building. Lazarus Fane was orchestrating his men in an effort to get their operations up and running. He was yelling and there was a deep seething anger in his voice. Smith had been with Fane since the beginning. He knew every facet of the man. Cicero had watched him grow quieter, more relaxed the past few years. Eldon had awakened something in Fane that Smith hadn't seen in a long time. He liked it. He welcomed it.

"Mr. Fane," he said. Smith walked over to him. Fanes eyes were icy, his lips drawn tight, his scar had gone white. "We need to do some traces, but I think what I have here should produce some results."

Lazarus spoke through clenched teeth. "I knew you'd bring me something. I've always been able to count on you to do whatever needs to be done. That's why you're going to be taking the lead on this. When I give orders, I want you to handle them. I don't want any mistakes. You don't make mistakes. That's why you're getting the job. I grew lax over the last few years. That won't be happening anymore. First and foremost, I want Eldon dead! I want his body dragged through the streets, I want every bone in his body broken," Fane's rage had sent his voice echoing through the building. "I want parts of his body shoved down his throat while he is still alive enough to choke on them."

This was the old Lazarus Fane, the one Smith had grown to admire over the years. "And," Fane continued, "I want Carter found. I want her and those crystals brought to me. That bitch crossed me and she's going to wish she hadn't. She'll see everyone around her die before she does. Then, it's her turn. I made another mistake bringing her in on this, thinking I could get her to do the research I needed. I should have known the only way to get her to cooperate would be with a gun to her head. Even that is arguable. I don't care how you go about it. Use any methods you decide to employ. Just get my crystals and the research back here. You will be compensated appropriately."

Cicero smiled. He would have done Carter for free. He still owed her for his broken face and a shattered knee. That had been years ago, but he had never forgotten the rock she'd grabbed smashing into the side of his face, the force of her kick sending his knee in a direction it was never meant to go. Yes, he would enjoy this. Carter was a walking dead woman now. Some payback was going to feel good.

"What about resources? Hunting either one of these two down isn't going to be easy. We're going to need access to confidential information. Lots of it," asked Smith.

"Anything you want, just ask. You'll have it," confirmed Fane.

"Well, first we need access to credit records. I've found two card numbers. One I believe belongs to Eldon and another one that I think is a close associate of his named Jason Hand. We need histories, billing addresses even if they belong to accountants. I think we can squeeze them easier than his closer associates. And we need to be able to track current purchases. It'll be easier to get on their tail. Those need to be our priorities from this information I just obtained." He handed Fane the folder he'd brought from the messenger office. "You'll notice that each of these slips is signed by a Jason Hand. Now I realize that these are a few years old, but even if he doesn't still work for him, he could be persuaded to part with what knowledge he does have. Also his name was listed in the service's current account records so odds are good, he isn't retired."

Fane spoke, "Do you have an address on him?"

Smith smiled. "Yes, one, his tracks aren't covered quite as expertly as Eldon's. If we begin searches for Mr. Hand, we might turn up quite a bit. I think we can come in through Eldon's back door."

"It's certainly worth looking into," said Fane. "You've done well. It's good to see you haven't lost your touch."

"My aim's still good too."

Fane smiled at the remark.

Cicero's report had calmed Fane down somewhat. "Good," thought Smith. They all needed clarity now. Clear thinking, good planning was the only thing that was going to salvage all of this. Things were going to get much worse before they came to an end and they would need clear heads. There were two fronts here, both led by extremely clever people. Smith wasn't about to underestimate either of them.

He didn't dare. Fane had put him in charge and now he had to get results. This was how he liked it, an "any means necessary" order.

"I'm going to need about four men. I want to check that address I found for Hand," said Smith. "If he's there I want to make sure we have enough man-power to make sure we get him. Also, he might not be alone. I'm sure all of Eldon's people have to be on alert, waiting for us to make a move. They may all be travelling with escorts or bodyguards."

"No problem, take who you need. We don't want any mistakes. Make sure they are well armed. You know Smith, this could even be a trap. That information could have been planted just so we'd walk into it."

"Yes Mr. Fane. I am aware of it, but it's what we have. Also if we wait trying to decide whether we can trust the information, they could be gone and we lose what we could have gained."

Fane nodded. Smith was right, but he knew Smith would be cautious. If anyone could smell a trap, it was Cicero. "Stay in touch. I want updates on everything," said Fane. "We will re-headquarter in Michigan. There's still equipment there. The property holding is buried so finding us there won't be easy. Call, after the raid. We should be set up so that we can track those card numbers."

Smith nodded and went to round up the men he wanted for the raid on Hand's address. Smith planned to go in hard. Whoever was there wouldn't get a chance to do anything about it. Fast and hard, that was the way to do it. It was late, it was dark, it was perfect.

Lazarus Fane would wrap things up here and head back to Michigan.

* * *

Jason Hand didn't like leaving his boss at a crucial and risky moment like this. It was his job to protect him and he took it seriously. Most of his adult life had been spent in the employ of Eldon James. He didn't know anything else. If something happened because he wasn't there, he wouldn't forgive himself. He'd never disobeyed orders and he wasn't going to start now, but he didn't have to like it.

He went to his office. He needed to begin an electronic search. It wasn't going to be easy and he'd need a lot of people working on it. He'd need special people working on it. He made a call on his computer. It was across the internet and it was coded.

Samurai's Ghost picked up the call. "Go to code IM." Samurai's Ghost was a hacker of the highest ability. Hand and Eldon had used him on several occasions and they made sure the pay was excellent. "I have a tough one for you," messaged Hand.

"If it wasn't you wouldn't have contacted me. What's the job," Samurai sent back.

"I'm looking for electronic transactions under a name that would have some relationship to the author Jim Harrison."

"Is that all?"

"For now."

"I'll get my group on it right away. I'll IM as soon as we have something. Should only be a few hours."

Jason signed off. The Ghost would find something. He always did. He liked problems. There was no information that he or his digital geniuses couldn't access. Now there was nothing else to do but wait.

As soon as the information came through he'd have to leave. He'd make a fast trip to his house, get some things packed. He'd need the helicopter for that. He made a call to the pilot. "Pete here." A voice on the other end. "Pete" was Peter Bradley, an ex Marine that Jason had served with in Iraq. He had saved Jason's life, back there in Iraq. Jason was trapped and Pete had flown through heavy fire to get to Jason and get him out. The bullets had been flying and Pete had ignored them. He did the same thing on the way out. No one was to be left behind and Pete took those sentiments to heart. When they got back home and were discharged, Jason had put Pete's name in for the job of pilot for Eldon James' private helicopter. It paid well and Pete had always been appreciative and dependable.

"Pete, get her warmed up. I'm in a hurry." Jason told him.

Twenty minutes later and he was at the Manhattan Heliport. Pete was waiting to takeoff as quick as Jason could get inside and buckled in. They took off and flew out over the water.

He was on the way to his Long Island house. The sound of the helicopter blades was hypnotic and he realized how much the events of the last few days had tired him. It was going to be a long time before he would be able to rest too.

Below him was his estate. Working for Eldon James over the years had provided him with a well above average lifestyle. Someday he might even get the chance to actually spend some time here. The rigors of his job demanded most of his time. When he got lucky, he was able to spend a night or two within the red brick walls. He signaled for Pete to put them down.

The helicopter settled down in the open yard behind the house. Outdoor lights illuminated it. He jumped out and ran to the house ducking the rotor blades. The Pete kept the motor running. Jason dashed inside and went straight to his bedroom and hastily threw some clothes in a carrying bag. He went to a safe in his wall and grabbed some cash in case he might need to get information while he followed Carter's trail. He then grabbed a pair of automatic pistols that were housed in a dual shoulder holster at the back of the safe. He pulled them out and checked them. The clips were full. He put them on under his coat and then grabbed his bag, slung it over his shoulder and headed back to the chopper.

As he was leaving the house, he saw movement across the lawn at the perimeter of the light. "Damn," he spit. He knew that Fane's people had somehow found his house and they were moving in. He heard a shout, but he couldn't make out the words over the sound of the helicopter. He crossed his lawn in record speed. There were a couple of cracks and Jason knew he was under fire. He ducked as low as he could get and still carry the bag. Another crack and he saw Pete jump. He'd been hit.

Jason leaped into the passenger side and told Pete to go, even before he'd belted himself in. The pilot grimaced, the bullet had struck him in the side, but the craft began taking off in spite of his wound. Pete looked over at Jason who was looking at him intently. "Are you going to make it?" he yelled at Pete over the chopper blades. Pete grimaced nodding his head back at Jason.

As they rose Jason could see more men running onto the grounds of his home. He was angry. He shot at some of the men and then shot into two of his windows. It would trigger his alarm. Police wouldn't be long in arriving. He ordered the pilot to head back to Manhattan. The chopper flew with a slight wobble, barely missing the trees on the edge of Jason's property as it gained altitude. The wound was affecting Pete's flying.

He knew that they had to get back to New York quickly. Jason wasn't sure how badly wounded Pete was. If he should lose consciousness, Jason had no idea how to fly. Pete got them up and heading back to Manhattan, the men on the ground had fired a few random shots as they were leaving but it didn't appear that they had actually caused any damage to the craft itself.

He thought about the invasion of his home and property. There wasn't much information there that would lead them to Eldon James, but it appeared they knew enough about him to trace his house. How had they gotten it? Where had he slipped up? He'd always felt he was the one who was protecting his boss, but now, he seemed like the weak link in the chain. He was disappointed in himself more than anything. Now that his house was compromised he didn't dare go back there. Fane's men would be watching it now, watching for him. What else did they know? When he got back he'd have to tell Mr. James. Eldon James would be in danger.

Jason kept a close watch on Pete as they came into the city. They really didn't dare go out of control here. Buildings, cars, they probably wouldn't survive a crash. He began to breathe easier as the Heliport that was their destination loomed ahead. Pete was bringing the chopper down. Jason could see the perspiration that had soaked Pete's face. He was barely holding it together. It was then he saw the fluid slowly moving across the floor of the cockpit. It was blood, a lot of it.

They touched down with a jolt. Pete turned off the motor. It was the last thing he would ever do. Jason jumped out and went around to help him out. He unfastened his seatbelt. Pete fell out unconscious. Jason caught him as he fell and got him on the ground. The blades of the helicopter slowed as the engine died. Jason ran into the building to get help. When he returned, Pete was dead. His last act had been to make sure Jason had made it safely back. Just like he had before.

Jason clenched his fists. This was so senseless. Pete had had nothing to do with any of this. He wasn't involved and now he was dead. His friend, his comrade was dead and it was Fane's fault.

He had to pull it together. There'd be questions if they didn't get the body and the chopper secured. There'd be questions aimed at Eldon James. Everything they'd worked for would unravel.

He pulled out his cell phone and called directly to Eldon James. It was late but he knew his boss, he'd be there at his office, brooding, planning. They'd have to get the body out and all ties to him destroyed. It would have to be tonight. It would have to be now.

As he thought, Eldon answered and Jason began telling him of the evening attack. "I'm sorry to bother you so late sir, but we have a big problem." He told his boss as quickly and succinctly as he could about the raid on the house and the death of Pete at the heliport. Eldon spoke," Don't worry, this can work to our advantage. I have an idea. I want you to call the police."

* * *

Alicia Case made her way back to Manhattan. Now that her deception had been discovered by Isabella Carter, she would need a new assignment. She had a cab take her back to Mr. Fane's office. It wasn't there. She stood, shocked, as she looked at the shattered shell of a building that was the result of Eldon's explosion. It was gone, all gone.

She asked her cab driver to wait for her and went to a pay phone on the corner. She tried the number that she'd had no answer from before. It rang. Then there was an answer. Relief filled her. Alicia had been about to panic. She was told where Lazarus Fane had moved the office. It was down on the waterfront. She hated that part of town, but once she was at her destination, she would be safe.

When she was back in the cab she gave the driver the address. "Are you sure?" was all he responded. She confirmed it and he pulled away. Twenty minutes later they were in the dark warehouse district that made up the New York waterfront. The cab pulled up in front of the address she'd given him.

Alicia could see the lights on inside the building. She paid the driver and went to the door. She was immediately let in. "I'm here to see Mr. Fane," she announced.

One of the men at the door looked her up and down, grunted and then nodded and escorted her to Lazarus Fane. Her appearance before Lazarus was quite a surprise, one he didn't need as he tried to get out of the city and re-setup elsewhere, but quickly he smiled and said, "Miss Case, what are you doing here? I thought you were with your classmates. At least I believe that's what I'm paying your for."

He was very cordial and put his hand on her shoulder leading her to his hastily created, makeshift office. "Please, have a seat, can I have someone get you something?"

"I've had a long day and a long ride here. I could really use a bite to eat and something to drink," she answered.

Lazarus called one of his men and requested that they get Miss Case a bite to eat and a soda. Then he turned back to her. "So what brings you here? I believe you were doing a job for me."

"I need a different one," she began.

"Oh?" Fane asked. "How so? I thought the one you had was perfectly good."

"It was. Dr. Carter confiscated our cell phones so I couldn't stay in touch. That's why the last time I sent a text it was cut off. She decided we were leaving the university and we were going right then. No contact."

"Go on," Fane urged, still forcing a smile.

"She had us all pile into two cabs and we were on our way to somewhere. She wouldn't tell us where we were going," she said.

There was a knock at the door. One of Fane's men brought in a bag with a chicken sandwich, fries and a cola. Alicia thanked him for getting it and began eating while she was talking. "I didn't know it, but we were on our way to a train station in New Jersey. I think someone was trying to follow us, because the Professor gave the driver 100 dollars and we sped up and raced to the station. When we got there I tried to call you from a payphone to report in but I was caught by this guy named McKenzie that was travelling with us. He told Dr. Carter and they left me behind. I'm sorry Mr. Fane, but it looks like you'll have to put me somewhere else."

Fane smiled, put her somewhere else. Yes, that was it. "Did you find out where they were going?"

Alicia shook her head as she sucked on her soda with the straw.

Fane called one of his men back in. "Well, that's too bad," he said to her and then he turned to the man. "We don't need her anymore. Tie her up, throw her in one of the empty rooms in back. We'll kill her later. If we can buy her loyalty, so can someone else."

The man grabbed the stunned Alicia. The soda and half-eaten sandwich landed on the floor. The struggling girl was dragged away as Lazarus called for someone to come and clean up the spill. Smith would be back soon, he would enjoy this little chore.

≈ 9 ≈

Jason was puzzled, but did what his boss asked and called the police. They weren't long in arriving. James had explained his plan to Jason and it made sense to him, he knew what to do and then disappeared back into his office. Jason escorted the police out to the helicopter.

A detective introduced himself to Jason, "I'm Lt. Murphy. What happened here?"

"We were attacked," began Jason. "My pilot had taken me to my house in Long Island. When we got there we were attacked by several heavily armed men. They shot my pilot and killed him, but he got me back here safely before he died. He was a hero. He saved my life."

"Where in Long Island did the shooting take place?" Murphy asked.

Jason gave him the address. Murphy handed it to one of his officers. "Check on this," he told him.

"I'm afraid to go back there," said Jason. "I have no idea why they would do this."

The officer returned. "It checks out Lieutenant. Long Island police report answering an alarm that went off at that address. Neighbors reported shots and there were bullet holes in the windows. There was definitely gunfire there."

The detective looked at Jason for a minute studying him. "Is there anything else you can tell me about this? Do you have any enemies? Anyone want you dead? Attacked by several men doesn't sound like a random burglary. It seems fairly well organized to me."

Jason looked thoughtful for a moment. "Well Lieutenant, there is one person who has approached me, trying to get me to give up some of our corporate secrets. I refused even though he was offering a lot of money. I don't need money and I'm loyal to my company. It takes good care of me. I thought that was the end of it. You don't think they're connected do you?"

Murphy scratched his head. "Well we have to investigate every possibility. You don't recall the man's name do you?"

"Let's see," said Jason. "I think it was, um, Smith, a Cicero Smith."

"He gave you his name? Isn't that a bit odd?"

"Well I was going to have to contact him if I took the deal. Besides, he said he was working for someone else. He was only a go-between."

"Well, we'll run a make on him, with a name like Smith, it was probably an alias anyway."

"Really officer, I thought when I told him "no" that was the end of it. I never dreamed they would resort to something like this."

Again the Lieutenant scratched his head. "They may not be connected, but it seems to be the only lead we have. Are you sure there isn't anything else?"

Jason shook his head and watched as they wheeled the body of Pete away. "He was a good man. I liked him. He had a family, you know. And he was a veteran, decorated in Iraq."

He watched the police leave and wrap up their investigation of the scene. After the heliport had emptied, he went back to the office and reported to Mr. James. "I believe it worked. It shouldn't be long and there will be a warrant out for Cicero Smith."

Eldon smiled, "That should add some extra heat onto him and Lazarus. With the police looking for him on the charge of murder, that should limit his usefulness considerably."

* * *

Cicero Smith watched as the helicopter rose from the yard of Jason Hand. He swore under his breath. They'd almost had him. A few minutes earlier and they would have had Hand for themselves. He saw the bullets hit the windows and knew the alarm would trigger. They only had a few minutes. He looked again at the chopper that was now clearing the trees. The tail swung and he saw the registration numbers. Quickly he memorized them. He still had a trail to follow.

Rapidly, he and several men searched Hand's house, but there was no time to do a good job of it. They turned up nothing, then there were the sirens in the distance. Time to go. He gathered his men together and they were gone as quickly as they had arrived. This kind of operation was nothing new to them and they were professionals.

There was a faked delivery truck on the street that they all piled into and were gone. Three minutes later they passed the police going the other way. "Good," he thought, "clean getaway." All he needed now was to run down those numbers and find where it had landed. To fly in Manhattan, it would have to have registered its origin and destinations.

They headed back to the waterfront and their temporary place of operations. Fane came right up to him. "What did you find? Did you get him?"

"Yes and no," Cicero answered. "He was there when we arrived, but there was a helicopter waiting for him. I have the chopper's numbers. We should be able to get the flight plan and I'd be willing to bet that its delivery point will be near where Eldon is located. I thought you were leaving?"

"Something unexpected came up." Fane almost mumbled.

Fane smiled. He knew the truth of it. They might have Eldon right where they wanted him. Across the room came a yell from one of Fane's computer operators. He had been packing their computer equipment when something came over his laptop. "Mr. Fane, you better see this."

Lazarus walked over to the man with Smith close behind. "What?" he yelled. Smith leaned over his shoulder and saw what had disturbed his boss. Cicero Smith was wanted for murder! It was right there in front of them, posted on the police website, a police photo and the warrant.

Fane whirled on him and demanded, "What is this all about?"

"I'm not sure, but Arnie must have got him."

"Arnie? What's an Arnie?" said Fane, thoroughly confused.

Smith pointed to one of the men that had been along on the raid. "Arnie. When we saw the chopper was going to take off a couple of the men opened fire. I saw the pilot slump. I didn't think we hit him because he flew away. It appears we may have."

"Appears?" yelled Fane. "Appears?"

"It had to be Eldon," said Cicero. "I didn't think they dared bring the cops in on this, but obviously they have. They must have done it without involving your brother sir."

"Of course they did it without involving my brother. The man whose house you attacked, this Jason Hand, must have reported this as a personal attack trying to explain away a body that had landed in their lap," said Fane. He began to calm down. "You're going to have to be scarce for a few days 'til this cools down and I have an idea how you can do that. We'll make sure the cops find nothing but dead ends.

Smith followed his boss to another part of the building, a quiet deserted part of the building. Smith felt like he'd let Fane down just as he was giving him the space to operate the way he wanted to. He'd botched this one, badly.

Fane opened the door to a small room. There was a young girl there, tied to a chair and gagged. It was Alicia Case. Fane turned to Smith, "This was our informant that was inside Dr. Carter's class."

"What happened?" asked Cicero.

"It seems she was found out, right as they were leaving a train station."

"A train station, where? We were watching Grand Central."

"Union Station," Fane let the words roll off his tongue. "I should have thought of that. It's what I would have done."

"Has she said where they were going?"

"Oh she's said a lot of things. She's been very cooperative thinking that we would let her go and give her a new assignment. Kids, they say the funniest things." The look in the girl's eyes was one of terror and desperation. She understood the position she was in." Unfortunately," continued Fane, "Carter never told anyone where they were going, including our little informant here. She does confirm that the good doctor does have the crystals with her however. This leaves you with two chores. One, get rid of her." Fane nodded towards the captive.

Smith smiled.

Alicia's eyes flashed and got wide as she realized she was living her last few minutes. Fane was wiping his hands making small audible smacks like he was brushing some invisible dirt off from them. "Two, you're going to go to Jersey to the train station and find out where they went. It also gets you across the state line so that things can cool down here over this murder charge. If you find their trail, follow it. Don't show up in Michigan without Carter or the crystals. If you do come back without Carter, it better be with the crystals and Carter dead!" Fane's voice rose at the end with his frustration. "Just to be clear, the latter is a perfectly acceptable solution.

"In the meantime," Fane went on, "we will find the records of the helicopter and find my brother. With this murder charge, I'm afraid you're going to have to be out of that. I'll oversee the operation personally. I owe him a long slow death and I want to be sure he gets it." A light came into Fane's eyes that frightened even Smith. He wouldn't want to be in Eldon James' shoes, though he had to admit, he would have liked to be there to watch. He hadn't had that much entertainment for a long time. Well, he'd have to make up for it with Carter. Pulling a trigger on her would be one of the easiest things he's ever done.

Fane turned to leave, "Get rid of her," was all he said as he went out the door. Smith went over to the chair and untied the rope that held her to it. There was another one that still bound her hands and her arms like the coils of a python. Another rope ran to her ankles like a hemp shackle restricting her movements. She tried screaming against the gag, but it died in the rag. She went limp hoping Smith wouldn't be able to carry her, but she was wrong.

The rope offered easy purchase to haul her out of the building into the darkness of a waterfront night. Here, there were no lights. No one would see her die. Smith dragged her to the end of the pier. The water was deep, reflecting the blackness of the night. The girl still struggled in a vain effort to defeat her bonds. Cicero dropped her and her gag came loose. As he reached down to replace it, she bit him. Out of reflex he hit her hard, muttering "Little bitch." It dazed her and he got the gag back on. Then, Smith threw her in the water. He watched as she sank in the watery blackness. The last thing he saw was her eyes filled with the fear of death, her attempts at screaming deadened by the gag as she was swallowed by the river. Smith walked back toward the building, smiling, rubbing the bite wound on his arm. He would have liked to toy with her a little longer, but he didn't have the time. He had work to do.

* * *

The train had crossed the North Carolina border heading south. Isabella watched everyone and everything. So did McKenzie, but it really did appear that they'd gotten out of New York without their destination being discovered. The students occupied their time with quiet conversations and time on their laptops. Jeff and Bob seemed to be in perpetual conversations about the crystals.

McKenzie sat across from Isabella. It was one of her more relaxed moments, she didn't have many. Mac decided to venture into unknown territory. "So Doc, what's between you and this Lazarus Fane? I figure I might as well know a little history. It's not like we don't have time right now."

She looked up. "That was a long time ago. It's not a pleasant memory to dredge up."

"It's a long train ride, we should talk about something. I could use a little enlightenment here." He pulled out a flask from inside his jacket. "Maybe this'll help."

She cocked her head. "Scotch?"

"Yup, is there anything else?"

Isabella nodded, "Many things, you should switch to rum, probably keep you in less trouble. No thanks, anyway."

"Look who's talking about trouble."

"Point taken."

"C'mon, what's up with all of this? What happened in Central America? Who is this Fane? What'd he do?"

She leaned back in the seat and let out a sigh. "It was 12 years ago. It was supposed to be one of those crowning moments in life. At first it was, but before it was over, it would be the biggest disaster of my life. In some sense I feel like I can never make up for it. Yet in many ways, it made me who I am, for better or for worse.

≈ 10 ≈

21 Years Ago, Central America

"When word of this gets out, things are going to get dangerous," commented Isabella to the native worker standing next to her. "Keep your eyes open for looters and robbers." Her companion nodded. The city was their heritage, it would be protected. This American woman had returned to them the home of their gods.

They stood on a high bluff overlooking the crowning achievement of her young career, the discovery of the lost Mayan city of Itchen Balam. Spread across the landscape below, exposed to the world for the first time in over 500 years, the light of the sun once again shines upon the great temples and palisades of the Mayan Gods.

It had taken weeks to clear away the jungle growth, expose the ancient stones of the temple and begin to reveal the streets of the once great metropolis. Isabella's fingers tightened on her ever present machete.

She descended the hill down to where the workers were doing surveys and attempting to recreate a picture of what the city looked like so long ago. The jungle sun beat down on the workers making the heat oppressive.

"Bella," shouted Tom her assistant. His blonde hair ruffled by the tropical wind, blue eyes and ever grinning face seemed excited about something. She walked over to him, quizzical look on her face.

"Our initial surveys show that this could have been the largest of all of the Mayan Cities. It may also be the oldest."

"What brings you to that conclusion?"

"Weathering on the scoring of the stonework. Bella," he looked at her hard and serious, "I'm guessing as old as 5,000."

"That's impossible. We won't be publishing that conclusion until it's been verified. But keep at it." She smiled, "If you're right, it changes everything."

She had learned a long time ago to trust Tom's instincts. They'd been students and then colleagues, together since college and he was a prodigy in the field. There was no one more qualified, she could have had working on this project with her. The two had been a team and accompanied each other on every dig. If this was any one else's discovery, it was his. He'd worked hard and long to help prove her conclusion of the location for Itchen Balam.

She walked past the other workers and climbed the one temple that they had been able to clear the jungle completely away from. Climbing the steps always felt so good. There was an ease and comfort to it. She felt at home.

She reached the top, inside the alcove where the priests and priestesses performed the rituals and ceremonies to the gods. An altar of red stone was there where the countless sacrifices had taken place. Here above the jungle she could see for miles. There were tree covered mounds and hillocks that she was certain covered the rest of the city. Yes, this place was old, maybe older than all the rest of the Mayan cities. She could feel that it was different than the other Mayan cities she'd been in. Maybe it was because she felt like it was hers, after all she'd discovered it.

She began to descend the far side. Away from the workers, where the jungle still tried to encroach. The trees and vines still were thick at the bottom on this side. It was where she would eat her lunch. She liked the feeling of protection she got from the thickness and isolation. Besides there were some carvings she wanted to look at closer, heads of the feathered serpent Kukulcan, the Mayan God of Gods.

As she reached the bottom, something flashed in the jungle. There was movement and then it was gone. Her hand went to her machete. She held the handle tight. There was dangerous wildlife all around. Letting down your guard could get you killed. Her eyes scoured the thick foliage, but nothing more moved.

It didn't take her long to find the carvings after she reached the bottom of the stair. They were off to the right and still partially vine covered. The ground was rough with broken stones and difficult to walk on. These sculptures seemed odd to her because they were only on one side of the stair. Usually, Mayans would adorn each side of the stair identically instead of being side-by side, only a few feet separating them.

The faces of Kukulcan were well preserved and had borne the weather and jungle well. She could make out all of the details of the sculpture. The great gods faced the jungle they had watched grow around them for hundreds of years. The stone carvings seemed as eternal as the gods they depicted.

She took off her knapsack and hung it over the lower jaw of one of the sculptures and took out her water bottle. She smiled and said "No offense great god, but if you could please hold my knapsack for a moment." The jaw moved and the pack dropped to the ground. She backed up, eyes wide with astonishment! The water slipped from her hand. Between the sculptures, stone was grating. A hidden doorway was opening up. Isabella looked at the doorway, looked at the stone head and then reached for her pack and took out a flashlight.

She waited a few minutes marveling over her accidental discovery before entering letting fresh clean air replace the old and bad that had been inside the secret chamber. Then she cautiously entered. Inside there was a long hallway.

She gasped as the light hit it. The walls were lined from top to bottom with human skulls. There were hundreds of them, mud plastered one on top of the other, forever standing vigil over the entrance of the chamber. It was a frightful sight, this passage of skulls, yet her curiosity drove her on.

Proceeding at a slightly downward angle the hallway ran until she was about what she guessed would be the heart of the pyramid. She would get measurements later to confirm it. In front of her was a huge room. The walls were lined with carvings, etched into the stone, that she concluded told tales of gods and past histories. Great carvings of statues stood in relief in the walls. The room was stark and beautiful. It stirred something in her. There was an altar in the center of the room and she could see how the stone was worn at its front by the thousands of priests and priestesses that had worshipped at it over the centuries. This chamber was dedicated to the gods. It was a place where secret ceremonies and rituals had been held away from the sight of the common Mayan. It had been a place of great power...and it seemed familiar.

A sense of Deju Vu was nagging at her. She searched her brain to remember if she had read of anything like it before. She came up blank. As far as she knew, nothing like it had ever been discovered. She shook it off and started exploring the Mayan carvings and statues. They were perfectly preserved and contained rare detail. She became convinced that she had been the first to enter since the Mayan clergy itself so many centuries before.

The great statues watched her as the skulls had in the hallway. One could almost imagine some life into them. She thought about what those stone eyes might have witnessed over the years and in the back of her mind, she had some idea.

The priests and priestesses proceeding in, the room lit by torches. The head of the priesthood, all decorated in his finest ceremonial garb standing before the altar, shouting entreaties to the gods, working himself into a fever pitch hoping to invoke the magic that would grant the city the favor and blessings of harvest and game. Some rituals maybe even communicated with some of the gods themselves. The great Mayan shamans, whose magic that was supposed to have been so powerful, invoking the jaguar and the serpent. She could almost see them there through the mists of time.

She walked up to the altar and stood overlooking the chamber. Before her would have been the supplicants, awed by the power of those men that spoke with gods. She shifted her foot and her toe kicked something. A stone plate fell away from the back of the altar. She shined her light seeing a small alcove revealed. Isabella bent down to look. Inside was another skull, but this one was made of quartz!

She set the light down and picked it up. It seemed to glow with a light of its own. As she looked into the skull's eyes, she seemed to hear something: "Welcome home priestess."

* * *

Four thousand miles away, Lazarus Fane sat in his office reading a newpaper. A particular article had grabbed his attention and it wasn't letting go. It read:

"A previously unknown Mayan city was discovered last week by University of Michigan post graduate, Isabella Carter. Her historic discovery is the culmination of years of cooperative research by her, University of Michigan, New York University, and the Museum of Natural History. It is still too early to tell what discoveries and cultural information will be revealed in the excavation of the lost city named Itchen Balam, but speculation is that it should be considerable and will probably shed new light on the Mayan culture.

Isabella Carter is also notable for being the great- great-grand niece of the famed Howard Carter who in 1907 discovered the undisturbed tomb of Tutankhaman, the richest find in all of Egypt. Her parents were John and Annabelle Carter, renowned antiquities and relic experts. They disappeared in a plane crash in Central America seven years ago."

Fane leaned forward and paged his secretary. "Get Cicero Smith in here right away." There were never any formalities with Fane. He expected everything to be done right now. That's what he paid people for. He stood up and paced his elaborate office. The walls and shelves were decorated with archaeological discoveries from around the world. Dozens of lost cultures were represented: Greeks, Romans, Incas, Mayans, Chinese, Sumerian, Egyptian.

Fane adored his collection.. Why should they go to a museum when they could belong to him? What he didn't want he sold on the black market to other private collectors. He'd made a fortune looting tombs and temples, desecrating holy shrines, and stealing relics from the hands of museums. This was his passion, his blood, his life. Fane was the worst kind of collector, he was obsessed.

He looked up when Cicero Smith came through the door. He walked over to the desk and showed Smith the newspaper article. "Pay off the right people. Get me this site."

Smith nodded. "I'll take care of it, sir." This would mean a big bonus for him. He'd worked for Fane for years and he'd seen him like this before. He would be satisfied with nothing less than success. Failure would mean the end of his career.... And very probably, his life!

* * *

Isabella sat looking at her find in her tent. It was late and her workers were bedded down for the night. She had told no one about the crystal skull. Its beauty captivated and fascinated her. It seemed to glow with an inner light she couldn't explain, like there was almost a life in there. It felt warm to the touch and she was compelled to look into its eyes.

Over the years, several of these skulls had been found in Central America and there was much speculation to their origins and purpose, all of it ending in mystery and inconclusion, legend and stories, whispers of strange occurances surrounding them. She put it back in her knapsack and settled down into her bed. She thought of the Mitchell – Hedges skull that currently resided in Canada.

It wasn't long and she was asleep. A dream came to her that was vivid and real, a rare one that she would always remember. She was traveling through the jungle, barefoot as she could feel the earth under her feet. She followed a long worn path, yet it seems like the undergrowth was closing in as if it hadn't been traveled in a long time. Ahead she saw light flickering so she continued onward, the path leading directly to the light. She entered a clearing and behind it was the temple she'd discovered. In the center of the clearing was a fire and she could see figures around it dressed in the very elaborate, colorfully feathered, ornate Mayan clothing and headdresses. She walked towards the fire and saw that they were all watching her, no, waiting for her.

Somehow she knew these were the ancient gods of the Maya: Yum Cimil, Kinich Ahua, Yum Kaax, Nacon, Tzultacaj, Ix Chel. They all stood waiting for her. Their faces were human, but their heads were decorated to represent the figures that had become so prominent in the sculpture of the ancient Mayan cities. They smiled and looked at her and pointed to the temple stairs. She gave them a bow as she walked past to ascend the stairs.

The stairs were cool and smooth to her feet. She climbed them with ease as if she'd done it a thousand times before. Ahead of her she saw something at the top. It was another figure. It waited patiently as she climbed. When she reached the top, she knew who she stood before, Kukulcan, the god of all Mayan gods.

He appeared to her as a man, not the beast or creature of the carvings. His face was human, but his headdress was that of a serpent's head made out of jade and rubies. Ornate feathers laid down to the rear of the headdress forming the illusion of scales out of feathers. Fangs were painted on his face to further cast the image of a feathered serpent.

Before him suspended in air was her crystal skull. It hovered and glowed. Kukulcan spoke to her. "Long ago you were a great and powerful priestess, a loyal believer and servant of the gods. In exchange you were granted favor and grace. You belonged to the jungle and the jungle belonged to you. That mantle awaits you and our favor is once again yours."

He reached out and touched her and she felt strong and full of energy. Even in her dream she felt a bit dizzy and light. Kukulcan pointed to the crystal skull. "This is your gift. It was yours and he has been waiting for your return. He is your connection to me, to all of us." He turned and entered the room at the top of the temple. He opened a secret alcove next to the altar and pointed inside. "These were yours and they still await you. Long ago this city was your home, finding your way here was no accident." Inside she saw the ceremonial robes of the priestess. Next to it sat a beautiful ornate headdress with jade and shell jewelry. There were pots of paint that the Mayan clergy had used for their faces and body in their rituals.

Kukulcan turned to face her once again. "Welcome home priestess, but beware, danger comes to you on the wind."

Isabella woke up. It was dawn and her dream hung over her with a clarity unlike anything she'd ever had before. She remembered it all, in detail. None of it was lost as most dreams are upon waking. She sat there contemplating it when she heard a commotion outside her tent.

"Bella," Tom stuck his head inside of her tent. "You better come, it seems we have a visitor."

* * *

She stood and went outside. She could see the man crossing the clearing coming towards her. He was one of the local natives. He used a tall walking stick and was dressed in only a loincloth. He had the long nose and flat face of a true descendant of the Maya. His hair was straight, long and black, the feet were bare. Around his neck was a thick necklace made of beads and large seeds. As he approached, some of her workers kneeled as he passed, an obvious sign of importance in any culture. She smiled and went over to him.

Isabella had been rigorous about learning the language of the locals. It had been part of her preparation for coming here. Fortunately she had found the dialect reasonably easy to pick up on and articulate. When the old man spoke, she understood him.

"You had the dream last night," he said to her. "The gods of this place spoke to you." He waved his arm in an all-encompassing flourish.

She was surprised at this revelation but tried not to show it. "How did you know that?"

The native smiled, "They spoke to me as well. You must accompany me."

"I can't go anywhere right now. I have my work here. I have to get the crews started on their jobs," she countered.

"I can wait." The native sat on the ground and began waiting.

Isabella stood for a moment looking down at him in exasperation, then spun on her heel and began her morning routine.

It was nearly noon when she returned to him. The sun was high and the heat of the day was bearing down. The old native seemed not to notice. She stood over him and spoke, "I'm here. What do you need me for?"

"You must come with me. I am to be your guide."

A couple of Isabella's workers had wandered over. They were local natives she'd hired onto the project. One of them spoke, "You should go with him, Ms. Carter. He is a great man among our people. If he wishes you to go with him, he means to honor you, not harm you. He is a good man." He accented his statement with an inclination of his head towards the ever patient old man.

"How long will I be gone?" Isabella asked.

"That will be up to you," he smiled.

"Do you have a name?"

"It is Yetlkan. I will be your guide."

She went back to her tent and threw a few things into her pack. She left her "Gift" inside. Her next stop was to leave Tom in charge of the dig.

"You can't go off into the jungle with some strange native, alone," he protested.

"Just keep things moving here. I'll be fine. And yes, I do realize how this seems like a really bad idea. But, the people here have been really good to us. They could have gotten rid of us anytime they wanted and we wouldn't be able to do anything about it. I think we can show them a little trust. Besides, it's not them I'm worried about. This discovery is a prime target for looters. You keep your eyes open. I'll be back as soon as I can." With that she turned and walked back to the quietly waiting Yetlkan. He then led her into the jungle, the foliage closing around them.

Yetlkan moved through the jungle with a fluidness that came with a lifetime of its travel. He moved quickly and quietly, more agile than his age reflected. Isabella was pressed to keep up.

It wasn't long and they entered a village. Most of the natives were wrapped in bright cloths or nothing at all. Many looked up at her, a quiet interruption in an endless daily routine. He led her to one of the grass roofed huts, presumably his.

The notion was confirmed when they entered. He immediately bade her to sit on one of the thatch rugs on the floor of the room. She accepted. He placed himself across from her, a small pile of glowing coals were in a firepit between them.

Yetlkan stirred the coals and looked Isabella in the eyes. He studied her closely as Isabella's patience grew thin.

"Why have you brought me here?" She was becoming impatient.

"I was told to."

"By whom?"

"Those that were in your dream,"

"What do you know about my dreams?"

"I know that the gods of this jungle spoke to you. I know that you found the secret place that only one of the priesthood would know. I saw you that day when you found the sacred place. I know what you found there, what was waiting for you."

"Were you spying on me?" she said not disguising a certain amount of indignation.

"No, watching over you. I knew when you came, you were "she" returned," said Yetlkan. "You were once a priestess, a part of the inner sacred circle. You were Otomie."

Isabella was taken aback. She couldn't believe what she was hearing. "And how do you know this?" She tried to keep the irritation out of her voice. She didn't succeed.

"You must believe me. There are things I must show you, things you must learn," There was an urgency in his face. One that made Isabella realize that he was earnest in his belief. "I know what you carry in your pack. I am supposed to show you how to use it."

"You know what the skulls are?" she responded. He had her interest now. Even if he didn't know how to actually use the skull, she wasn't sure if they were meant for any actual use, but this would at least enlighten her to what the traditional belief was. She had an opportunity for some valuable insights. It was a rare opportunity.

She pressed, "Tell me about the skulls."

"I must show you," he pointed to her pack.

She reached in and pulled out the crystal skull. It shone inside the dusky hut even without the light. Isabella marveled again at its beauty, its glassy flawlessness. She carefully placed it in front of her on the rug she sat on.

The crystal's face gazed on Yetlmak. "You must look into it. When there is a need it will show you things. You must open yourself up, open your thoughts."

Isabella turned the skull towards her and looked into the pockets that were the eyes. She looked at the crystalline depths, there seemed to be an infinity in there, a space encased in pure clear quartz. It was a beautiful world unto itself.

Yetlmak began to speak in a low voice, trying not to disturb Isabella's gaze. "In your dream you saw the old gods. They spoke to you. Do you remember how the great god touched you, how you felt when he did."

"Yes," she spoke quietly. "He said this would be my way to speak to them, through this. He also said that 'I am the jungle and the jungle is me.' What did he mean by that?"

"The jungle is a place with many dangers, and yet the creatures that learn about the ways of the jungle, are wary of its dangers, become masters of it. They become a part of it and it no longer holds the dangers it once did. You must study it, watch it and then learn from it. You must understand it."

"And why must I learn it?" she asked.

"Because it will save your life. The life you have ahead of you, great priestess, is different than the one past. You will travel a different path, yet you will always carry your past with you. Do you remember what else you were told?"

"Yes, a great danger comes on the wind."

"Yes, can you see it, the danger? Can you see it in the skull? Can you see what comes?" he asked anxiously.

"No," said Isabella. The skull was definitely a bit hypnotic, but it was revealing nothing to her. As near as she could tell, it hadn't even said "Hi." It wasn't a good sign. She sat the skull down. Her head was beginning to swim.

Yetlkan stood up and went outside his hut quickly. Isabella could hear him speaking to some women of the tribe, but she was unable to make out what was being said.

He returned quickly and retook his position across from her. I'm having some food brought for us.

This appealed to Isabella. She'd skipped lunch. Some food would be welcome.

It wasn't long and there was a selection of fruits and meats brought in. It was accompanied by a jug of native local brew. She'd have to be careful with that. She'd heard stories about the tribal concoctions.

Yetlkan waved his hand motioning for her to start and she dug right in. As she would pick up a fruit or a piece of meat, he would explain what it was and what its uses were besides just food. Most of the fruit contained some medicinal property.

Isabella smiled, guess her doctors were right about it being good for you. Most of it was sweet and juicy. The meats turned out to be mostly fish, wild pig and reptiles. Isabella hesitated when it came to her first iguana. She gingerly tasted it, drawing her lips back as she did. It was good. A few sips of brew to wash it down and then everything was good, really good.

Suddenly the room seemed to slant. She reached for the rug trying to steady herself. Everything was beginning to move, shifting in different directions all at once. She looked across the firepit, Yetlkan was smiling.

"This will help," he said. "It will open up your sleeping mind. You need to let it flow freely."

His words were becoming more indistinct, harder to follow. Her eyes rolled as the walls of the hut flew around and then disappeared. The world around her seemed to warp and twist. Yetlkan watched her as she laid down on the mat, flat on her back, eyes wide and staring. Her jaw moved as if she were speaking, but no words came out.

Isabella drifted in a swirling darkness. The time seemed endless and unmoving. A limbo, then, in front of her was the pyramid of Itchen Balam. She was on the backside of it, near the offset heads of Kukulcan. Her hand reached out and she pulled down on the stone jaw that released the door to the sacred room. It opened and she began her walk down the corridor of skulls. The countless eye sockets stared, the jaws grinned, the white bone gleamed and shone white.

She felt unafraid, she'd been here before. She walked forward and entered the sacred room. It was as she had found it, empty and quiet, the stone altar standing, waiting. She walked towards it, ran her fingers over it. The cold stone send static shocks into her hands. Isabella smiled.

Her gaze was drawn to a place along the wall behind the altar. There was a flat surface between two carved figures. She cocked her head slightly as she looked the wall over intently. It seemed familiar to her, not just seen it before familiar, but intimate, countless times familiar. It shouldn't have been.

Isabella studied the statue on the right, third feather from the top, she pushed, the feather moved. Stone grated on stone. Dust and pebbles fell as the wall began to slide open. She stepped back and watched as a chamber revealed itself.

Into the opening she walked. The walls were honeycombed with large pockets, placed within each was a mask or headpiece. She knew instantly that these were the ceremonial adornments of the priests and priestesses of the long abandoned city. Jade, carnelian, rubies, emeralds, shone throughout the room. Once, brightly colored feathers, now were broken and faded from the ravages of time. The room was a marvel and a glimpse into a world long gone, a world she was supposed to have been a part of.

She turned and looked back out into the main room. They had worn these and gathered there. Distantly she thought she heard whispers, voices speaking in the Mayan language. Faintly she thought she saw them moving, raising their arms in supplication, beseeching the blessings of the gods. They prayed for the good and prosperity of the village. Much rested on the shoulders of the priesthood. Isabella could feel their concern, she felt as if she could touch their emotions, ride their fervor, bask in their ritual. She seemed to become a part of it, integrate with the vision and float into her body once again. It had been a journey that opened her mind and formed new paths of vision.

Yetlmak watched over her in his hut. She'd moved little, but her breathing was steady and even. In the distance, outside his hut, Yetlmak heard voices. They seemed excited, agitated. It distracted him from his vigil over Isabella. He looked away and when he turned back, Isabella had stood. She turned to the door of his hut and opened it.

Down the village path strode a Jaguar. It growled and tossed its head at any of the tribe that it felt might be too close. The great cat walked with kingly ease towards the hut. It saw Isabella standing there gazing at it, unfrightened by its bravado.

Isabella stepped down. The villagers watched as the cat approached her. They were certain that her death was soon to be witnessed. As the cat approached, Isabella crouched, nearly sitting on her heals. The Jaguar, sacred animal of the Mayans, stopped in front of Isabella. It let out a long, low growl and studied her intently, the cat's eyes looking deep into hers. Another growl and a toss of its head, it laid down.

Isabella remained still. The animal continued to stare, its tail twitching behind it. The villagers were astounded. They were witnessing a vision, a sign from their gods. Had the priestess indeed returned as Yetlmak had said? Were they witnessing a blessed return?

Suddenly the cat stood up and walked away. It returned to its journey through the village and then disappeared into the jungle. Isabella stood and returned to the hut, moving past Yetlmak who had witnessed it all from his doorway.

She returned to her position on the mat, remaining silent throughout. Yetlmak returned to his vigil, but he knew that it was all passed now. The vision had been powerful and strong, the village was witness. Their lost priestess would be one of the tribe, the resurrector of the past was among them, their city would be revealed and they would be whole again.

It was morning before she was able to hike back to the site. Her head felt a little fuzzy but it was quickly clearing. Along the way Yetlmak showed her things. Plants were pointed out and she was told their importance. At one point he reached down and snatched a snake expertly grabbing it behind the head. "This one will kill. One bite and seven heartbeats, death. See the yellow stripe next to the red, that's how you know. There are others that look like this one, none have the yellow next to red."

She learned much of what he said. It was part of her training, to take in oral cultural accounts and recall them for her notes later. But she was happy when the jungle opened into the familiar clearing of Itchen Balam.

Tom came running across towards her. "Glad you're back. It's a jungle out there."

She smiled, "Glad to be back. I need to hit my tent for a while."

Isabella turned and thanked Yetlmak. He smiled and then was gone into the jungle.

* * *

"Miss Carter, you better come quick." One of her workers poked his head inside the tent flap.

She got up and went outside. She could hear the sound of a helicopter in the distance. "I knew it wouldn't take long for trouble to show up." She muttered under her breath. She wasn't expecting supply drops for a week. This was an unscheduled landing and she didn't like it. There was something that wasn't right about it.

The chopper broke the treeline of the jungle and hovered over the clearing. The blades threw up dirt and dried leaves. The tents shivered from the artificial storm. As it settled to the ground the engine was cut and the wind subsided. Several men emerged including one that was dressed in a khaki suit and tan bush hat. He led the group and started walking right straight towards Isabella.

"Are you Isabella Carter?" He asked "My name is Lazarus Fane.

"I know who you are." Isabella replied distastefully. "Your reputation precedes you."

He reached into his coat and pulled out some documents which he handed to Isabella. "This site is now mine. I've been granted complete control by the Mexican and Yucatan Government. You'll find the paperwork in order."

Isabella was livid. She shook she was so angry. "You've got no right. This is my discovery and I've been guaranteed the opportunity to continue developing this site. I'm here in an official capacity for two Universities with the blessing of the local government. You'll just have to leave."

"Actually, I have the right and yours has been revoked," Fane responded coolly. "As I see it, you have three choices, you can join my team and continue on, but in my employ or you can gather together yourself and your team and leave, still alive, or I can simply shoot you all. As I see it there are plenty of options, none of them do I find displeasing"

"I'd never work for you. I know who you are Fane and what you do. Anything you found here would never see the light of day. Whatever you didn't want personally would disappear on the black market. You're the worst kind of looter, one that uses the guise of respectability, one with no ethics. And as far as killing us, you wouldn't dare. There would be too many questions. Too many people would come looking for us." She spat back at him, her face flushed with anger.

"I'm sorry to hear you won't be working for me, I could have used you. As far as killing you, it's amazing how many questions a few thousand dollars here and a few thousand dollars there will satisfy. It's just good business. It keeps the wheels of progress moving. You know, the jungle can be a ruthless place. Anything can happen, looters, wildlife, any number of accidents and mishaps can occur. You know, they rarely find the bodies down here."

Behind them Fane's men had been milling around the camp and the tents. Isabella's argument with Fane had distracted her for a few moments and one of Fane's men came running up. "Senor Fane, Senor Fane." He shouted.

Shock came over Isabella's face. He was carrying her knapsack. Fane turned and faced the man. He was obviously a lackey he'd hired after reaching the Yucatan. He handed the knapsack to Fane. Fane reached inside and drew out Isabella's crystal skull. A look of greed and passion crossed his face. An "Oh my," escaped his lips. His hands trembled as he held it. In the sunlight the beauty of it shone with a radiance that nearly blinded. Fane became mesmerized momentarily.

Isabella heard a noise behind her and realized that Cicero\][poi Smith had moved behind her standing between her and Fane. Now she knew trouble was going to begin. Fane looked up at her, his eyes wide and anxious. "W W W Where did you find this?" he could barely get the phrase past his lips.

"I'll never tell you." She spat

"Take them," shouted Fane.

That was Smith's cue. He reached out to grab Isabella's arms from behind and got a grip on them. She lifted her leg and kicked backwards connecting with Smith's kneecap sending it in a direction it was never meant to go. Smith yelled in pain and let go of one of her arms. Isabella spun brushing the ground with her free arm and managed to grab a rock. Using her momentum she kept on with the swing connecting with the side of Smith's face. As her back was toward Fane he pulled out his pistol and cracked her on the head at almost the same moment Smith took the force of her blow. Smith fell to his knees. Isabella fell unconscious.

It must have been several hours before she came to. Her head pounded from where Fane had cracked it. As she opened her eyes the sun blinded her making her head pound all that much more. Fane came walking up. She could barely make him out through the haze that clouded her eyes. "I see you are awake now." He commented with that always even controlled voice of his.

"Did you have to hit me so hard?" She hissed.

"Well, judging from Mr. Smith's face here, that would be a yes." Through the haze she could see where the right side of Smith's face was swollen and bandaged. His right eye had closed completely. He looked at her with murder in his eye. "So far, he's lost three teeth. Fortunately, I provide dental to all my employees. Now I believe I was in the middle of asking you a question when you so rudely interrupted me."

Isabella couldn't help but manage a small smile over Smith's current discomfort, but that was all she could manage. While she was out, they had expertly bound her so there would be no repeat of her previous performance.

Fane knelt down in front of Isabella and shoved the crystal skull in front of her face. "As I asked before, where did you find this?"

The sunshine reflecting off the quartz skull was intense, but she looked deep into it even with the pounding in her head. "Her skull" was what Kukulcan had called it in her dream. She had been called Otomie. "I won't tell you." She answered.

"I'm going to ask you one more time. Then I'm going to start shooting your workers one by one until you change your mind. Where did you find this?" Fane's patience was running out quickly.

Isabella still looked at the skull held in front of her. It was almost hypnotic. A phrase came to her. "Remember, you belong to the jungle and the jungle belongs to you." She straightened up as best as she could bound and looked at Fane, defiance etched across her face. "I'm not going to tell you."

Fane stood up. "Ok if that's the way you want it. We'll see how long this lasts." Fane pulled out a gun and shot Tom in the head. Just like that, no hesitation, no ceremony. Suddenly, out of nowhere he lay dead, next to her.

Isabella was stunned with disbelief. It had happened so fast. Tom was kneeling there, then he was on the ground bleeding out of a large hole in his head. She was in shock, she was angry and struggled against her bonds but to no avail. She screamed at Lazarus. "You killed him. You shot him for no reason."

"Oh, I had a reason, and now do I have to repeat the process. Are you going to tell me where you found this?" He began again." I can move right down the line killing them all one by one."

Isabella could see that all of Fane's men now carried guns. They were helpless and outnumbered. She saw no way out. "Don't hurt anyone else. I'll tell you whatever you want to know. Just leave them be."

Lazarus leaned down and smiled, "Now that's more like it. See, that wasn't so hard was it? You know, when you look at me that way, you remind me so much of your mother."

It took a moment for what he had said to sink in, but it did. "What do you mean, looked like my mother?" she hissed.

A tight smile crossed his face as he explained, "I knew her. And your father. They too got in my way, wouldn't cooperate."

"They were killed in a plane crash," she yelled at him, tears in her eyes, anger seething through her.

"Yes, they were," Fane continued, barbing and wounding her with every word. "They thought they could report me to the authorities. The two of them had no idea that I let them go. The plane was rigged to crash. Place money in the right hands, the outcome of the investigation is assured. So you see, your parents crossed my path too and they didn't fare so well. Don't make the same mistakes they did," his voice was low and steady. "I might let you live, let's say, for old time's sake."

He motioned for one of his men to come over. "Stand her up."

The lackey bent and cut the rope that bound her legs. She could now stand and walk, but her hands were still bound. She stared at Lazarus with undisguised hatred. She looked at the body of Tom, the brilliant, wonderful, laughing, never hurt a soul, Tom.

"If I show you where I found the skull, I have your word the rest won't be harmed?" she asked Fane.

"There'll be no reason for them to remain as hostages," he assured her.

Fane ordered two of his men, both armed with AKs to watch over the rest of Isabella's crew. Then turned towards Isabella, "Show me."

Isabella saw her crew huddled together as she walked towards the temple pyramid. She had to do it for them. No one's life was worth all of this. No one's life except for Lazarus Fane's. She'd never really believed he'd do it, actually kill one of them. But now, Tom was dead. If she hadn't refused, maybe he'd still be alive. If she'd just given in.

Yet, then, would it have only delayed the inevitable, postponed only briefly what Fane intended to do all along. Deep down inside she knew the inevitable outcome, they'd all die. Their corpses would become a part of the jungle. As she lead the way, the irony struck her of the phrase of Kukulcan, "you are a part of the jungle and the jungle is part of you." She almost laughed within her anger, shock and grief.

Isabella rounded the pyramid leading Fane to the side that hid the sacred room. The jungle growth began to close in as they approached the border of the clearing. She led on feeling numb and battered, but her anger wouldn't let her be beaten. Her mind was looking for any way out of the situation.

The man next to her fell to the ground for apparently no good reason. She looked down at him and then saw another fall. Lazarus whirled at his men shouting, "We're being attacked!"

Random rounds were fired spraying the jungle foliage to little effect. Isabella studied the jungle, she knew they were out there, the tribe had come, had watched over her. With still bound hands she manuevered herself away from Lazarus and his men.

Blowgun thorns were finding their mark. Suddenly hands pulled Isabella into the jungle. Lazarus swore and hissed to his men "Back to the clearing." The men turned and ran back into the open spaces of the clearing. The men that were guarding the remainder of Isabella's crew were unconscious and the prisoners gone. Fane kicked and stormed, yelling, "You bitch. I'll kill you." A dart pierced his neck and he fell face down into the dirt.

Isabella was pulled back into the jungle. She saw the smiling face of Yetlmak and several of his tribesmen. Their faces were painted in bright colors and their hair was decorated with parrot feathers. Something flashed in her mind, masked Mayan priests kneeling next to her. Then it was gone. "The rest of your people are free," he said as he cut free Isabella's hands. She shook them and nodded "Ready."

They raced quickly through the jungle back to the village. She moved easier through it, becoming more accustomed by the minute. She felt her muscles stretch, her footing was sure. She pictured in her mind the Jaguar, long and sleek, graceful and strong. Her senses felt keen and sharp, seeing and hearing the smallest things. Her reflexes were taut, ready for any threat. There was a comfort in all of the trees and foliage, wrapping and surrounding her with their protection.

Yetlmak watched her as they travelled. "You are one of us once again, Princess. You feel it now don't you?"

Isabella looked around at the descendants of the long dead tribe that had claimed her for their own. Had her discovery of Itchen Balam merely been subconscious memories from a past life? She felt different, changed. "Yes, I feel it," she admitted.

Ahead was the village. They'd be safe here. There were too many natives. Fane could stumble around the ruins for months and never find anything. There would be a resupply helicopter in a week. If she wasn't on site, there would certainly be questions, an investigation. Then she could bring that murderer to justice. U of M will back her, after all, Tom was a student. They will have to do something just to save the University's reputation.

She followed Yetlmak to his hut. Once again she sat on the mat across from the shaman. It was time to make plans.

Lazarus Fane had picked himself up out of the dirt with the help of Cicero Smith. The unconsciousness induced by the darts only lasted a couple of hours. Fane looked around. He hadn't lost any men, though most looked nervous about their situation.

It wasn't lost on any of them that they were in the open and the surrounding jungle hid things, everything. Quiet, silent death could strike them any moment and they were nothing but a target.

Several hours of tense waiting gave away to no more attacks and Fane and his men began to breathe easier. "It appears they have what they want." he commented to Smith.

"Maybe," Smith said cautiously. "They could be waiting until dark and the camp is asleep."

"Well maybe we can kill two birds with one stone," he grinned wickedly at his pun. "They can't have Carter and we can't have them attacking us. I want you to take some men and make sure those natives won't attack again and bring Carter back here."

"You want me to use lethal force?"

"I don't care how you do it, Smith. Just get it done."

"Alright." Cicero Smith grinned, he lived for these kinds of moments and working for someone like Fane insured he would have them. "It'll be a pleasure."

He left the tent that had been previously Isabella's. It was late in the day and they would need to be in position before it became dark. He picked out five men and armed them with AKs.

Lazarus watched as the jungle swallowed them. He was quite satisfied with himself. It was the quickest and best solution. Then he could move ahead with finding the treasures Itchen Balam had to offer. He looked at the crystal skull that Carter had found. What other treasure had been lying there with it? Gold? Jade? Emeralds? When the jungle was removed, there would likely be several places that held caches of priceless artifacts. Again he looked at the skull, the rarest of the rare. It would have to go into his personal collection. There would be plenty more around here he would be able to profit from. The skull would be his.

* * *

Fatigue quickly overcame Isabella in Yetlmak's hut. The incidents since Lazarus Fane's arrival had taken its toll. She was tired, grieving and angry. His death had been so senseless. And there would have been more if it hadn't been for her adopted tribe and their rescue.

Yetlmak knew of her sadness and encouraged her to rest, let it all pass. "In time," he told her, "there would be punishment for the evil that was done. That was the way of the jungle."

She managed a slight smile, "I thought that was survival of the fittest?"

"That too," he said. "Remember, fittest doesn't always mean the biggest or the most savage. The smallest snake can kill the great jaguar. The fish of the stream can devour the great ox in moments. Survival is cunning and senses. Seeing the smallest movement, hearing the quiet crack of a twig, smelling the scent of a predator, feeling the vibration of the ground as something approaches, these are the things that mean life in the jungle. You have those senses. You must learn to trust them, rely on your instincts. It is the instinct that is triggered when the senses detect things that we may not be conscious of. You are a child of the jungle, you must learn to listen to yourself. When you do, you will be the fittest."

Yetlmak smiled, "You're tired, sleep now. We will talk more, when you're rested."

Isabella curled up on the mat. She felt comfortable here. It was a refuge from the horror of Lazarus Fane and murder. She needed to think, needed to plan. She needed sleep.

* * *

Cicero Smith led his men quickly through the jungle towards the village. If they could get close before darkness fell, they would be set. He'd wait until they slept, well into the night. Less chance of resistance then.

It was hot and steamy. Bugs swarmed and harried them through their hurried trek. Smith grumbled, "Goddam bugs," and slapped one that was feeding on his face. Above, monkeys paid them little attention as they moved from branch to branch.

Smith had never liked the jungle, but since working for Fane required him to endure all climates, it was simply another job for him. Get in, get the job done and then, back to civilization to wait for the next job. Though truly, he did enjoy his job. Smith was a problem solver. He removed obstacles by any means necessary. If it meant some killing, collateral damage, sacrifices as hinderances to a means to an end. Dead, there's no one to argue against your side of the story. Usually things tie up quite neatly that way.

It would be the same here. Every step Smith took was a reminder of the damage Carter had caused to his knee. It matched the throbbing in the side of his head. He'd take pleasure in killing her. They'd say the natives did it, we came across the bodies when we got here. They were all looters and when they found nothing, they killed everyone.

* * *

Isabella once again found herself standing in front of the ancient Mayan pyramid. Again she was greeted by the ancient gods. Again Kukulcan spoke, "Welcome once again. Long ago you were a priestess and a warrior. You were strong and spoke your mind, fought for what you believed. You followed the ways of the Jaguar, cunning and fierce. You live in a different world, but you haven't changed. You are the same priestess that walked these steps long ago. You are the same priestess that brought down the corruption of Quetamoc, stopped the bribery of sacrifices. There are no more temples, there are no more sacrifices. We are diminished to a memory, our people and their ways lost to time."

"Ahead your life will be trial and triumph. You will know great sorrows and perils. You must dig deep within and discover the warrior, once again let the spirit of the Jaguar flow through you. Feel the power within. Fill yourself up with the energy of the jungle. Open your senses and use your instincts. You will be that warrior once again. Remember the Jaguar, his strength is in his senses, his cunning. He is rarely seen but always felt. Deadly and dangerous, he strikes only when he is confident, his foe careless, unaware. Become the Jaguar, recall the warrior and none will be able to stand in your way."

Suddenly he moved his face closer to hers and said with urgency, "Jump you're in danger!"

Isabella woke up with her body already in motion. Her surroundings in Yetlmak's hut were a blur yet she saw Cicero Smith with a gun which he was swinging at her. It glanced off without doing any damage as she rolled away. He then swung the gun up and emptied it into Yetlmak. He laughed commenting, "Stupid old bastard." under his breath.

Isabella raged with anger and grief, yet her instincts told her to "get out" and get undercover of the jungle. Inside she wanted to tear out Smith's heart with her bare hands. She leaped at him under his gun muzzle and stuck her shoulder out and made sure it impacted his injured knee. The impact again forced it backward and Smith howled in pain as he went to the floor on his back. "You bitch!" he screamed.

Isabella let her momentum continue to carry her towards the door. The moment her feet touched ground her legs started churning and she was out the door into the night.

She was surrounded by gunshots and screams. Fane's men were shooting anything that moved. She took it all in, the carnage, the death. Then she ran into the jungle disappearing into the foliage.

* * *

Cicero Smith came out of the hut limping and cursing every member of Isabella's lineage he could conceive. He screamed for one of his men that was standing close enough to hear him over the constant noise of the gunfire. The men had run out of natives and were now unloading into the livestock. "Carlos, Get your ass over here."

Carlos, one of the men Fane had hired in Cozumel, nodded and walked up to Harrison. "What can I do for you, boss?"

"Where'd that bitch go?" he said through gritted teeth, the throb in his knee getting worse by the minute.

"I don't know. I didn't see her." Carlos knew Smith had a short fuse.

"How could you not see her? What are you blind?" Smith looked anxiously around hoping for a glimpse in the darkness, but there was nothing. She was gone. "Well, she won't last long out there alone. Maybe a cat'll get her, tear her apart slowly, eating her while she's still alive." He almost smiled. The thought almost cheered him up. The throb in his leg reminded him otherwise.

"Get the men, Carlos. Let's wrap this up and get back to camp. There isn't any damage left to do here."

* * *

Isabella kept running until she couldn't hear the sounds of death from the village. She slumped against a tree and collapsed under some large ferns with exhaustion. She laid there with the sounds and visions of death replaying in her mind. The horror wouldn't leave her. It was like being tangled in thick spider webs that you couldn't wipe away. The memories clung and crawled across her skin, tormenting her with their evil. She kept seeing Yetlmak and Tom, yes there was Tom, now lying in the jungle somewhere with a bullet through his head. All dead, they were all dead.

And then there were her parents. Fane had all but admitted to having killed them as well. She hadn't known it, but he'd always been there, lurking out there, causing her agony and grief her entire life. He'd killed everyone who had been important to her. He was even taking away her greatest accomplishment Itchen Balam. She would be nothing more than another lost soul that had vanished in the jungle, forgotten and Fane, Fane would walk away from it all like he had with everything.

He'd get away with it, murder, massacre, theft, bribery. He'd gone on his entire life, killing and stealing, beyond the law, destroying everything that was dear and now he was doing it to the only thing she had left: herself!

She heard a low growl and started, then she realized it had been her. Something inside of her shifted. Her breathing became regular, controlled. She slowly stood up in the newly gathering light of the morning. It was the sounds of the jungle that surrounded her now. She let them flow over her as they washed away the evil of the previous night. Fane was an evil man that was a bully. He got what he wanted no matter who it hurt. This hadn't been about her...but it would be now.

Isabella stiffened. She wasn't going to simply lie there and let the bugs and beasts devour her. She might be able to find her way to another village, but someone from the university would eventually come. Fane knew that, but without her he'd be able to explain away his story without anyone to refute it. He'd win again. He'd get away with murder, again.

Not if she could help it. He'd taken everything away, Isabella had nothing more to lose...and everything to gain. She felt quiet, calculating. Her senses were clear and she reached out with them as Yetlmak had taught her. There were the sounds, movements off to her left, scrambling, small monkey. Impressions came to her and she read them. To her left was the direction to Itchen Balam. To her right was the village of the people that had helped, now dead in pools of blood. But the village was her best option. There would be things there she would need, could use.

As she quietly walked through the jungle she mentally prepared herself for what she would see. As she walked to Yetlmak's hut anger and rage seethed through her. The carrion eaters had already started their work. She controlled her emotions. It would be her downfall if she couldn't.

She entered the hut. The body of Yetlmak lay motionless, eyes open staring towards her. She walked over and moved him. Laid him flat and crossed his arms on his chest. She closed his eyes. Then laid one of his furs over him.

She looked down at Yetlmak, no longer able to hold back her grief. "Oh great Kukulcan, he was a faithful man, he believed in you, they all did and they believed in me. Care for them, they are of the last of their kind, faithful to the old. Care for them. They are your children."

Isabella looked up. "Their murderers will be joining them soon." She stood and then,"I could use a little help, if you don't mind." She listened for a response. "Well it never hurts to ask," she muttered to herself.

She began rummaging through pots and baskets. Facepaint, she needed some facepaint, and a blow gun. She was sure he had darts somewhere. She grabbed another pot and she found some darts. They were small slender thorns with a reddish color. She set them aside.

More pots and then she found some pigment, green, red and blue. Then in another jar, black. Isabella, began to cover her face and arms in different shades, simply covering her skin, not concerning herself with art. The colors blended in making her feel primal, tribal.

She continued to look through the hut. A blowgun, she needed a blowgun. She found it in a shadowed corner. She picked it up.

In a corner where she had left it, was her machete, sheathed and undisturbed. Isabella threw it across her shoulders, like a sash, the machete itself, across her back. Her face was set stone, emotionless. She left the hut and disappeared into the thick trees, on her way to her city, Itchen Balam.

* * *

Lazarus Fane saw Cicero Smith limping across the compound. He was being supported by two of his men. His knee had swollen to the size of a football and he couldn't put any weight on it.

Lazarus shook his head. "She better be dead."

"They're all dead," sputtered Smith. "She will be too."

"What do you mean 'will be?'" Fane shouted.

"She's out there, somewhere. She' got no provisions, no weapons. She can't come here. She can't last."

"You didn't kill her?"

"No, I thought I was making that clear." Smith was getting irritated now. He needed to get off of his leg.

"What happened?" Fane growled.

Smith directed the two men who were supporting him to get him to a chair. They did, outside of Lazarus' tent.

Cicero began. "I thought I had her. She was sleeping and I tried to bash her head in with the butt of my gun, but she jumped just as I brought it down, like she knew I was doing it."

"She was playing possum on you," retorted Fane.

"I don't think so. If she would have known, she never would have let me kill the old Indian she was with. She hit me and ran off into the jungle. Nobody saw where she went. End of story."

"You didn't leave anybody there in case she came back?"

"Came back to what? The place is a cemetery. There's nothing there for her."

"Listen Smith," Fane hissed. "I hired you because you're good at cleaning up messes. Right now, you don't seem to be getting the job done. Don't make me re-evaluate your job performance. Got me?" He got into Smith's face with his final words and rested his weight on the hand that was now wrapped around Smith's swollen knee.

Smith grimaced, "Yeah, Boss, I got ya."

Fane stood back up, "Good. You sure she's lost in the jungle?"

"She hasn't got a chance."

* * *

Isabella stood on the rock bluff that overlooked Itchen Balam. She'd always liked this spot, she was able to look over Itchen Balam clearly from there, admire its granduer emerging from the jungle as they cleared it.

Now it had a different purpose. She could see Fane and his men moving around the camp. The men were spread out away from each other watching the main camp perimeter. She wasn't sure how she knew, but she was certain they thought she was dead. It was her advantage. She'd be able to move undetected until she was ready. A plan had formed as she had walked to the old Mayan city.

It would require patience and silence. It would require the right moment and then...some luck. She noted the exact locations of each guard and then wound her way down the bluff, then circled the ruins.

She moved cautiously, her senses on the alert for any movement. A guard wasn't far away, she could hear his movements, tell the difference between it and the wildlife moving around her. The sounds of the wild had a regularity to it, a pulse, a rhythm. The guard moved clumsily, randomly, without grace. She could smell him too, essence of sweat and tequila.

His mind was wandering, frustrated. He wanted to be on a cot sleeping, not out in the hot sun.

Isabella was suddenly confused. How had she known that? She mentally reached out again. This time she got nothing. She moved quietly through the ferns and underbrush away from the guard. It wouldn't be far and she would be near the entrance to her secret room.

She crouched peering through the foliage at another guard. This one was out of sight of the others. He'd wandered out of view searching for shade in the intense sun. Isabella watched him and studied him. He was tired and unhappy too. His guard was down, he was sleepy.

She brought the blowgun to her lips. Her lungs exhaled. The dart shot out and missed the guard by a few inches. He never noticed.

Isabella inhaled again, put the dart in the gun and blew the dart. This time the guard slapped his neck, an indication she'd hit him. It wasn't long and he dropped face first in the dirt.

Looking back towards the camp, she saw nothing, no one had moved or begun to venture her way. Quietly she separated herself from the jungle and crossed the cleared ground to where the guard lay. He still breathed but it was irregular. Isabella wasn't sure if she'd hit him a with a knockout, or curare, a deadly poison. But then, she didn't care either. If he died, it was one less problem to deal with.

She rolled him over. There was a sidearm in a holster slung on his belt. She opened the leather flap and pulled out the gun. It was something she'd never held before. It was heavy and strangely warm from the heat of the day. She'd expected it would be cool, even cold to the touch. She turned it over and found there was a kind of comfort in it. Her fingers seemed to fit perfectly around the handle and into the trigger. It seemed tailored. She moved the safety back and forth. She knew its purpose.

Without further hesitation, she pulled the belt and holster from around the guard. Isabella strapped it around herself and replaced the gun in the holster. *Now to the secret room,* she thought.

* * *

Lazarus Fane, had calmed down and sat next to Cicero Smith. Smith's face was swollen and he could only see out of one eye. He looked at Fane, "We can search this place top to bottom but I don't think we're going to find anything."

Lazarus was more sceptical. "I'm certain that where that crystal skull was, there will be more treasure. We just have to find it."

One of the workers stuck his head into the tent. "Come quickly, there is something happening."

Lazarus flew out of the tent. The worker pointed towards one of the pyramid temples. The sun was just peaking the top of one. There seemed to be something there. It was directly in line with the bright sun making it hard for eyes to discern anything. It seemed to be a figure in robes, with a headdress. In the bright light it looked like a mirage from the past. It seemed as if an ancient Mayan stood once again upon the great altar of the gods.

"Whatever it is shoot at it." Ordered Fane.

The man next to him looked at him in horror. "You cannot shoot a god. We are being given a vision of the ancient ones."

"Shoot it!" screamed Fane.

Many of his men were looking on. Unmoving. Seemingly in shock.

Then Cicero Smith hobbled out of the tent. He raised his pistol and shot. The apparition vanished.

The workers began to mumble. Though Fane had hired them, most were still of Mayan descent. The incident had effected them all. Profoundly.

Lazarus Fane wasn't buying any of it. "Search that temple. Find whoever or whatever that was."

Some of the men hesitated, but Smith held his gun on them and motioned for them to follow. With the swollen knee, he decided he would remain behind and watch over the camp. A desertion of the camp just might be what someone was hoping for. He looked around at the jungle. "I'll bet that bitch isn't dead," he mumbled under his breath. He was wary and on his guard.

Lazarus led his men to the base of the temple. "Spread out. Make sure you cover everything. Fane turned and began the arduous climb to the temple top. His men surrounded the base and some even entered the jungle. They kept weapons at the ready as they walked.

As Fane reached the top, he could see the surrounding jungle and lost city. He could see his men moving below as they combed the grounds. They were turning up nothing. That was when Fane realized he was hearing nothing. Silence. The birds and the insects were making no noise. It couldn't be because of the gunshot earlier. It would quiet things momentarily but never for this long. He looked to the horizon, the sky was blue. There was definitely something that was not right.

* * *

Isabella had taken refuge inside the temple's secret room. She had formed an idea on how she might even the odds. She needed to frighten Fane's men. They were mostly cutthroats from the backstreets of Merida but down inside they were descendants of the Maya and all she needed for her plan to work, was enough of a scrap of that for their Native beliefs to come out. She needed to put doubt and fear into them.

She opened the chamber that held the ancient regalia of the Mayan priests and priestesses. Though they were old and tattered, she was able to find one that still was holding together. One she could wear, if only briefly. It would be all she'd need.

Isabella smiled to herself. Wearing the old robes seemed natural. There was even a headdress. The feathers held some of their color. She placed it on her head.

There are moments when the past meets the future or vice versa. They meld together to create a moment. One where the present or the past are cast out. Rejected completely.

As she walked past the wall of skulls, she could feel all of the hatred and anger towards the interlopers. Those that had killed the offspring of the ancient. As she approached the secret door to the outside, it grew ever stronger. She opened the door and a priestess of the Maya greeted the early morning light for the first time in 500 years.

The sun would be rising at the peak of the temple soon. She needed to be there at the right moment. She climbed the stone steps gracefully without fear. As Isabella climbed, she knew she was being watched. She could feel the eyes, sense the anticipation behind them.

She climbed to the rising sun and she reached it as the sun reached the moment, Fanes men would be blinded and dazzled by an apparition they would never be able to quite make out. Isabella saw Fane wrestling with his man and Smith coming out of the tent.

When Fane fired his shot Isabella was already dropping to the ground. The bullet whizzed by and then came the sound. The apparition had disappeared.

She knew Fane would immediately begin a search so Isabella made fast time getting back to her secret room. She closed it behind her at the same time Fane reached the base of the temple.

As she walked inside, things had changed. There were several Natives there dressed in warriors regalia. She still wore the garb of the priestess. On the floor lay the body of Yetlmak. As she saw it tears welled up and she dropped to her knees next to her teacher. He'd had taken her under his wing and all she had brought him was death. And Tom too. They were people she cared deeply for. Her anger was renewed. She looked up at the warriors that had brought the body of Yetlmak to the cave. They looked down and saw a priestess of old honoring the old man in the way of the true Maya. They all knelt. It was then she realized that they were hers.

Some were survivors from the village Fane and Cicero had slaughtered. Many had escaped to the jungle and hid. It explained why she felt she was being watched. She was. Right now, the Yucatan jungle held many hidden surprises and they were all allies of Isabella Carter.

She rose and returned the robes and headdress of the priestess back where she had found it. As she walked past the altar, where she had found the crystal skull, she looked. It was where it had been when she first found it. Deep in the night, camouflaged as she was, she stole it from Fane's tent and returned it to the secret room. She was reasonably sure that he hadn't realized it yet or there would have been an uproar that would have been heard all across the peninsula.

* * *

Lazarus Fane came down off the temple worried. Something wasn't right and he knew it. He called in his men and realized several were missing. It didn't bode well. Fane rarely made mistakes but he was starting to think that turning Smith loose on that village may have been one. He wasn't about to make another. He'd spent considerable time in thick jungle like this all over the world. Experience can save your life.

He trotted back to the camp. Cicero Smith was lying moaning a bit over his swollen knee and face. The pain was terrific and his ability to walk was severely impaired.

One of Fanes men that was outside the tent fell to the ground. Lazarus could see a small thorn sticking out of the victim's neck. He turned to Smith with urgency on his voice, "Get the helicopter warmed up. We may need to leave." After a pause, "Quickly."

Cicero leaned up and started to get up. He was going to need a crutch. He saw a suitable stick in the woodpile that would work. "Grab that stick," he said and pointed past Fane.

Lazarus grabbed it and tossed it to Smith. "Now get going. We don't have much time."

Smith got up on his crutch as Fane whirled out of the tent and ran to his. Like magic a long thorn appeared in his bush coat. It hadn't penetrated to him. Keeping his head down he ran into his tent. He'd stashed the skull under his cot. It was gone. There was a sinking feeling deep in his guts. It was gone. He kept tossing that thought over and over. It was gone. Another of his men falling down snapped him back to his senses. He could hear frantic movements outside the tent. Then, there was the scream.

Fane came out of his tent. Most of his men were on the ground, out cold or dead. He didn't take time to find out. One of the survivors of the massacre had just killed one of Fane's men who had taken special glee in the slaughter of the unsuspecting. He was removing his heart. It explained the scream. Fane shot him. He looked over to where the helicopter was and saw Cicero Smith just reaching it.

Fane had gained nothing here except defeat. Cicero Smith had gained a lot of injuries. It was time to accept the losses and leave. He suspected the local Natives had taken back their skull. It was an incredible loss. He ran towards the helicopter. Then, hesitated for a moment. He didn't want to leave without it. That was when something moved between him and the helicopter. It was green and red and blue. Its dark hair hung over its face. It carried a Machete in one hand and a gun in the other. He raised his and fired, but the target was no longer there and the bullet ricocheted off the helicopter.

Smith yelled "Damn, you almost shot me. I got enough damage. Let's get out of here."

As he turned he saw her.

Isabella had attacked the encampment and now Lazarus was trying to run away. He'd seen to the murder of dozens and now he was running. She got between him and the helicopter. As he raised to shoot she moved, the bullet missed. She shot at Lazarus. It was now her chance. The bullet struck him in the shoulder. Causing him to stagger from the impact. She tried to let go with another, but there was only one bullet and she'd spent it. She had only one thing left, the machete. She threw it. It didn't kill Fane, but it sailed by close enough to leave a long gash along his face.

Cicero Smith was strapped in and he had some leverage. Fane stumbled to the helicopter. Smith grabbed him and pulled him aboard nearly dragging him into the seat. Fane was bleeding hard from the wounds. He lifted off as quickly as he could.

Isabella watched the helicopter take off. She could only hope that Fane would die from his wounds. The sooner the better.

Less than a week later a resupply copter came in. Isabella knew the pilot and told the story to him. Of course she had an entire village of witnesses. Even so, the Mexican/ Yucatan government deemed that there was insufficient evidence to go forward. Apparently, Lazarus had lived to pay off those in the right places. Again.

Jason Hand had a message waiting for him at his computer. It read "Dalva Wolf, seven tickets on a train in New Jersey. Second purchase: food in South Carolina. Third purchase: Everglades Airboat Transportation, Okeechobee, Florida. Please deposit usual fee to account." It was signed Samarai's Ghost.

Jason grinned. He knew they'd do it. He had a location. They had buried themselves somewhere in the Everglades. Smart really. Nobody would think to look for them there. He went to Mr. James' office with the news. Hopefully this would be a short trip.

* * *

Isabella Carter, Aiden Mckenzie, and the four remaining students climbed into the airboat. The big propeller fired up creating a cacophony that you could barely think over, let alone talk. They were going into the heart of America's largest wetland.

Why, eluded McKenzie. What could possibly be out here? There were only reptiles and birds, dangerous ones at that. They didn't bother McKenzie, but it didn't seem likely they were going to solve any mysteries with the alligators. He leaned over to Isabella so she could hear, "So what's up doc? You need a new pair of shoes? Thinking maybe we needed some quality time in a swamp? What the hell, we doing here?"

She turned so he could hear her. "I needed to get you somewhere there wasn't any scotch."

McKenzie showed her the flask he had in his duffle. "Where…"

"South Carolina," he said before she could finish. "That train ride was getting a little trying. But level with me Doc, why here?"

"There's a friend of mine, has a research facility out here for the wildlife and botany. We were classmates at U of M for a while. He went into his field, I went into mine. He has all of the same equipment we need to finish our studies on the crystals." She leaned back. It was hard to talk like that.

The lush swamp flashed by as the airboat followed trail after trail through the reeds. It was like a wetland highway system. It took years to learn them and if someone tried to negotiate them that didn't know them they became hopelessly lost in minutes.

The passengers in the boat watched the flamingos, egrets and cranes that could be seen along the banks fishing for the minnows that were their staple diet. The glades teemed with life. Even at the speed they were going, they could see how overwhelming the population was.

They rode for over an hour traveling deeper and deeper into the heart of the Everglades. It was not someplace that was going to be easy for anyone to get if either Fane or James figured out where they were going. Isabella seemed like she knew what she was doing.

McKenzie was starting to feel like he was just along for the ride. All of the students had fields of expertise. He was a diver who happened to be in the right place, or the wrong place, depending how you looked at it, at the right time. He was beginning to feel like he had nothing to contribute. Though he had to admit, the airboat ride was a good time.

The boat came out into some open water and ahead they could see an island with some buildings on it. They were heading towards them. The airboat throttled back and pulled into an old wooden dock. The operator climbed down from his seat in the back and jumped on the dock. As soon as he had them tied, he lit up a cigarette. The long ride had lowered his nicotine level drastically.

The group climbed out and Isabella led them towards the building. A man came out to meet them and the two stood eyeing each other for a few minutes. She spoke first, "I need your help."

Almost immediately he responded with "What kind of trouble did you bring with you?" And he started to look around, thinking there might be someone out there lurking in the swamp.

"Hopefully none, but you never can tell, it's early yet," she responded.

He laughed nervously. He had images of his facility getting blown up for some unknown reason. "Well, come on inside," he motioned them to follow.

The inside was air conditioned and cool against the hot humidity of the Florida wetlands. He took them into his offices where Isabella introduced them. "This is an old school colleague of mine named John Micco." He stood up and shook everyone's hand. So far, so good. No explosions, no gunfire.

"So what brings you here?" he asked trepiditiously.

"We need to use your equipment to scan some objects," Isabella replied.

"They must be one hell of a find to bring you way out here."

"They are," she assured him.

"OK, Everything here is at your disposal. Just do me a favor. Leave the buildings standing when you leave."

"I'll do my best," she answered.

"I've seen your best. It's why I'm worried. Hell, it's why I'm out here."

McKenzie displayed a quizzical expression. "Something we should know about Doc?"

Isabella ignored him and asked John, "Could you show us to your microscopic scanners. What we're looking at is very small, deeper than cellular."

John looked surprised. "Anything you'd like to tell me about?"

Isabella smiled, "Show us the way and we'll show you what we've got."

Micco's lab was magnificent. Magnetic resonance scanner, CT scanner, laser scanner, computer imaging, everything they needed. Jeff and Bob went straight for the computers while Karen and Sandra set up their laptops for the comparative studies with the original crystal. Isabella brought out the package from Egypt that had been housed in her pack. "I want these scanned first and all the results downloaded onto the portable drive. We'll analyze what we have later as time allows. We don't know when and how fast we may have to move."

"I knew it," said John. "There is trouble following you."

"Well, I'm hoping I lost them."

He looked at McKenzie, "She's going to get me killed yet."

Bob Peters spoke up. "This program I've written should isolate all of the symbols, first in their correct order then it will data base them numerically as to amount of usage. The program will also give us three dimensional image views so that we can view the symbols from every direction. This should work on a model similar to building a DNA strand and genetic coding only in this case we're looking at language strands throughout the objects.

Isabella laid out the crystals on a lab table. Sandra picked up the first one and placed it onto the bed of the laser scanner.

"Now as the scan begins, it will build a digital three dimensional image of the crystal and the embedded symbols," said Jeff.

"As soon as that is done I want the imaging saved in the drives. After we've done each of the scans, then we can begin to analyze language and meaning. Our first priority is to get the primary source information saved. Save first, analysis later," said Isabella.

Micco watched as the first imaging began. As the symbols began to appear, he pulled up a chair and sat down. "All this is on a quartz crystal?" he gasped. Then he pulled his eyes away and turned to Isabella, "How old?"

"We're not sure, but we think older than any recorded civilization."

Isabella grinned the impact of the discovery had hit him. The possibilities of the encryption had captured his curiosity. Anything was possible with these and the knowledge these could add to history was intoxicating.

Micco watched with amazement as the model of the crystal was built. Layer after layer, symbols upon symbols, the characters of a lost language accumulating before his eyes. He understood Isabella's passion for her work, the discovery of something new, something unseen before. He compared it to when he found a species of plant or wildlife that was uncatalogued. The excitements of his own discoveries had carried him away.

He was a Native American, a Seminole and as one he had an affinity for nature and its workings. It was why he had become a biologist in the first place, but in his soul there was also understanding of lost culture. John understood rediscovery of the past. It was something that was close to his heart. His tribe, like all native tribes, were trying to rediscover theirs as well.

When the first crystal was mapped, they began on another one. There were twenty in all, twenty tiny doorways to an unseen past. The next big step would be trying to read the language. It would be an almost insurmountable job to piece together linguistics that very likely hadn't been spoken in thousands of years. Without some form of Rosetta Stone, nearly impossible.

Isabella moved back and forth watching the images. She was intently studying the characters and their alignments. She couldn't help herself. Her mind tossed placements and order back and forth searching for sense. This was what she did the best. Then a thought occurred to her.

She picked up the crystal that they had finished scanning. She held it in her hand and closed her eyes. Her mind opened and Isabella reached out. The crystal felt warm in her hand. Deeply she thought trying to penetrate its secrets. An image began to form in her mind. Pyramids, unfinished pyramids. She could get nothing more.

It was a shot, she thought. Isabella picked up another one and went through the same routine. There was a sphinx without a head. It was then she knew she was definitely getting some impression from the stones, but was it simply because they had lain in the harbor of Alexandria so long? Had they absorbed some of the energy of their surroundings?

A long sigh escaped her lips. It had been worth a try. She knew nothing more than she had a few minutes before.

McKenzie had been watching her carefully. Everyone else had been absorbed with the revelations of the scanner. "Any luck Doc?"

Isabella shook her head. There was obvious disappointment on her face. McKenzie knew she had hoped to get something. He spoke to her. "Let's go outside for a minute, get some fresh air."

She nodded and they went outside the research facility. McKenzie saw that she appeared tired. "Why don't you get some rest Doc?"

Isabella shook her head. She had to see this through. "I'm alright. I just hoped I'd get some impressions from the crystals that would help get to their meaning. I know it was a long shot, but hey, you got to try."

McKenzie smiled at her. "You're always trying, Doc. Maybe if you relaxed for a bit it might help. Let the kids in there do their jobs. I don't think anybody is going to find us here, at least not right away and if they do, I'm sure we'll hear them coming with a deafening roar. My ears are still ringing from that ride."

She laughed. It was something he hadn't heard her do much. Everything had been so serious since they had met in Egypt. That seemed so long ago now. "Still, why don't you go inside and take a five. Maybe it'll give you a clearer perspective. Actually, I think I could use a break myself. Buy you a shot Doc?" He took out his flask and offered it to her. She took a pull off from it followed by a cough as the rough alcohol went down.

"How do you drink this stuff," she grimaced. "Tastes like something you'd use for sterilizing wounds."

"Slowly," he said, "and I have. Sticking with you Doc, you never know when that might happen."

"Listen McKenzie," she began.

McKenzie interrupted, "I wish you'd call me Aiden or Mac. There's no need to be so formal anymore. Hell, I've slept on your couch."

"Ok Mac, I need you. I think this is all getting dicey enough that I need your help. You've pulled my fat out of things so far and well, I don't think we could have gotten this far without you. I appreciate that you've got my back."

"Thanks, Doc. Happy to help."

She turned and went back inside. McKenzie stood there. It was what he had needed to hear right then.

* * *

Cicero Smith walked up to the window at the train station. The woman clerk smiled and asked, "Can I help you?"

"I'm hoping you can. I'm looking for my daughter. She left on a trip with four other students, two males and a two females and their teacher with an escort, a man and a woman. This is a family emergency and it is very important that I get a hold of her."

"Doesn't she have a cell you can contact her on?"

"Yes, but it appears she has it turned off, strange, I know, so I decided to see if everything was alright. You never know these days."

"Well, unfortunately we don't keep records of all of our passengers, just the ticket purchasers. You say there would have been six of them?"

"Initially there were seven but one it appears missed the train."

"Oh yes, I remember now. The one that missed was wandering around in here until she could get a ride back to Manhattan. I recall who they are." She went to her computer and called up the ticket purchases. "Yep, here it is. Seven tickets purchased by a Dalva Wolf. They took the train that runs south."

"How far does that go?" he asked.

"All the way, Florida. But they could have disembarked anywhere between."

Cicero nodded his head and thanked her. He had what he needed. He walked away from the counter and called Fane. "I've got their trail. They took a train south and the tickets were purchased by Carter, she's using the alias of Dalva Wolf. I need a trace on card purchases under that name. I know the direction they went, but I don't have a destination. When you have that information, get back with me. I'm already heading for the Jersey airport. I'll need some men to meet me and a private charter."

* * *

Lazarus Fane hung up the phone to Cicero Smith and went over to one of his employees. "I need you to run a credit card check on the name Dalva Wolf. I want everything you can find as quick as you can get it."

He then went over to another also seated at a computer. "Do we have that helicopter flight plan info yet?"

The man that was seated there replied, "Yes sir. Here it is." He handed Fane a printout. "The helicopter has been a standing charter to an Eldon James. Here's the address they had on file."

Fane studied it for a moment and then under his breath he mumbled, "Got you." The address made sense. It was an exclusive high security building. He turned back to the man on the computer. "I want a list of all of the companies housed in this building. I need to be sure which one is his, but I'm reasonably certain, it will be the one on the top floor." It just made sense. Eldon would want to be on top. There would be no halfway for him.

"Mr. Fane." It was the other man now. "We have three purchases under the name of Dalva Wolf. The last one is in Florida. Okeechobee." Of course. Why hadn't he thought of that, John Micco. He was the Seminole biologist that had built a research facility in the middle of the Everglades. It was currently being funded by money brought in by tribal casinos. His expertise was biology but he was a former classmate of Carter's and he would have the equipment she would need. He was doing well out there in the middle of nowhere. This would be hard to reach. That was why Carter had chosen it. Extra planning was called for with this one.

Fane patted him on the shoulder. "Good work," he commended him. He then got on the phone "Smith, you're going to the Seminole Biological Research Facility in the Everglades. You might want to pull it up on Google Earth with your handheld to see what you're up against. You might have to be creative with the logistics of this one. We have contacts in Florida. There will be men waiting for you when you get there. Everything will be set up from here." He ended the call. Things were looking brighter. Now all he had to do was call Captain Riley.

* * *

Lieutenant Murphy's desk was a mess. There were files of open cases everywhere. Even though much of police information and evidence was done on computers, there still was actual paperwork involved. In truth it was even worse, they wanted paper and digital versions of everything. It had actually become twice the paperwork. This annoyed Murphy endlessly, as it would any cop. He now had to investigate twice as many cases with half the time to solve them. It irked him. It wasn't what a cop was supposed to be all about, paperwork.

Captain Riley poked his head out of his office door. "Murphy come here, I need to speak to you. Bring that file of the helicopter pilot shooting." He then poked his head back in just as abruptly and shut the door. Murphy was reminded of videos he'd seen of prairie dogs popping their heads out of their holes. Then next thing poof they're gone, just like the Captain.

He got up and went into the Captain's office. "What's up Cap?" he asked as he handed the file to Riley.

"Sit down, Murphy," began the Captain. Murphy obeyed. "I just got a call from the Long Island police. They're taking over the investigation of this case. The shooting occurred in their jurisdiction, they are investigating a break-in that's connected to it. You're off the case. We're handing over all information we have on this. The problem is now theirs. We already have too many cases we aren't going to solve anyway, one less on our hands isn't going to hurt."

"But Captain, I did a rundown on the name that Hand guy gave me, Cicero Smith. We've got a lot of dope on this guy. It looks like he's suspected of dozens of crimes, but they've never been able to get anything on him. Every time we bring him in he gets released. We have all the usual info, mug shots, fingerprints, DNA swab, identifying marks, the guy pays us regular visits. The problem is we've never been able to book him for an extended stay."

Well," said Riley, "write it up, bring it to me and we'll send that along with the rest. Either way, it's not ours anymore. I need you to focus on your other cases."

Murphy got up and went back to his desk. More paperwork.

Inside Riley's office the Captain was smiling. The Cicero Smith problem was all taken care of. He had the folder. When Murphy finished his report, he'd have that too. The warrant had been cancelled earlier. At least one of his children would be going to college now.

≈ 12 ≈

Jason Hand stepped off a plane into the heat of Fort Meyers, Florida. His next step would be to rent a car and drive to Okeechobee. It would take under two hours. He even thought he'd rent an airboat from the same place Dr. Carter had. On the plane, he'd come up with a plan. Maybe they had been approaching this all wrong. When Mr. James had been in Egypt, they had the information that she was working with Fane. That she had been trying to acquire them from McKenzie strengthened the appearance. Even though she and Fane were known to be bitter enemies, it hadn't made much sense to him. It was only later they discovered her real purpose in Egypt. The failed hit on her and McKenzie had been a mistake. Now with their exit from New York it had become apparent that this had become a three way struggle. Lazarus had had her under his thumb somehow. Maybe it didn't need to be this way. Maybe she could be reasoned with, though he was certain she'd never part with the crystals.

That was why he had decided to offer her a deal. One that he prayed she'd take. If she didn't, then there might not be anything else he could do for her and her students. His boss would get those crystals at all costs. He believed too deeply that what he was doing was the right thing, not just by keeping them away from Lazarus, but from humanity itself. The information that was on those crystals had to be kept from the world at all costs. If she wouldn't give them up right then, maybe she would come back with him, listen to his boss' reasoning and see the truth of what she was doing, the danger her research presented to the world.

He'd never met Carter before and maybe that could be his advantage. He wouldn't be recognized as an immediate threat. If his boss had come, just the sight of him might have sent them on another flight for solitude and safety. Time was running short. She would solve the riddle soon and then there would be no hope. The information would be unleashed upon the world. He needed her to stop now, preferably without bloodshed. He knew she believed she was only doing what was right. Maybe if she understood that Mr. James was the good guy here, not some black market racketeer that wanted to make millions off the discovery. Eldon James stood to profit nothing.

Ninety minutes later he was in Okeechobee swatting mosquitoes and paying for a ride into the heart of the Everglades.

* * *

Isabella was tired. It was the second day and they had all of the crystals scanned. The work had gone on nearly nonstop. When one student got tired another would take over while the others slept. Micco's facility was set up for extended stay research which included a kitchen and a well stocked pantry, the joys of which McKenzie had discovered almost immediately.

As self-appointed cook, he'd kept everyone fed as the research had moved ahead. It wasn't that he wasn't interested, he simply had no idea where else he could help.

Isabella on the other hand, had become buried in the images of the scanned crystals. This was what she did the best. She focused on different combinations angles and directions. She was working in the dark and she knew it, but there were rules that written languages followed. Most used letters were likely vowels of the "E," "A," and "O" variety. Then "T," "R," and "S" would be the most commonly used consonants followed by "N," "M," and "D."

The program Bob had written had tracked, numbered and catalogued the usage of each of the symbols. Isabella was using the data for her basis of analysis. The program had also coupled most commonly used character combinations that would represent words. They found several of those combinations repeated and those were numbered and catalogued. The problem was, without some basis for a starting point, some clue to the text, it was all guess work and nothing was falling into place.

Bob on the other hand still believed that they were all on the wrong track. He still believed what they were looking at was some type of format coding for some form of computer language. Since she had had no luck on her own, Isabella had given Bob her blessing to follow his own theory. If he was right, he might be able to write a program that could analyze and assimilate the unknown language into a readable computer image. She believed that they should follow every course of investigation that had any possibilities. Bob was a genius when it came to computers. She felt that if anybody could do it, it would be him.

That was when the visitor arrived. An airboat had pulled up at the dock and tied up. Jason Hand had arrived. He walked up the dock towards the building, the ride had left him with gratitude he was once again on dry land.

John Micco and McKenzie had spotted the boat as it approached. They came out to meet it. McKenzie was wary and kept his hand on the revolver he had hidden in the back of his pants, though he figured if trouble was going to be involved, coming alone would accomplish very little.

John approached Jason with his hand extended. "Hello, I'm John Micco. I'm the head researcher here. Is there something I can do for you?"

Jason smiled and returned the handshake. "Good to meet you. My name is Jason Hand and I'm looking for Dr. Isabella Carter. I need to talk to her. It's extremely important."

"There isn't any Dr. Carter here," replied Micco. McKenzie had stepped back and to the side slightly so that he could watch Jason's every move.

"It's alright," Jason continued. "I don't mean her any harm. I know she's here. I was able to track her and her fake card. I hope you realize that means I'm probably not the only one. Now can I see her?"

Micco sighed, he knew it was only a matter of time before trouble would arrive. "Come on. I'll show you where she is." He led Jason into the building. McKenzie brought up the rear so that he could watch Hand's every move. He didn't trust him at all. Hand hadn't said who he was working for and it bothered McKenzie. Was it Fane? James? Or some new faction that had gotten involved that they didn't know about.

Hand was led into the lab, but Micco and McKenzie insisted that he stay at the door. They didn't want him seeing anything associated with the research. Isabella looked up and frowned. She came over to the door.

John spoke up, "He insisted on seeing you."

"You know me?" she asked.

"No, we've never met, but I'm sure you've heard of my boss Eldon James."

Both Isabella and McKenzie went for their guns. "Last time we heard from your boss, he was trying to kill us," said McKenzie.

"Yes, that was regrettable and it was a misunderstanding," said Jason. "He once sent you a note saying he would be in touch. I'm here to extend an invitation.

"So, what you're saying is the two bullets aimed at us were for the people in the next room? Come on. Taking us for stupid will only get you killed," replied Isabella, a definite tone of acidity was in her voice.

"That's not what I mean," backpedaled Jason. "We thought you were working for Lazarus. We couldn't let him get control of the crystals. We've realized our error since. I just want to talk to you."

"I'm not buying it, Doc. There's something about this guy that smells and it's not just the swamp and gasoline from his ride here."

Isabella concentrated for a moment, reached out with her mind trying to get a feel for the newcomer. He believed what he was saying, that much she could pick up. "It's OK, Mac. Let's hear what he has to say. If we don't like it, we can shoot him later. I'm sure John here has some hungry alligators we can feed the body to."

McKenzie grinned big. "I like that plan."

Jason however wasn't that thrilled with it. "Even if you don't like what I have to say, could you maybe refrain from the killing part. The idea of my own death is a bit unsettling to me."

"Not to me," said McKenzie.

They went to Micco's office. Isabella wanted Jason away from the research and the students. She didn't want him to see them. Her students were worried enough as it was and she was worried enough about them.

Isabella came in last and closed the door behind them. "OK, here's your chance, talk."

"It's like this," he began. "You're on the run from what you perceive is two enemies. Mr. James is not your enemy. As I said, before, it was a misunderstanding. We want the crystals, yes, and we are willing to go to extreme measures to get them. But we are only willing to do that as a last resort."

"It didn't seem like that in Egypt," said McKenzie. "I lost my job, I was kicked out of the country. I've got no reason to like or trust your boss."

"I have to agree with Mac," said Isabella. "It seems to me your last resorts come long before exhaustion of possibilities."

"I need you to come back with me, speak to Mr. James," he continued. "Understand why he wants the crystals, see that his motives aren't like those of Lazarus Fane. I guarantee you safe passage. Consider it a flag of truce."

"Why can't you tell us yourself what he wants? It would save us all a lot of trouble. Better yet, why didn't he come himself?" asked Isabella.

"I'll answer your last question first. Mr. James is in a war with Lazarus Fane. In an attempt to disable his network of criminals, he blew Fane's office up. It was also a message to Lazarus to back away from the crystals or the next one wouldn't come with a warning."

Isabella was visibly shocked by the news. "Eldon James blew up Fane's office?"

"Yes, not long after you left."

"Oh my god," she sat down. When she could find words, she continued. "Let me guess. Lazarus is coming after your boss with a vengeance."

"Yes, how'd you know?"

"It's what I would have done."

Now it was Jason's turn to be puzzled. "Why?"

"You're not an archaeologist are you, Mr. Hand? When you see the displays in a museum, they're just interesting curiosities to you aren't they? Well, to Lazarus Fane they are objects of a deep love. He doesn't have a family, he has his collection. That office was full of unique and priceless museum quality artifacts that any curator would have sold his first-born for. There were the finest items handpicked by him from every ancient culture known to man. All of them were priceless and irreplaceable. Your boss did the equivalent of blowing up a room in the museum of Natural History. He blew up Lazarus Fane's one true love, a lifetime worth of work and acquisition. Right now, I would bet, your boss is a walking dead man."

"Well, he didn't waste any time responding," Jason went on. "He sent a Cicero Smith to kill me. They attacked my home and shot..."

"Cicero Smith?" asked Isabella. "This is only getting worse by the minute. You do realize he's Lazarus Fane's number one killer and frequently his right hand man?"

"I'm beginning to. I was able to get him charged with murder before I left. I hope it will get him out of the way for a while."

"You really don't have a clue do you?" Isabella had sunk lower in the chair. "Cicero Smith is a killer. Fane is a very powerful man. The charge won't stick for long. All your murder charge probably did was sent him following you which will of course lead him right to us."

"Well, I have to admit, finding you wasn't all that difficult, Dalve Wolf. If I can do it, Fane can too. Trust me, it wasn't that clever of an alias. Anyway, that's even more reason for you to come back with me. We can protect you. Which brings me to your first question, why won't I just tell you what he wants? I don't understand it like he does. He has a vision of the consequences of your research that threatens us all. He feels that because of a chance meeting in the Caribbean, he has been chosen for this task. Mr. James is an extremely powerful man too and he has used all of his resources in locating these crystals. He is using his connections in every possible way to keep them from the possession of those like Lazarus Fane and others that would pervert the information on them for profit and power. You're badly outnumbered and outclassed here. There's you, these two and four students. You obviously know how many men Fane has at his disposal. We can tip the scales for you. We can provide protection for you."

"From the sounds of things," Isabella responded, "going to New York and stepping into a war zone doesn't seem liked the 'A' choice to me. So far, we were doing fine here until you showed up. Now I'm thinking maybe we're going to have to move again. Besides it doesn't sound like you're doing that good of a job protecting yourself if Smith is after you and attacking your home. It seems sloppy to me. It's only a matter of time until you're dead. I've been dealing with Fane for a lot of years. I know what to expect. But then again, I'm not stupid enough to blow up his office. "

She turned to McKenzie, "I'm thinking maybe you'd better keep a close watch outside. He's probably right about if one's on our trail, then Fane or Smith is probably not far behind. John, do we have an escape plan."

Micco shrugged, "Until you arrived I never thought I'd need one. I'll work on it though. I have some people I can call."

"Listen Hand, I've heard your proposal and I have to admit, I'm not even remotely inclined to take it. I have no reason to trust your employer and after Egypt I really don't have a reason. You seem as though you can be trusted to keep your word, but New York is a quicksand pit. You don't step in one on purpose."

Jason asked, "Can I see how far you are on your research?"

"Not on a bet."

It was the answer he'd expected. It had been worth a try. His only other solution was going to be to steal the crystals or kidnap her. The latter seemed like an insurmountable job at the moment. Stealing the crystals was probably the better option. He had his guns. They were probably unarmed and wouldn't take any chances. He had never met them before, they wouldn't know what to expect. He had no idea how badly he'd assessed the situation.

* * *

Lazarus Fane was looking at a list of offices located in the building he suspected of housing Eldon James. His focus was on those on the top floor. He knew if his brother would have his lair anywhere, it would be there. Next to him were blueprints, the architectural layouts. A quick call to city hall had produced those in short order. Fane was trying to come up with a strategy. One that would be successful without having to exit through an army of SWAT officers.

He wanted Eldon dead, true, but he wanted to be free when it was over to enjoy his victory, then put a bullet through the head of a particular archaeologist thorn in his side. He was amazed at how these people had become such nuisances to what he had conceived was a perfectly simple, straight forward plan.

Now he was being forced to spend way too much time conceiving and exacting revenge, when all that had to happen was everyone just doing what he said. He hated it when people didn't pay attention. Now he was going to have to risk an attack on a populated office building, just because Eldon had been stupid enough to cross him. But, it had to be done. There was no letting this one go. He thought for a moment. Had he ever let anything go? Nope. Perfect record by his recollection.

This was one operation he was going to have to orchestrate himself. He would have to see Eldon dead to be sure of the success of this one. The problem was that none of the offices were registered to names he could identify that would belong to Eldon. Granted to operate in the dark as he had, Eldon would have had obscure dummy corporation names, but even then there should be some clue to determine his hand at the helm. Lazarus wasn't finding anything that left him with any certainty. Actually it was the opposite, he had doubts, too many of them. He was going to have to find some way to assure himself of Eldon's presence in an exact location. He needed to be sure of where Eldon's office was precisely. Otherwise the ground to air hand held missile launchers would only stir up a hornet's nest, a big one.

There was always the option of landing a crew of hired mercenaries on the roof and having them drop over the sides and come in through the windows with ARs blazing. Then he could walk in behind them and try to identify the pieces.

No, that would still attract too much attention too quickly. This had to be more subtle, surgical was what the military called it. Hit and run. All they had to do was remove Eldon. After that everything else would wither and become a non-issue. He could try something devious like poison, or maybe curare. Again, Lazarus shook his head. Tit for tat really called for blowing Eldon into smithereens. He wanted them to have to stuff what was left of him in a jar to have to bury him. Although, blowing him up seemed too quick, too painless. There should be some agony involved in this payback.

The thing he needed was more information, some reliable intel that could assure him that what he was hitting was his real objective. The fact that he had doubts, told him that this could be sloppy. There had been enough of that. What he really needed was someone on the inside of Eldon's inner circle. What he needed was a traitor, one that was in financial trouble. Those were the best kind. They could be manipulated and blackmailed. They wouldn't need money if there wasn't something hanging over their head.

The only name he'd been able to find associated with Eldon was Jason Hand. After Smith's attack on his house, Fane didn't think Hand was an option. There had to be someone else, someone that could get in and not arouse suspicion, someone that could enter Eldon's domain under an official capacity.

One of his men interrupted his thoughts with a knock on his office door. "What?" asked Fane.

"There's a Captain Riley here to see you about some files you wanted," was his answer.

"Send him in," said Fane. "Send him right in."

The Captain came through the door with the files and the report he'd gotten from Lt. Murphy. "Here you are. It's all taken care of. Everything concerning the Cicero Smith incident is right here. Anything else I've personally removed from the database."

Fane was cordial. "Thank-you Captain. Your help has been invaluable. I will make an electronic transfer to whatever account you decide."

"Well, I do have a retirement account that I would appreciate a deposit into. It's one that I've managed to keep off the books if you know what I mean."

Fane nodded, "I understand perfectly. How would you like an even bigger deposit?"

The Captain was immediately interested. It showed on his face, but he was cautious. "I don't want to do anything that would ruin my career."

"I understand Captain. What I have in mind is something that isn't in any way illegal. I just need some information gathered and then report it to me. Nothing more."

Fane handed him the report on the building suspected of being Eldon James'. "I need you to go back to this building under the pretense of gathering just a bit more information on the shooting incident. Try to interview not just Jason Hand, the person that filed the charge, but his boss Eldon James. It is important that you talk to James himself. Insist on it."

The Captain looked at the address and scowled. "This is wrong. This isn't the same address where we picked up the body of the pilot." He reached down and opened the police folder on the case and read quickly Lt. Murphy's report. He then laid it out in front of Fane on his desk and pointed at one of Murphy's entries. "See here. This address and this one don't match. You're looking in the wrong place. Here's where the actual call came from."

Fane leaned back in his chair and let the news sink in. He had been planning an attack on the wrong building! Somehow the flight address had been changed. Whether it was before or after the fact it didn't much matter. He'd almost blown everything.

He leaned forward. "Captain, you've just saved me a lot of trouble. Will you do the job for me?"

Riley nodded. There was nothing to it, a simple routine police interview, piece of cake. "Sure, why not?" he said.

Fane stood up and shook his hand. "You'll see just how much my gratitude can be worth." When Riley had left, Lazarus let out a long sigh. He'd almost blown up the wrong building.

≠ 13 ≠

Cicero Smith hated Florida. As far as he was concerned this place was little more than a breeding ground for vampiric insects. He had five men with him. None of them were happy to be there. The sign at the place they stopped advertized Helicopter Flights into the Everglades. It was just what he had been looking for.

There was an open clearing where the jungle growth had been cut back to create a rough landing area. As they were getting out of the car a smiling dark skinned man, probably an Indian, Smith guessed, came out and started walking up to them. He'd heard this was Seminole territory.

The Seminole lost the smile when he saw six guns pointed at him. Smith backed him up into his house. Cicero asked the man if they had enough fuel to get to the biological research facility. The Indian nodded. He had his men tie him and then they went outside and fired up the choppers. Two of the men Fane had sent him were pilots. One thing he could always count on was that Fane was thinking of all the necessities.

In minutes they were in the air and heading out over the Everglades of Florida. The helicopters would get them there in no time. The Seminole had used an old trick, he had inhaled and tensed his muscles while he was being tied. When he relaxed the ropes were loose. He was out of them in no time.

* * *

Something was nagging Isabella inside her head. There was something that wasn't right. She couldn't quite put it all together, but she had learned from long experience to never ignore these kinds of feelings.

She had been contemplating the things that Jason Hand had said when an unease had come over her. They had a fox in their midst and she wasn't sure whether he'd try something desperate or not.

McKenzie was watching Jason closely. It reassured her that if he did try something, he'd be on it. That was when John Micco returned. He came through the door looking grim. "I was in contact with some of my people on the outside. It appears we have company coming."

Isabella bolted towards the door, "Do we have any idea who?" she asked.

"Not exactly, but they've stolen two helicopters from an Everglades aerial tours. They mentioned the facility as they were committing the theft."

"Smith!" she hissed. "McKenzie, get everyone together and wrap up what we've got."

"On it Doc."

She turned to Jason Hand, "It looks as if you'll have to wait a little longer to try and steal those crystals. Right now you might want to contemplate how you're going to save your own ass." She didn't wait to see the look on his face. She was in motion.

"John," she shouted. "Do we have a way out of here."

"One," he said, "but I don't know how well that's going to work against helicopters."

"Any weapons?"

"A couple of rifles and a few of these," he had a small round thing that looked a little like a grenade.

"Is that what I think it is?"

"Kind of. They don't have as large of a charge. We use them to stun some of the larger more dangerous wildlife down here. They work the same way though. Pull it and throw it. I have a box of these in my airboat. Like I said I don't know how well we're going to do against choppers."

"How do you get this stuff?"

"I'm on the rez, we can get anything."

"You don't happen to have any ground to air missles do you?"

"No, but call ahead next time. If I knew you were coming, I'd have stocked up."

"Any loads for those rifles?"

"Plenty."

"At least we can fire back with some range."

Micco looked skeptical. "Have you ever tried to shoot anything from a moving airboat?"

"Nope," she grinned, "but I'm always open to new experiences."

"How come your new experiences always include the possibility of getting killed?"

"Just lucky I guess."

Isabella went to make sure McKenzie had the students on the move. They were scrambling in the lab, closing up laptops, Jeff was deleting information from the main computers, Sandra was locating and packing the crystals. It was an organized chaos that almost seemed to be becoming a routine with the students.

Karen smiled at her teacher, "We were expecting this and we've talked about it. Always be prepared."

Isabella couldn't help but admire how her students were adjusting to the moment. Hopefully they would be able to hold it together when the shooting started. That would be the real test. "Mac, get them to the boat. I need to find out what Hand is going to do."

Jason was standing out front of the building watching the sky. When she came out he turned to her, "I don't hear anything yet. You might have time to get away if you go now."

"That's exactly what we're doing and you're coming too."

"No I'll stay here and draw their fire so that I can buy you an extra couple of minutes."

Isabella grabbed his arm, "Listen, I've got four students that have never been through something like this. You've got guns, right?" He nodded. "You know how to use them right?" he nodded again." You're coming with us. I need every experienced hand I can get. You'll have to wait 'til this is over to pick up where we left off. Right now, you're on the team."

"OK," was all he said and he followed her through the facility to the back and then out to the moored airboat. McKenzie scowled but didn't say anything. The students were in the middle while Micco was on his elevated seat with his boat controls. Isabella hoped the back of the airboat would shield the students somewhat. If there was a chase, the choppers would be pursuing from behind.

The air was filled with the sound of the boat's propeller as John pulled away from the dock. The boat skimmed the surface picking up speed. Isabella and McKenzie were watching intently to the front and sides looking for any sign of Cicero and the stolen helicopters. Jason watched behind the best he could with the prop blocking his vision. Jeff, Bob, Sandra and Karen waited for something to happen.

Isabella was the first to spot them. They were coming across the glades to the north flying in the direction of the facility. She saw them alter direction and turn their way. She nudged McKenzie and pointed towards the black spots in the sky. Looking back she saw Micco yelling into a microphone headset that was attached to a radio transmitter. She pointed. He nodded. Jason saw what was going on too. McKenzie shouted at Jeff, "Pass me one of those rifles and some shells." It was done.

Jason had a gun in each hand. Isabella had hers pulled too. McKenzie loaded the rifle and then waited.

They threaded in and out of the reeds going at break-neck speed, Micco navigating the waterways expertly.

The helicopters had picked up their pursuit and had fully committed to the chase. Micco saw them coming. Maybe his lab wouldn't get blown up after all, just them. Suddenly he preferred the lab.

The boat kept on in a straight direction while Micco kept yelling into the radio. Both choppers were coming up from behind and along each side. Micco kept the throttle open as bullets started whizzing by. Both McKenzie and Isabella were crouched in the front, McKenzie trying to get a near steady bead with the rifle.

The men in the helicopters appeared to have only handguns so their range was limited, but they had altitude as an advantage. They still had to get fairly close for any kind of accuracy. The guns were firing, but hitting something was left to luck.

The choppers were closing in. Jason, Isabella and McKenzie were all firing now. They seemed to have little or no effect. Ahead as they skimmed across the water, they could see tiny splashes where the bullets struck the surface.

Micco took a sharp turn and went off in a different direction, but the helicopters were right back on them in a couple of minutes. The momentary respite allowed them to reload and begin firing again. This time the helicopters began to encroach on the sides of the airboat. The passengers in the boat could see the faces of their hunters well.

Again Micco made a sharp turn. Again the choppers regained their positions. Karen Arntsen reached behind and under her seat, where she was almost lying horizontal with her classmates to avoid the bullets. She got to her knees and threw something at one of the helicopters. The chopper wobbled and weaved losing its position and then seemed to lose some control. There was a flash in the cockpit, it angled to its side and the blades bit into the water. The craft spun, flipped sending a sheet of water into the air and then buried itself in the water and reeds of the everglades.

Everyone was baffled until Karen grinned and showed them the grenade pin that was still around her finger. She crouched back down. The other one was still hot on their tail. Micco was again making a beeline. He headed straight for a cluster of reeds ahead. As they drew closer the chopper again was right alongside. Isabella could see Cicero Smith inside. He was aiming right at her. He was smiling.

Out of the reeds ahead came airboats, lots of them. The helicopter was hit with a hail of bullets. Spiderweb cracks appeared in the glass that enshrouded the cockpit. The helicopter pulled up and went straight up in the air. It climbed fast. Men and guns were in all of the airboats and they continued firing at the climbing chopper.

It gained altitude until it was out of range of the bullets. Micco raced past the small army of boats and throttled down. He smiled, they'd made it. His plan had worked.

They were escorted out of the swamp back to solid ground. When they were out of the boat Isabella went over to Karen. She had always been the quiet one. It's the quiet ones you have to watch out for. Karen smiled, "Pitcher in high school. All state."

Isabella looked around, grim, they'd come out of it in one piece, but they might not next time. Micco put his hand on her shoulder. She spoke, "Nice plan. I didn't know you could get together such an army that quickly."

He looked around at his Seminole neighbors and answered "You mess with one of us, you mess with all of us."

"Well I'm definitely glad they came to our rescue. We might not have made it without them."

A man came and tapped Micco on the shoulder. John scowled for a second and then said to Isabella, "Someone wants to speak with you, all of you." He motioned at McKenzie, Hand and the students.

He led them away to an old one level, three room house. As they went in there were Native blankets, crafts and artwork decorating nearly every space. An old Seminole sat in a chair watching them come in. "He's one of the tribal Elders and he says he must speak to you. He has a message for you," continued Micco. "His name is Yaha, it means wolf in our language."

Isabella kneeled down and dug into her pack and brought out a paperback book. It was a copy of the *Woman Lit By Fireflys*. She handed it to the old man. "I'm sorry," she said. "I do not carry tobacco or any of the other sacred herbs with me to give."

He took the book and smiled, "You know our ways. The spirit had said you would. It is alright, I like these stories." He set the gift aside and John got out the ceremonial pipe. The rest formed a semicircle around the elder and sat on a large rug in front of him. The pipe was packed with tobacco and herbs. "We must smoke to invite the spirits into our circle. They have told me they have a message for you." The pipe was lit and passed around. Everyone took a puff to complete the circle and begin whatever Yaha had in mind. Isabella sat in the fore, everyone else following her lead.

The old Indian seemed to drift for a minute, McKenzie fidgeted uncomfortably thinking the old man was dozing off, but Isabella motioned for him to be still and he was. Then Yaha's eyes opened and he spoke to Isabella. "The spirit of your teacher has entered the circle. His spirit now roams the world that is beyond but he still watches you, tries to guide you. He says you have lived in that place of darkness too long, that jungle made by men, your feet no longer touch earth. You have forgotten what it feels like to be a part of the southern forest, to know the ways and movements of the jungle. The Jaguar within you must awaken as it did so long ago. Remember who you are and who you were. Remember that Kukulcan, Ixchel, and Tzultacaj walk with you always. They guide your footsteps. You are surrounded by warriors with great abilities. The four are young and brave. You must trust in them and use them as you would the dart and the blowgun."

The old man then pointed to Jason Hand, "Inside of you is the spirit of the bear, great and strong. You do not know this and you must welcome this part of your nature. Before you is a great void that will threaten to consume your spirit. When this comes you must cling to the Jaguar, it will guide you from this place of darkness."

He then pointed towards McKenzie. "You are the hawk. You fly from place to place, circling, searching. You see the world from a different place and your eyes are sharp and keen as are your talons. You see the jaguar and the bear as they prowl below. Dangers that are ahead are yours and yours only to see. When the darkness comes, it will be your talons that saves all."

Yaha had finished. He'd said everything he'd needed to. The group left his home and stood outside. Isabella stood straight and tall. She felt the hot Florida breeze caress her face as she seemed to be looking somewhere distant. Her hair was dancing with the breeze. All eyes were on her when she spoke. "I'm through running."

Behind her was an audible "Yes!" from Jeff Barnes who held a clinched fist. They were all looking at him. "Hey, I'm sick of this crap."

≈ 14 ≈

By some miracle, Cicero Smith's helicopter pilot hadn't taken a bullet. His other man wasn't so lucky. Smith had pushed him out of the chopper somewhere over the Everglades. The pilot was looking for the first piece of solid ground outside the swamp they could find to land on. It turned out to be a pasture of Hereford cows. The two climbed out grateful to be once again on solid ground.

They had flown in the general direction of Fort Meyers which was away from Carter and the crystals. "Damn her," he cursed. She always seemed to have a knack for escaping his bullets. He remembered the time in Central America when he had gone in to clean out a village near that lost Mayan city she had discovered. The natives had been giving Fane trouble trying to run him off. Somehow the natives had gotten the idea that Carter was the reincarnation of one of their priestesses.

She had apparently been studying the culture under the tutorage of the local shaman. That was where Cicero had found her and him in a trance looking for visions from the gods. Smith had fixed that. He'd put a bullet through the old Indian's head. That was his mistake, he should have done Carter first. She had leaped up and flown through the air and tore at him like some jungle animal. Her face had been painted with some local dyes that added to the illusion.

He'd tried to get to his knife, but her actions had been so fast and fierce that he couldn't. Fortunately one of his men had come in and tried to crack her on the head with the butt of his rifle. It must have been a glancing blow because instead of lying there unconscious, she was gone. They had killed a lot of Indians that night.

Fane had been pleased with the job they had done until the next night. When it got dark, men died. One by one so that the others heard the screams of their comrades as they died in the darkness and wondering who would be next.

During the day, the few men that were left complained of seeing the ghost of a Mayan priestess walking through the ruins. Eventually they had to pull up stakes and leave. Carter had beaten them, but with the massacre of the village, she was left alone. The bitch always survived.

They made their way to a road and caught a ride. They were picked up by a travelling bible salesman who keep rattling on about how the apocalypse was coming and that how everyone should be right with god before the end came. Smith thought of pulling his gun several times and simply ending the righteous jabber, but decided he needed the ride more and the highway was too busy to chuck a body out of the door and expect it to go unnoticed.

Smith wanted to get to Ft. Meyers and a motel with a shower. Then would come the fun, talking to Fane and explaining how badly things had gone. Why had he ever involved Carter? You'd think he'd have learned by now that nothing goes right when she's involved.

The motel they pulled into had a giant flamingo on its sign and was painted in pastel pink and green. Smith wondered, *why was this entire state decorated in pastels? Why couldn't they use real colors.* God, he hated Florida.

He took his shower and then procrastinated his call to Fane by flipping through some channels on the room's TV. Finally he gave in and punched his cell. The voice that answered put him right through to Fane. The voice on the other end asked, "Have you got them? Is she dead?" Cicero had to admit that no was the answer to both questions. "I got shot up by a tribe of Indians," was the only excuse he had. He told Fane he figured she would head somewhere else now and he had no way to track her. Here she was under the protection of the Seminoles and he'd already had a taste of that. Fane said, "Come back. Everything has been taken care of here and I have something for you to do. We can pick up her trail from here." Cicero put down the phone and lay on the bed. All he wanted was rest. He'd go back tomorrow.

* * *

Isabella, Jason, McKenzie and the students had been put into a nice hotel on the reservation. Micco had put it on the tribal card so that it wouldn't send up a credit flag for those that were searching for the group. They all sat together at a table in the restaurant.

Isabella was talking to Jason. "I want to meet with James. You said I could talk to him essentially under a flag of truce, so I can come and go, right?"

"You have my word. But, there's something you need to know. Eldon James is Eldon James Fane, Lazarus' brother."

There was dead silence. Jason spoke first, "I thought you should know."

"Damn right we should know," blurted out McKenzie.

"Mac, It's OK. He told us before I walked in there. Thanks for being honest. Will he keep his word?"

"I think so. He hates his brother, it's why he dropped the last name. I have to admit, these two have taken sibling rivalry to a whole new plateau. They've initiated a war over these crystals that is going to leave a lot more dead before it's over."

"Listen," said McKenzie, "if he's a Fane, I don't see how we can possibly trust him. I mean, there's got to be some similarities, runs in the family kind of thing. Looking from our perspective, when one wants something, their motivations may differ, but I've got to say their methods seem to be identical. They get what they want at all costs, even if they have to kill to do it."

"Mr. Hand," began Sandra, "If the professor goes in there without the crystals, he's going to be angry, her life is going to be on the line. And, if we give him the crystals everything we've done, the research, escapes to keep them safe, the idea which all of us here hold to, that a discovery like this belongs to all humankind, that the greater good outweighs self-interest, will be a waste."

It was Jason's turn. "Normally I would agree, but if the information on these crystals are even part of what we think they are, it is going to rock every facet of human culture to its foundations. It will change religions, science, everything we believe to be true about the evolution of man and society will change. You aren't just on the verge of another archaeological discovery here, you are on the verge of changing all of human history. This can't be taken lightly. If this is dropped on the world at once, the disruption would be monumental."

He turned to Isabella, "That's why I want you to talk to Eldon. He is passionate about this and he is not his brother. I've been with Eldon for a lot of years and I know him to have the best of intentions. This discovery has frightened him to his core. I've never seen him so deeply committed to something. He believes he is right and I have to admit, he makes a very convincing argument. You said I was obviously not an archaeologist. You're correct, I'm not. But, I do believe, just because you are an archaeologist doesn't necessarily mean you're right or the world is ready to bear any kind of revelation about itself."

Bob interjected, "What you're talking about is censorship, suppressing our findings."

"No," said Jason, he looked at Sandra as he made his point. "What I'm talking about is self-interest outweighing the greater good. None of you can tell me, except maybe Mac here, that you haven't thought about what this discovery would do for each of your careers. As grad students this could single-handedly secure plum positions on graduation. Isabella, I'm sure you know what this would do for your reputation. Are you sure your motives are as pure as you make out?"

Isabella responded, "You make good points for sure, but I've had discoveries before. This isn't new for me."

"Not like this," interjected Jason.

"Granted, you're right, not like this, but calling into question the integrity of that of the students here solves little. And I find it a little annoying, but I understand why you've made the point. We've gotten off track here and I want to get back on. Make no mistake, when I go back, I intend to end this." The emphasis in her voice got her everyone's full attention. She looked at Jason pointedly, "I'm not going to be giving anyone these crystals. Neither Eldon or Lazarus is going to get control of them and they are definitely not going to continue to try to push us around. If I have to I'll put them down like diseased dogs. They're going to work with me my way or I'll get them out of the way."

McKenzie couldn't help but smile at this. Jason leaned back in his chair. The students seemed ready for anything. "Jason," she continued, "make a call to your boss. I'm coming to see him. Flag of truce right?" Jason nodded. He'd done all he could, the rest would be up to Eldon.

Isabella addressed the rest. "We leave in the morning. I have a plan."

≉ 15 ≉

Captain Riley approached the building in the report. He was confident that this would be fairly routine. He'd ask a couple of questions about the shooting to this Eldon James and then report back to Fane. All he had to do was confirm his presence. He had no idea why, but truthfully, he didn't want to know. The less he knew about Fane the happier he was.

He entered the building and went up the elevator, top floor. It was a quick ride, mercifully, he hated elevator music. The door opened and he stepped out. The reception area was spacious with a lone desk where a woman was working on a computer. He went up to it and introduced himself. "I'm Captain Riley with the NYPD. I need to speak to a Mr. Jason Hand and Eldon James."

The woman smiled politely and said, "Mr. Hand is unavailable right now. He's on a business trip and his schedule doesn't say when he'll be back."

"That's fine," replied Riley. "May I speak with Mr. James. This is official business." He took out his badge and showed it to her.

She nodded and picked up the phone and punched one of the buttons. She spoke, "There's a Captain Riley here to see you sir. He says it's an official visit. Yes, sir, he showed me his badge, gold sir." Apparently, thought Riley, this James was a careful man.

He heard a click and a door opened where there had seemed to be wall paneling before. "You can go in Captain," the receptionist invited. Riley stepped through into James' office. A man dressed in white on white met him.

"What can I do for you Captain?" asked Eldon. He motioned towards a chair. "Have a seat."

Riley did. "Would you like some kind of refreshment?" Eldon asked.

"No thank-you," Riley relied. "I won't be long."

Eldon went behind his desk and sat down. "So Captain, what's this about?"

"Well, I was hoping I'd be able to talk to Mr. Hand too, but I'm told he's out of town."

"That's correct," confirmed Eldon.

"Well maybe later," continued Riley. "I'm here in regards to the helicopter pilot shooting. Mr. Hand claimed that the actual shooting occurred at his house and not at the heliport, is that correct." Eldon nodded. Riley continued, "Mr. James, is there anything associated with Mr. Hand's job that would precipitate this kind of occurrence?"

"Well, Mr. Hand performs a myriad of jobs for me. He travels all over the world and as we are a corporation, there is going to be those that aren't happy with how we conduct business. This could have come from anywhere. Mr. Hand is a good and effective employee as well as a good man. We've received no threats, and if he had I think he would have come forward with it. We want all of our employees to be safe here and I back them up 100 percent."

"Has he ever had any difficulties like this before?"

"I'm sure if he had, your department would have heard about it. We are always happy to cooperate with the police." Eldon smiled at Riley looking him directly in the eye, and then asked, "Wasn't there another officer assigned to this case? A lieutenant?"

"Yes, but I felt that this visit warranted someone higher ranking. I know you're a busy man and look at it as a sign of respect."

"Of course." Again Eldon gave the Captain the polite smile.

"Well I think I've taken up enough of your time, Mr. James, I want to thank-you for seeing me." Riley stood up to leave and Eldon stood and came around from behind the desk.

"That's quite alright, Captain Riley. If there's anything more please feel free to contact me."

Riley left the office and went down to the street. His next stop would be to Fane and then back to his own office. It had been a piece of cake like he had figured. Routine. Easy money. It was a good day.

* * *

Lt. Murphy stood looking at the body. Drowning victims always looked unnerving to him. "Her name is Alicia Case," the coroner was droning. Then he looked up. "Murphy, she was a student at NYU."

It was a jolt to Murphy. The wet ropes that had bound her lay on another table next to a wet rag that had been a gag. This was not good. It would be a bombshell. They had to solve this one. There would be too big of an outcry from the community and the university about students being safe. When word of this got out the media would be all over it. Even the mayor's office would have something to say about this one.

He let out a long sigh. This one would have to be top priority. The prosecutor's office would insist on it. "We did have some good luck," went on the coroner. "She apparently bit her assailant before she died. We found bits of skin lodged in her teeth."

Murphy walked over to the table and the dead girl. "They say dead men tell no tales. Hopefully this girl will tell us everything before long. Run a DNA profile on the skin and match it in our database. If we're lucky, we'll score a match."

"Already on it," he said. "I do it as a matter of routine, now."

If they could come up with a match, that would save a lot of work. The problem was that the DNA pool was so incomplete. Getting a match was still hit or miss, but it was a chance. Currently, it was their only chance. Right now, she was just another body pulled from the river. There was no idea of motive, no clues as to why? There hadn't been rape involved, just murder. "Send your report to me the second you get it. There's going to be some screaming about this one and I'm going to need answers, fast."

"I know," said the coroner."As soon as I have it, you'll have it."

"Thanks," said Murphy. He walked away shaking his head. Girl students trussed up and thrown in the river, he just hoped it wasn't the start of a trend.

* * *

Isabella, McKenzie, Hand, and the students caught a cab from JFK airport on Long Island. They had decided to avoid La Guardia and go straight to Jason's house. They had concluded that after the ill-fated attack no one would be looking for them there.

Micco had seen them off that morning. He seemed sort of sad to see them go. "You really livened things up around here," he'd said to Isabella.

"At least your facility is still in one piece," Isabella had retorted.

"Thanks for that. Good Luck back in the city."

Micco had shaken hands with them all and then he hugged Isabella. She winced slightly but returned the affection. "Take care of yourself John." She'd watched him until they made the turn in the boarding tunnel. It had been good to see him again. She had always been sorry that she couldn't return the affection he'd always wanted to give her.

It was about 40 minutes and they were at the Long Island house. They got out of the two cabs they had hired and went to the house. Jason disabled the alarm and they went in. "Spread out and make yourselves at home," he said. "This place is rarely used, it's probably about time there was some life in it."

"I'm thinking food," said McKenzie.

"Help yourself," replied Jason, "There's plenty here."

"I think this will work fine for a base of operations for now." Isabella sat down. The students had spread out around the room and were already involved in their own pursuits.

Bob, particularly was tapping away on his computer. He looked up and saw his teacher watching him. "I think I'm close to something." He said. "I've been writing this program that I think will integrate some of the symbols into binary traditional coding so modern computers can read it. The more I do this, the more I really think this is formatting code. I'm reasonably sure that whoever wrote this had some form of computers similar to ours. The difference is like when one computer can't read a file from another because it was from an older restyled operating system or like how an Apple program won't work on a computer loaded with Linux or Microsoft. I think we're dealing with the very same principal. I'm close, I know it."

Isabella walked over and watched him over his shoulder for a few minutes. He was typing equations and language codes faster than she could keep up. It was what Bob did. It was a second language to him. Truthfully it might even have been his primary language and he was very fluent in it. Jeff and Sandra were sitting next to each other studying the scanned symbols turning them over and over and up and down, sideways, vertical, every direction they could.

Jason and Mac were cooking. The smell was filling the house rapidly making everyone realize how hungry they were. Eating regularly had been out of the question and now that they had slowed down for the evening, the realization had come over them all.

Karen sat studying the crystals themselves. She had taken it upon herself to have Micco's computer's create a molecular model of the crystals. It had bothered her that they were flawless, the same size. Quartz in its natural state wasn't uniform. Like all natural things it varied. There were factors in its formation that were uncontrolled, heat, pressure, all of it from the formation of the earth. The uniformities shouldn't be there unless they weren't natural. It was something that had been bothering her for quite a while. The problem was that it had been difficult to focus over the last few days. Now as everything had settled down for the moment. She was about to expose the secret.

The crystals were grown. It was something they could even do today with the current technology. Use a shard of quartz for a seed and then grow in a matter of days what it would take millions of years to do naturally. These were an ancient version of the same thing.

"Professor Carter, these crystals were cultured," Isabella came over to look at what her computer was displaying.

"Are you sure?"

"Yes, you see here in the computer analysis of the crystals they're all identical, but just as importantly, no impurities. If they were grown naturally there would be traces of other minerals evident that would have been absorbed when the crystal grew. So what we're looking at is a manufactured data storage system. These weren't gathered and then etched. They were being produced on a mass scale. At one time these may have been as popular as CDs or a record collection."

"Great work," complimented Isabella. "We'll crack these things yet.

From the kitchen came the chorus of "Food" from McKenzie and Hand.

* * *

Cicero Smith walked into the Sault Ste Marie waterfront building. It was different here than in New York. There was an Icy feel to the air that made him shiver a bit. He was grateful to be out of Florida. He needed to regroup and this was a good way to do it. Lazarus Fane was in his office. Cicero went straight to it.

"So what happened down there?" Fane asked. "I'm almost beginning to think you're losing your touch."

"I'm still not completely sure, except that it appears Carter had a lot more allies down there than we counted on."

Smith spent a few minutes relating the tale from his perspective. Fane listened intently and when Smith finished, he commented. "I think what you underestimated wasn't Carter but the person she went to see, John Micco. He's a Seminole Indian, but more importantly, a prominent member of the tribe. Once he was involved, the entire reservation was involved. Plus you said you stole the helicopters from an Indian? You were doomed to failure right from the start." Fane's voice had taken on a tone of definite irritation.

Smith winced uncomfortably. It was true, everything he had done lately had seemed to backfire or there was some miscalculation that had come back to haunt him.

Lazarus studied him for a minute and then, seeming to be satisfied, gave Smith his new orders. "I have obtained information where Eldon is located. The source is 100 percent reliable. The job I have for you is what you do best."

Cicero grinned. He knew what the job was and he knew he'd better not blow this one. If he did, he'd better disappear where Fane couldn't find him because Fane wasn't going to take this one lightly. No, he had to succeed.

"Here's the address," said Fane. "Eldon is smart and wary. You'll have to come up with something clever and you will have to do it fast. If he has time to react, he'll have you pegged in a heartbeat."

"Got it boss. I'll get right on it. I have an idea how I can get in there without arousing any suspicion." Cicero got up. He'd need some time to prepare.

⚍ 16 ⚍

Lieutenant Murphy got a call from the Coroner. "I thought I should get back to you as quickly as I heard. We got a match on the DNA sample. We were lucky and it came right up. It's someone by the name of Cicero Smith."

Murphy sat bolt upright. He'd been sleeping, but he was wide awake now. The name Cicero Smith had stuck with him. It was the name that had been attached to the killing of the helicopter pilot. This was something he could sink his teeth into. Since he'd called the suspect's name up on the computer something hadn't set right with him. There was accusation after accusation, but nothing had ever stuck. The guy was teflon.

There had to be someone protecting him, someone behind him that allowed him to walk every time. There was either lawyers funded by someone with serious cash, or there was someone on the inside. Likely it was the first option, cash and lawyers.

He'd find out soon, strong coffee, some breakfast and a call to Long Island to get the folder back. He'd nip this guy in the bud before he could kill again. The best thing Alicia Case could have done before she died was provide the evidence of her killer. She may have died, but she was testifying anyway.

* * *

It was morning and a miracle was happening. Jason Hand had got up and was making coffee for everyone. His sight was blurred and he needed to focus. Isabella wasn't far behind him and saw he was already in the process of creating the beverage that was so necessary to getting her synapses firing. That was when she noticed Bob.

Bob Peters had been working all night. He looked it, but he hadn't been able to stop. He was muttering to an invisible companion, "I've almost got it. It's almost there, it's almost there and hit the "enter" button. He sat back watching, his hands poised over his computer like he was trying to grasp something invisible.

On his screen came an image. It was that of a half built pyramid, but the image was skewed, shuffled slightly, but it was there. "I've got something!" he shouted.

It took a moment for his declaration to sink into the fog that encased Isabella and Jason's brains, but it did. Isabella came over blinking her eyes, fighting for clarity and cocked her head slightly looking at what was on Bob's computer. "What happened," she said, "someone upload a bad picture on the internet." She still wasn't getting it.

Bob had leaned back. "I did it. It's part of what's on one of the crystals. Somehow I missed something in my coding, but it's there. I'm close. This particular crystal for some reason has something to do with pyramids. This is all I've been able to bring in so far, but it's something. It proves I was right. The symbols we've been looking at is code for an unknown operating system. It's not an actual language as we see spoken languages, it's a computer language."

Isabella let this soak in. It wasn't easy without coffee, but Jason brought her a cup of fresh brewed and she at least had hope of future comprehension. She took the hot cup, sipped and went back studying Bob's screen. "So you're saying that on one of the crystals is the image of a partially built pyramid?"

"Yes," said Bob. He was filled with excitement and was actually shaking slightly. "I haven't been able to bring up any text yet. I think I may have made some small errors in the program I wrote. I'll have to go back and rewrite it until I get it to display everything. I know there's more information in there on this one crystal. It's just not displaying it yet. I don't know where I went wrong but,…"

Isabella interrupted, "From where I stand you went very right. This is amazing work. I can promise you, there's definitely a passing grade in this."

Bob had one of those smiles a smack in the head couldn't wipe off his face. "I need to figure out where I went wrong. There should be more to this."

"It's OK," said Isabella. "You've come a long way. Maybe if you went and got some sleep for a while, a new perspective on things, might help. This is truly amazing. You've reached into the past and pulled out a piece of it. We'll get there. You'll get there. Walk away from it for a while, let your mind relax."

Jason was looking at the pyramid. "Something having to do with a pyramid does make sense with its point of origin Alexandria."

Isabella pulled him to the side. "We're going to see James here in a while. Can I count on you not to mention this?"

Jason took a sip of his coffee. "Near as I can tell you haven't learned anything yet. It's just a picture of a half-built pyramid and a poor one at that. I don't see anything that's earth shattering here." He took another sip of his coffee and walked away.

A sleepy McKenzie wandered in. "What's new?"

"A fresh pot of coffee," said Jason.

* * *

Lt. Murphy was on the phone at his desk. He was talking to an officer at the Long Island Police Department. "What do you mean you never requested them?"

The voice on the other end was explaining, "We never requested the case. Our department had decided to let your precinct handle it since all of the witnesses seemed to be on your end. We never put in the request."

"But," Murphy tried to continue. "My Captain..." he let it trail off. And then, "Thanks for your time Sergeant. If I need anything else I'll get back to you." He hung up the phone. He went into the computer to call up Smith's file. It was gone. All of the information that had been there a couple of days ago was gone. He sat back in his chair. He let it soak in. He needed an address for Smith. There was nothing. He knew where he could get it though. Suddenly he was happy for paperwork. There would be booking files downstairs with the uniforms. They would have written up their own report. Those would still be there. They would take a few minutes to dig out, but they'd be there. These wouldn't have been databased. It was too big of a job. Nobody had that kind of time.

He picked up his cellphone and went to the Captain's door and knocked. "Yea?" came from inside. Murphy opened the door and sat in the chair.

"Captain, did you send that file on the helicopter shooting over to Long Island?"

"Of course, why? Didn't I tell you to drop that case? It wasn't ours anymore."

"Yep Cap. I just wanted to grab an addy out of it, but if it's gone, no big deal. Later Captain."

Murphy got up and walked back out into the squad room. He reached into his pocket and turned off the audio recorder on his cell phone. He would go downstairs and get the address he needed. He'd have work for a couple of uniforms anyway. Then, a trip uptown to Internal Affairs and the Prosecutor's office. So much to do, so little time.

≈ 17 ≈

Jason and Isabella got out of Jason's car in the underground parking garage below the building that housed the offices of Eldon James. McKenzie had stayed behind though not without ample protests. Isabella insisted that he needed to stay and protect the students while they continued on the work with the crystals. Jason had assured him that Isabella would be returning, he'd give n his word on it. McKenzie had finally relented, but McKenzie had the last word. "If she doesn't, I'm coming looking." He looked him in the eyes as he said it and Jason knew McKenzie meant it.

He had put his hand on Mac's shoulder. "It's OK I won't let anything happen to her."

They went to the elevator that went up to Eldon's office. They stepped out and Jason went up to the receptionist. "Welcome back Mr. Hand," she smiled. "I'll let Mr. James know you're here."

"And Dr. Isabella Carter," he said to her. The receptionist nodded and called Eldon. The door buzzed and opened immediately. Eldon stood there waiting to welcome them. "Welcome Dr. Carter, Glad you're back, Jason"

Isabella was gazing at the white on white wardrobe of Eldon's. "I'm thinking maybe you could use a little variety in your wardrobe," she commented. "Weren't you wearing this in Egypt."

Eldon smiled tightly, "I have several of these. But let's get to the point, shall we, did you bring me the crystals?"

"No," said Isabella, "I came to talk, not deliver. Jason thinks that after I talk to you I might be convinced to give them to you. I'm not inclined to agree."

Eldon walked around behind his desk. "Dr. Carter, you must give those crystals to me. It is imperative that Lazarus Fane never get his hands on them."

"Trust me he's not going to. It'll be over my dead body."

"That's what worries me. That doesn't accomplish the aim. Listen Dr. Carter, you might think you can keep control of the crystals, even die trying, but if you die and still have them, he wins.

He gets them and then so does every crack-pot dictator, terrorist, regime, super power, whoever is willing to pay the price. I can't have that. If you keep them and discover what is on them, you're going to make the information available academically. I can't have that either."

"So according to you, no one can have them except you. What makes you so high and mighty that you know better than everyone else? What makes yours the supreme logic?"

"Dr. Carter, let's look at this from another perspective for a moment. We don't know where these crystals came from, but we can agree that they are artifacts from some time gone by, correct?"

"Yes," said Isabella. Jason watched quietly as the two debated.

"If that is so, then by their very nature they shouldn't exist. There is no recorded culture or time in history where man achieved this level of technology where the crystals and the information on them could have been created. It is academically out of the realm of possibility and yet, there they are. You have satisfied yourself that these are not fakes, am I correct?"

She nodded.

"Then we have to take the next leap and hypothesize that they are the product of legends, namely Atlantis or Lemuria or some lost culture like them. Some people would claim aliens, but I think they are from an earthbound source, as I suspect you do as well. In the writings of the Greeks and the Egyptians there are allusions to other races in other parts of the world that co-existed with them in the early days of the rise of their cultures. There were tales brought back by those that explored the seas in those early times reporting of great civilizations beyond the known seas or in some cases the edge of the world. They were spoken about in whispers because the wonders of these places exceeded the capacities of their imaginations and challenged their beliefs of the world. In our world today we have parts of the earth that are highly advanced and then there are other parts that are as primitive as they were a thousand years ago. This diversity of culture and advancement is nothing new. Some regions rise while others fall or are left behind. It's the nature of society. So, having an advanced society while other portions of the globe are lagging behind is not unusual.

"That's all fine and I don't disagree with any of it so far. But you're not telling me anything I don't know already. You still haven't explained why it is so important for you to have the crystals and no one else."

"I'm getting to that. Whatever civilization created these crystals, it appears they had some influence on others that we are aware of, hence the discovery in Alexandria within the ruins of the library. That easily leads one to the conclusion that the Egyptians, if not the Greeks, were aware of their unique significance. Both civilizations refer to a place called Atlantis by name. Other parts of the world, ancient writings in India speak of a place called Lemuria. Some thought that when Ankor Wat was found, that it was a remnant of Mu, but tests have proven that it is far too new for that. Both places are described to have great technological wonders and more importantly a crystal based technology. These places fit the criteria for having developed a technology that might have designed these crystals. Even if they aren't the product of these two, though I think it is likely they are, someone created them. Human beings at some point have risen to a point of advancement that is equal to or beyond the point humanity is at right now. The fact that we can't prove it speaks volumes. The fact that there is no trace of them having ever been found, no archaeological evidence at all, except for these few crystals paints a very dark picture. Somehow they created something that was so powerful they were wiped out without a trace. Nothing. If we were to destroy ourselves now, with nuclear weapons, there would still be some kind of evidence that we were here, that we existed. For them there is nothing. Plato writes that Atlantis was destroyed by some kind of cataclysmic catastrophe that has it swallowed by the ocean. He claims that this was done by nature, but what if he simply couldn't conceive of anything else? The power they must have created to wipe themselves off the earth without any trace at all, entire civilizations, continents even, suddenly gone. Nothing is left, no writing, no ruins, no art, no evidence at all, wiped away clean. Somehow they destroyed themselves and all that they had accomplished. Mankind as we know it consists of children born out of destruction. Today we teeter on the edge of it again. To hand the world a tool of this kind of magnitude would only repeat that mistake of destruction. The information on those crystals can't be allowed to fall into anyone's hands."

He looked hard at Isabella. She responded, "You still haven't answered the question of why you?"

Eldon reached into his desk. "These were McKenzie's. With a flourish he tossed Mac's crystals on the desktop. "I should have them because I am the only one willing to do this." The movement was fast and accurate. He brought the hammer that had been in his drawer down on the crystals sending shattered shards in every direction.

Isabella felt herself getting nauseous. There was a sickening tightening in her stomach as she watched the useless fragments fall to the floor in front of her. Her mind raced with the tragedy and sacrilege. He had done it so fast, so unexpected. She hadn't had time to save them.

Even Jason hadn't expected this. He drew back repulsed by his boss's demonstration. He had always thought they would control the information. Screen it and then release what they deemed dangerous. Being around the research team the last few days had made him realize their importance. "Sir, is doing that absolutely necessary?"

"Weren't you listening to what I said?" Eldon was yelling now. His patience was gone. The emotion of the moment had gripped him. "Now, Dr. Carter, are you going to bring me those crystals?"

It took her a moment to speak. She was still recovering from the shock of the destruction. "If I had even considered it before, I surely wouldn't now."

Eldon looked at Jason. "Then hold her until she changes her mind. I'm sure we can find somewhere secure around here for her to think about it for awhile."

Isabella spun towards Jason and was about to say something, but he was first. "No, I can't."

"What do you mean you can't. You work for me remember." Eldon's voice had taken on a sinister edge.

"I can't," he said. "I gave her my word that if she came her she could leave under her own free will. I'm not breaking it."

Isabella glared at Eldon. She knew he was a Fane and he had shown it in the last few moments. Eldon stared at her. "I'll get those crystals. You can't keep them from me. Jason, get her out of here."

Jason took the cue from his boss and ushered her out the door. The office door closed and they went to the elevator. Jason spoke first, "I'm coming with you."

"Why, so you can report back to your boss our every move. No way. That's not going to happen."

"Listen," he said and grabbed her by the shoulders. He had no idea how close he came to getting hurt in regions that repair slowly. "I don't agree with what went on in there. I thought we'd analyze the information and then keep what was dangerous out of public hands. I never thought he wanted them destroyed. I could have done what he said back there. I could have led him and some men back to the house and this would have been all over. I didn't. And I won't."

She studied him for a moment. He was telling the truth, she could feel he was disturbed, even worried.

He continued, "I have an idea on how we can settle this, find out for sure what's on those crystals. Then we can see the information first, decide for ourselves how bad the impact will be and then make a decision that doesn't include destroying them. I need to go to my office to get my laptop. Come with me, please."

Isabella nodded. They stopped at the floor below and went to Jason's office. He disconnected a couple of USB connections and then folded it. He slid it into its case and then started to leave. That was when they felt the building shake. It was a sudden jolt and shifting that accompanied a muffled boom. The pair stared at each other and saw bits of dust and dirt fall from the ceiling. There was little doubt, it was an explosion!

⚡ 18 ⚡

Getting the jacket, hat and clipboard from one of the New York Messenger Service messengers had been easy. A pop on the back of the head had done nicely. Cicero Smith would go unnoticed as he entered the building that housed Eldon James. This had to work.

He approached the elevator keeping his hat down low. He'd stuffed cotton between his lips and his gums to change the shape of his face. It was an old trick but it was effective. Colored contact lenses changed the shade of his eyes. If anyone did look at him the description would be wrong. If he was picked up on a video camera, the elevator shoes would make him appear taller. The powder in his hair had given it a grey look, on surveillance he'd seem older.

He stepped off the elevator on the top floor. The receptionist looked up and smiled, "Can I help you?"

"Yes, I have a message for a Mr. Eldon James." He tried to alter his voice deeper.

"I'll take it," she said.

"It's special. I need to have him sign for it. I apologize for the inconvenience, but it's what they told me, can't leave unless I witness his signature."

She picked up the phone and explained the situation to the voice on the other end. When she hung up, she turned to Smith, "He'll be out in just a moment."

Cicero smiled and turned slightly so that he could get his hand on his gun without her seeing it. Eldon's door clicked and began to open. He rushed towards it bringing out his gun. He pushed through and saw the man in white on the other side. He relished the surprised look on Eldon's face as his gun fired into the chest. There was a delight in Smith's eyes as he watched the victim spin and fall to the floor face down. There was nothing to compare with looking into a dying man's face when he turned him over to face him. He thoroughly enjoyed seeing the deep red blood contrasting with the pure white of Eldon's attire.

There would be one last thing, the best part. He reached inside of his coat and brought out the surplus army issue hand grenade. He pulled the pin and shoved it into Eldon's coat. Smith grinned, "Your brother says 'hello.'"

Cicero knew from experience that he had five seconds to get out of there. He wasted none of them. He headed out the door. He glanced over to where the receptionist had been but she had run when he had fired the gun. It was smart too, because he would have had to take her out on the way out. Now he had to just get out of there. Not only to avoid the explosion, but to avoid the police which she would assuredly be calling. He went to the stairs instead of the elevator. It'd get him away from the explosion faster. Waiting for an elevator was too unpredictable. He'd gone down two floors when he felt the jolt of the explosion.

He couldn't help but have a satisfied grin on his face. It had been a job well done and a pleasure to do. God he loved his work.

* * *

Jason and Isabella bolted for the elevators. The jar of the explosion had set off a safety trigger and they weren't working. They went to the stairwell and ran up, skipping stairs as they went. Ahead of them was the reception desk and the blackened door to Eldon's office.

Jason stopped. "I can't look."

Isabella went forward and peered inside. Then she came away. The inside had been destroyed by the explosion. She got a hold of Jason. "We have to get out of here." The police will be here any minute. There's nothing we can do."

Jason looked at her, agony and anger decorated his features. "If I had only been there. I didn't agree with him, but he's been good to me over the years. Working with him has been my life. If only we had been there just a little longer, maybe we could have prevented..."

"It's done, we can't change it." Isabella interrupted. "All we can do is go after Lazarus now. Make him pay." She pulled Jason to the stairwell. He wasn't himself and they had to get out of there. They had to get back to the house. If Fane had hit Eldon, she and the students was the only problem left. They'd be next on the list and now he could give them his full attention. Fortunately, she didn't think Lazarus was aware they'd returned to New York yet.

The police passed them on the stairs. "Evacuating," was all she had to say as they rushed past to get to the scene of the explosion. The lower down in the building they got, the more people joined them in the stairways. It appeared an order had gone out to empty the entire building. When it came to explosions the police took no chances in New York. They got people out and asked questions later.

Once they were in the garage they went to Jason's car. Isabella drove. Jason was still dazed and shocked, though he was slowly coming out of it. As they pulled out of the garage, the street was chaos. All of the public services were showing up, Police, Fire, Emergency Medical. They worked their way through to side streets, then the going got easier as they got further away from the scene.

They were going straight to Long Island. She had to make sure they got there soon. Jason was starting to talk. It was a good sign. "You didn't know him. He wasn't evil like his brother. He really was trying to do good. He was trying to make our world better."

Isabella replied, "All we can do now is get Lazarus back. There's so much to get Lazarus back for. He's had this coming for a long time. We're going to go on the offensive. You'll get your chance. I'll get my chance. We're going to rid the world of that son of a bitch once and for all."

⚡ 19 ⚡

Cicero Smith had dumped his disguise and had made his way back to Fane's warehouse in Michigan. He came in with a feeling of triumph, accomplishment. This one had gone right, very right.

Lazarus was waiting for him. He already had heard the reports on the police and emergency band radios. He grinned at Cicero as he came in. "It appears they found one body in the wreckage. No other casualties. Nicely done Cicero."

Harrison smiled. He liked it when his boss was happy. "He was quite surprised when I pulled the gun on him and shot him in the chest. He lived long enough I'm sure to feel the full effect of the explosion."

Fane was ecstatic. "You're sure it was Eldon?"

"Oh yea. There was no mistake. You should have seen the blood on that stupid white outfit of his. He looked so pathetic laying there. He thought he was a big man, but in the end, he was just another victim."

"That was where he belonged, on a casualty list as a victim. He asked for this. He should never have screwed with me. He never really did understand what I was doing, what we could have become together. He always opposed me, tried to stand in my way. It's done now. No more. Now for Dr. Carter."

"I'm ready boss. It'll be a pleasure to take care of her."

"We still haven't located her, but it's only a matter of time. I want you to go get some rest. When we have her I'll call you. I want you clear, at the top of your game. She's never been easy to deal with. You know that. With Eldon out of the game we can focus on her, take our time and get it right. I've made sure we still have someone watching her office if by some chance she gets stupid and comes back to the city. She may think I won't be looking for her here in Michigan and try to hide right under our nose."

"Yes sir," agreed Smith. "You know how to get in touch with me. I'll be ready. I'm heading back to New York immediately."

"Smith, excellent work," Fane commended once again.

Smith turned and left. A bed and his New York apartment was calling him. Hell, he might even celebrate with a cocktail. Had he remembered to fill the ice cube trays?

* * *

Isabella and Jason pulled into the drive of the Long Island house. Outwardly everything looked quiet, undisturbed. Jason had snapped out of his initial shock and now all there was left was anger. Isabella asked Jason as they were getting out of the car, "Are you armed?" He nodded. "Let's go," she was out of the car as she said it.

They went to the house cautiously. Her eyes were watching everything, taking in everything. She was good at this and it was something that was almost instinctive with her.

Jason was looking around for signs of an ambush too.

McKenzie stuck his head out of the door. "About time you two got back here. I was worried. The news is all over the internet and the TV. We were worried you were caught in it at first, but then they said there was only one casualty, we knew someone was coming back. They won't say, but we had figured the casualty was James.

They went inside. Everyone was there. It was a relief to Isabella. McKenzie went on, "There's other news too. They pulled the body of Alicia Case out of the river."

It was a shock to Isabella and yet, it wasn't. It was typical of Lazarus. The other students were looking at her for her reaction. Jeff spoke, "I know we couldn't but I wish we would have taken her along with us. She wasn't bad, she just made a bad choice. She didn't deserve this."

Isabella had to agree. It was Sandra's turn, "What's with this guy. He just chews people up and spits them out? I don't get it. You read about people like that but you never expect to run into them. They're supposed to be a myth, like the Loch Ness monster or the Abominable Snowman. We knew Alicia, she didn't deserve to die."

"I know," said Isabella, "but where Fane's concerned there's always a body count. People who come in contact with him get killed. Tomorrow, that is coming to an end." She looked meaningfully at Mac and Jason. "I have an idea how we can find out where Fane is. It's getting late enough now that I think we should let all of this sink in and get our heads right. We're going to need them. If we're going to get to him, we'll have to be swift, accurate and cunning. If we slip up even a little, we won't be coming back. Fane won't let us live through this."

Jason had sat down at the dining table across from Bob. Isabella was right, they needed to focus and get past the chaos that death brings to a person. They needed to calm and settle the emotions so they didn't rule decisions into rashness.

McKenzie spoke up, "We're a team here." He turned his gaze meaningfully at Jason. "We work together. As I see it, we have an advantage here. They don't know we're here. If they did, we'd be under siege right now. With the death of Eldon, we're all Fane has to worry about. He's going to be looking for us, but he doesn't know where. Right now, he's scouring the world trying to find any kind of sign. Until one turns up, he's going to continue looking. That's our advantage. We have surprise on our side. That can even out a lot of odds."

Isabella had to agree and it was how she had assessed their position.

Karen said, "Car's out in the drive isn't?"

"Yes," confirmed Isabella.

"I know, I can see it," said Karen.

There a chorus of "What?" from around the room. "Better move it inside before Fane sees it." She answered their puzzled looks, "Google Earth."

Jason got up, "I'll move it. At least I'm supposed to be here. All of you stay inside."

He returned after a couple of minutes and resumed his place across from Bob. He was watching him and could tell he was frustrated. "How are you coming on your program?" he asked.

"I can't figure out where I went wrong. I keep going over this and going over it. I can't find where I made a mistake," answered Bob.

"Maybe that's your problem," said Jason. "You've looked at it too much. You can't see what's there anymore. How do you feel about getting another opinion?"

The lines in Bob's forehead pinched. "I don't see how we can risk that."

"We can with what I have in mind. I know someone. I guarantee discretion. He has your kind of talents for cracking codes and writing software. The only thing I would need is a partial string of the format that is on the crystals. We don't have to give it all to him, just enough to whet his appetite. He does jobs for me once in a while and I know I can trust him. Maybe he can see what you can't, put you back on track."

Bob was hesitant. "What do you think Professor? Can we risk it? Right now I'm stalemated."

"You're sure about him?" said Isabella.

Jason nodded. "Believe me, he'll do this with complete confidentiality. I was going to suggest this anyway. It's why I went and got my Laptop. I can only contact him through it."

Isabella nodded. "Alright. Go ahead."

Jason booted up his computer. He instant messaged Samurai's Ghost. Bob handed Jason one of the thumb-drives. "Just a piece," he said.

He sent the Ghost some of the information. Now they had to wait.

* * *

Cicero Smith put the key into his lock and turned. He opened the door and stepped into his apartment. The plane flight had been horrendous and he was anxious to sleep in his own bed. There was a man sitting there facing the door. Cicero reached inside his coat, but the man spoke up quickly, "I wouldn't do that if I were you." Three uniformed police officers stepped into view with guns drawn. Lt. Murphy continued, "But if you'd like to it wouldn't bother me. Otherwise, get your hands on your head." One of the uniforms reached around and took his gun away from him as he complied.

"What's this about?" demanded Harrison.

"Well," said Murphy who was enjoying drawing this out, "It's about a dead college girl which you killed."

"I didn't have anything to do with killing any college girl," lied Smith.

"Yes you did and I can prove it. I can prove it beyond a shadow of a doubt. You're going to fry Smith. If my suspicion is correct, this is only one in a long line of murders you've committed, but I've got you cold on this one."

"I want my lawyer," growled Cicero.

"Oh by all means, you can have one. You can have several. I don't care if you call the entire Bar of New York. They're not going to be able get you off from this one. You see. I've got the DNA. Somewhere your victim bit you. I suspect we'll find it when we search you downtown. DNA is a great thing, you see, it's indisputable. You're guilty, open and shut. Cuff him men. Read him his rights. Let's take out the trash."

Cicero was led away in cuffs. They'd even brought along a pair of leg shackles to insure he couldn't make a break for it.

* * *

It had been three hours since Jason Hand had sent the string of formatting to Samurai's Ghost when he got back in touch with them. A ping from his computer let him know he had an Instant Message.

The message on his screen read: "I need the rest of this but I have an idea how I can help."

Jason replied, "We need to meet to give you the rest of the information. It would be myself and the person who is writing the programming. Guaranteed discretion."

"You know I don't meet with people."

"The information is too sensitive. Even with a scramble, we can't risk the internet."

There was a pause. Jason waited knowing that this was a hard decision for the Ghost. He had sent him something that he wouldn't be able to ignore. Jason was certain he'd give in.

The I.M. came back. "You're certain there's no other way?"

"To do this you're going to need all of the information and we aren't willing to risk this any other way. We really need your help."

He relented. The next message gave them an address. They had it. Bob spoke to Jason, "A hacker?"

Jason nodded, "One of the best code men on the planet. If anyone can see what you can't, he can. Get your information, we're going for a ride."

Forty minutes later they pulled up in front of an older brick building. It looked like it had once been an office building, but it had since been converted to apartments. The pair went inside and climbed the stairs to the third floor. Jason knocked on a door. It opened a crack. Jason said quietly, "Blade Runner." The door opened.

The two stepped in quickly and the door was quickly closed behind them. The person standing in front of them looked to be about twenty years old, his hair was disheveled, and behind him on a table was a bank of computer equipment. He was tall, slender and had the complexion of a mushroom. "Welcome to the Ghost's haunt," he said. "Did you bring it?"

"Of course," said Jason. He turned to Bob, "Let him see it."

Bob took out his computer and set it up. It was hard finding a place to set it since there were dismantled hard-drives, CPUs, discs and spare monitors, in every conceivable space there was. He got it up and running and showed Samurai's Ghost what they had. He displayed the partial pyramid that he had translated from the crystal's formatting. Samurai's Ghost watched intently as the information formed itself through the software Bob had written. "I'm missing something," Bob began, "I can get some of it, but a lot of it is incomplete. I need you to see what I'm missing."

"Show me your original program," said Samurai's Ghost moving a box of chocolate covered Cheerios out of his way. Bob brought up the file that contained the software code. Samurai's Ghost looked at it analyzing Bob's format structure.

Jason stood looking around the room. There was a shelf full of Dungeons and Dragons books. Next to them was a collection of Lord of the Rings miniatures. "Got anything to drink around here?" Jason asked.

"There's some Dew in the fridge. Take your choice, there's green, blue, and orange," Samurai's Ghost said without even looking up. He was studying Bob's program intensely, reviewing algorithmic equations that were supposed to produce the imagery on the screen. "This is brilliant," he was mumbling under his breath. "You've taken a completely unknown computer language and made it readable. What made you decide where to start?"

Bob pointed to a string of symbols in the unknown language. "These kept repeating. They just looked like this string of code which correlates to the tiling structure of building images. From there I took what I saw would be the next logical step in building that program and essentially tried to think like the original programmer would have done. I came close but obviously, I misinterpreted something."

"How about if we try this." Samurai's Ghost moved one of Bob's code strings into another position. It helped. The image of the pyramid shifted and tightened. "I see," he continued. "Then if we put this here that should help even more." It was done. Again the picture corrected slightly. "What's this?" he asked pointing to a section of the original crystal formatting.

"I'm reasonably sure that it is a text accompaniment to the pyramid image," answered Bob. "Naturally, that presents a special problem when we don't know anything about the texted language."

"True, but text language display would still be a basic code string that would bring it up in its correct sequence, regardless of what it is. Essentially, what I'm saying is that text display code is the same no matter what language the computer has to display. The translator codes which take any known language and turn it into another are completely separate and different from the initial text display."

"I had thought of that," said Bob. "But, it isn't coming up so again I did something wrong."

"I think that together the two of us can create something that will work."

Jason had been aimlessly wandering around the apartment sipping on his Dew. "So how long do you think this might take?" he asked.

"It's hard to tell," said Samurai's Ghost. "It's not like we can suddenly push a button and say 'There you go it's done.' These things take time. We have to write it, try it and it probably won't work so we have to write it and try again. If you want to take off, go. I'll contact you when we're done." He looked at Bob. "Is that cool? You can crash here until we whip this."

"Sure," replied Bob. "It's kind of bugging me a bit that he's back there pacing anyway."

Jason nodded and headed out the door. He'd go back to the house and get some rest. Isabella had some plans for the next day and she wanted him sharp. Bob was more useful and safe where he was at. When he heard from Samurai's Ghost next, hopefully they would finally know what secrets the crystals contained.

≈ 20 ≈

The next day they were up early in the Long Island house. Isabella was explaining her plan to Jason and Mac over coffee.

"Do you think that's going to work?" asked McKenzie.

"I've known Fane for a long time. I understand how he operates, how he thinks. He wouldn't let that much of a loose end hang," she answered.

"We will need weapons right?" There was a hopeful tone in Mac's voice.

"I'm definitely not going to try this unarmed, but if things go how I've laid them out, we shouldn't need to use them."

"So you want me to drive? Are you sure it wouldn't be better if I was backing you up?" said Jason.

"Mac's been covering my back right along and he's done right by me so far, I say if it isn't broke, don't fix it. Are we set to go?"

The two nodded. They went to the car and set out for Manhattan. They'd take the expressway, that was quickest. Once they were on Manhattan, they headed for NYU. It was a bold move, but once the plan was in motion, they'd only have a few hours to carry it out.

Jason pulled the car up near the building that held Isabella's office. She got out and Jason pulled away. Isabella then went inside and walked straight to her office. She thought that she had picked up a shadow, but wasn't sure. That was good. It was what she wanted.

Isabella unlocked her door and went inside. She spent a few minutes rummaging through her drawers and then turned to leave. As she went down the hall, she realized she was right, she'd picked up a tail. She smiled to herself. Everything was going well so far. It was after she went outside and headed for the parking lot that she heard the voice behind her, felt the gun in her lower back. A gruff voice announced, "Well Mr. Fane will be glad to see you."

The man behind Isabella suddenly went rigid and there was another voice, that of McKenzie's. He'd silently come up behind the man while his attention was focused on Isabella. "Mr. Fane isn't going to get a chance to hear about this. There's a wire around your neck that's thin enough that all I have to do is tighten, it'll slice through your throat like butter all the way to your spine. Drop your gun and you might even live to tell about this." The man could feel it cutting into his flesh with his every movement.

He dropped the gun and suddenly Jason was in front of them with the car. Isabella climbed in and pulled her gun. She had it trained on the man as McKenzie pushed him in while he still gripped the wire. Then Mac followed him in.

Jason threw the car in motion and they drove away. "I told you Fane would still be watching my office. This tool fell right into our plan. We couldn't have trained a seal better," said Isabella.

Mac shoved a gun in the prisoner's other side, he'd twisted the wire together on the back of his neck so he could free up his hands. The wire maintained the pressure on the throat, a constant reminder of its presence. All Mac had to do was twist now and the man's life would be over. They left Manhattan and went back to Long Island where they could work in peace.

They pulled the car into Jason's garage and closed the door. The students had been told to stay inside no matter what they heard. Jason and Mac dragged their prisoner out of the car and threw him into a corner. Isabella came over and said, "Now, you're going to tell us everything we need to know. Where Fane is set up and how we can get to him."

"No I'm not," said the man.

Mac smiled, "I was really kind of hoping you'd say that." He planted a boot in the prisoner's stomach.

"You don't really think that is going to get me to spill do you? Fane will do a lot worse to me if I do."

"Oh that wasn't meant to get you to talk. I just need a little exercise. The car was a little cramped."

Isabella came close to his face, "Here's the deal. Either way, your career with Fane is over. You can talk and help us get rid of him or you can keep your mouth shut until you are so beaten that you'll be a cripple for the rest of your life and no use to anyone. Then there's the possibility, a very good one, that I'll have my friend here, who so delights in moments like these, slowly start twisting that wire around your neck. Believe me it will be slow. Think about this. You get away and you go back to Fane and admit to him that you had me and then it all went into the crapper. How do you think he might react to that? I suspect the only bonus you'll receive would be similar to the one he gave to that poor university girl. Can you tread water with your hands tied?"

Isabella could see some of her words had struck home. The look in his eyes reflected it. "Are you going to talk or do I tell him to twist? Your choice." McKenzie moved to grab the wire at the back of the man's neck. "It's a slow way to die," she continued, "but I've got all day. I set it aside just for you."

"What do you want to know?" the prisoner asked.

"I want to know where Fane's offices are now. I also want the layout of the place, in detail. Entrances, exits, how many men there are and where they're positioned. If you give me that, I'm going to do you a big favor. You're going to be kept here until I get back. Just in case you lied. If you did, you'll experience pain like you've never thought possible, because then I'm going to be very annoyed." Both Jason and Mac winced when she said this as if on cue. "If you tell me the truth, then there won't be a Fane to worry about and you can go your way."

The prisoner was thinking it over. Her arguments had made sense. Fane wasn't one to take failure lightly and he had definitely failed.

McKenzie reached over and was taking the wire in his hands to give it a twist. The man jerked away instinctively and then said, "OK, OK, I'll give you what you need. I'll draw it out on a map."

Isabella spoke to Mac, "Keep an eye on him." Mac grinned.

Jason went with her into the house to get something for him to draw on. "Are we really going to let him go?" he asked.

"Eventually. Why not? He's just a lackey, and I must admit, not a very smart one either. He was easy to get the drop on," she answered. "He won't be any use or danger to us when this is over."

* * *

Cicero Smith sat across from Lieutenant Murphy. Smith had come to a decision shortly after they had found the bite marks on his arm. The decision was that he would talk. Maybe he could work out a deal if he gave them a bigger fish, something like a trophy catch. He wanted to give them Lazarus Fane.

Murphy had no idea who this Fane character was, but he was willing to listen just the same. Smith described this shadowy figure that had fingers of crime throughout the world. How his dealings in the black market were infamous. He told how the trail of bodies that littered Fane's past would lead right to him and how Cicero had been forced to be his triggerman.

Murphy was having a hard time swallowing all of this, particularly the "forced to be his triggerman" part. That had been laying it on a little too thick. After listening to Smith babble on for several hours about this "super" criminal, he decided he'd had enough. He had an open and shut case on Smith and he had no intention of letting that go even slightly. He didn't think the prosecutor's office would either. The murder of the New York University student had gotten everyone up in arms as he knew it would. The media had wanted results, NYU had wanted results, and so had the mayor. Fortunately they had gotten results, results that had come rather quickly thanks to the lucky DNA match.

Right now everyone was touting the praises of the NYPD. Everything had been cleared up before anymore students had become victims. This was the kind of thing that made careers.

Things were looking seriously rosy right now. He saw no use in adding the proverbial thorn to it. He logged the name Lazarus Fane into his crime computer at his desk. He scratched his head. Fane was wanted by most police agencies in the world, particularly INTERPOL. There weren't any warrants, but he was wanted for questioning as a suspect in connection with dozens of crimes.

He sat back and sighed. This could complicate things considerably. He had to keep Cicero's story quiet until he could check it out. He went back to see Smith again. It was late and Murphy was tired. He wanted to go home and not have to go on the wild goose chase this nut Smith was trying to send him on. Smith had said he knew where Fane was at. He would go look. But, it was complicated. Smith gave him the address, but it was in Michigan. There were jurisdiction issues.

⚎ 21 ⚎

After a long plane flight, they had changed planes three times and each time the plane become smaller and ricketier. Isabella, Jason, and McKenzie were outside of the building that housed Lazarus Fane and his men. The warehouse was on the St. Mary's River. The Canadian border ran down the center of the river making it convenient for those no longer welcome in the U.S.

It seemed quiet. Isabella wasn't fooled though, there was danger waiting there. She knew this place, she'd grown up here and the stories of the waterfront were the stuff of legends. "His men are probably wearing vests, so shoot for the head or the limbs. It's a tougher shot, but it'll at least cause some damage."

She sent McKenzie away. He knew what to do. It was part of the plan. Jason and Isabella circled the building and went around to the front. There were no cars, the streets seemed abandoned. This part of Sault Ste. Marie was rarely frequented after dark. Isabella searched the waterfront for ways Fane could escape. It was a nasty habit of his, managing to get away, then turn back up when you thought you were rid of him once and for all. She had vowed that this would be the once and for all. That was when she saw it, floating, tied up to the pier.

It was a boat. Fane's avenue of escape. She nudged Jason and nodded towards it. Quietly they went over to it. No one was guarding it. They had gotten lucky. The pair jumped on board and removed the cowl that covered the engine. Jason pulled the wire that connected the starter and then replaced it so that it had to arc to connect. Isabella pulled the gas line. The toxic smell of the spilled fluid filled their noses. They replaced the cowl and climbed back onto the dock.

Isabella whispered to Jason, "If he gets this far, he'll have a big surprise waiting for him."

Jason nodded and grinned in the darkness, "It gives a whole new meaning to Big Bang theory."

* * *

Lazarus Fane was leaving. The arrest of Cicero Smith had been all over the news. There was talk of DNA evidence, guaranteed conviction, all of those things that spelled Smith's betrayal. Fane wasn't naïve enough to think Cicero was going to go down quietly. It was time to make a strategic exit from America.

He'd had the staff erase the computers and then dismissed them. He'd only left himself with a few bodyguards and he would release them as soon as he was on the boat. He could travel more discreetly by himself. He'd just assume one of his several identities he'd manufactured.

He called two of his men over. There were things he'd need that were packed and ready to go on the boat. That was when the door burst open. Isabella Carter and Jason Hand came through with guns drawn, ready to fire at the first movement.

Fane's men moved between him and the oncoming attack. They stood in front of him ready to take the bullets for their boss.

"Come on out from behind them Lazarus you coward," shouted Isabella.

"No coward, just a survivor, which is not what you're going to be," he retorted. His men had pulled guns and they stood facing each other. To their left Jason could hear men coming their way. They would come up on his side. He was between them and Isabella as they approached. He moved one of his guns in their direction. As he did one of the men in front of Fane moved his gun to shoot Jason. That was when the man's collar bone snapped.

McKenzie rolled as he hit the ground after planting both of his feet on the now disabled guard's shoulders, one on each side of his head. He'd come in from the back, disabled two guards and then had found his way to a catwalk that spanned the warehouse.

Isabella used the distraction and leaped, dropping her gun, her arms outstretched at the other guard in front of Fane. Her hands hit the startled man's face and she clawed as fast as her adrenaline pumped body would allow. She slashed over and over, her weight carrying the blind, bloodied, screaming man to the ground.

Jason turned his attention to the other men and began firing. He hit one in the thigh and he went down, but not before he got a shot off that grazed Jason's arm. Jason spun and came up on the last man who was running at him firing. Jason dodged and stayed low under the fire and contacted the man in a tackle that would make a football player proud. He pounded the man's head mercilessly with his fist and his gun until he didn't move any more. The wounded man pulled up his gun to shoot Jason but suddenly his head jerked back and a hole appeared in his forehead. McKenzie had grabbed Isabella's gun and finished the job Jason started.

Lazarus had used the fight to run for the door. Isabella stood up, hair stringing in front of her face, blood dripping from her fingers. She saw Fane hit the door and go through. She bolted in pursuit. McKenzie and Jason weren't far behind.

As Isabella had suspected Lazarus headed straight for the boat. Jason and McKenzie fired off a couple of rounds after him. Isabella stopped just before she reached the dock.

Fane jumped on the boat. There was the slight smell of gas in the air, but most boats had that. He looked at the key and then turned it.

McKenzie had been going to follow Fane onto the boat, but Jason held him back. "Don't, stay here, he won't get away,"

They saw the flame start at the rear of the boat and then a second later it built into a huge ball of orange, yellow and red flame. The explosion broke through the air and the concussion nearly knocked them down. Isabella muttered, "It's a good day to die."

In the distance they could hear the sirens of the police. It was time to go. The trio disappeared into the night. They made their way back to the rental car they'd parked several blocks away. They could breathe easier now. Fane was done, the students were safe, the crystals would cause no more deaths.

* * *

When they got back to the Long Island house, there was an instant message waiting for them. Samurai's Ghost said they had solved the programming problem for the crystals.

The students gasped as the trio walked in. The flight had been long. Isabella had tried to cover up a couple of facial cuts but had done a poor job of it, Jason was trying to hid his wound and McKenzie was limping. Jeff washed and dressed Jason's bullet wound while Isabella showered and McKenzie poured himself some scotch. The impact of the jump had twisted his knee enough that now, pain was setting in.

Karen told them about the instant message. As soon as he was able, Jason left to bring Bob back.

* * *

Bob and Samurai's Ghost had learned to work together well. Samurai's ghost had gained a great respect for Bob and his abilities. "I've never seen a program like this. You've taught me something and for that I'm grateful. It's not often I meet someone that is on a different level of programming than me. You're really out there."

Bob thanked him for the compliment. "I couldn't have finished it without your insights. You saw what I couldn't. It was both of us."

Samurai's Ghost picked up a thumb-drive. "What's your name?" he asked.

"Bob.."

"No not that one," Samurai interrupted. "Your real one."

"Nightstalker."

Samurai's Ghost handed him the thumb-drive. "Welcome to the Brothers of the Blade, Nightstalker. This gets you in contact with me and the rest of us."

* * *

Lt. Murphy looked at the carnage inside the warehouse. He had gotten permission to follow his leads to Michigan. If this could be tied back to New York, Michigan was usually willing to cooperate in an extradition. There were dead and broken men strewn about, butno criminal genius. Something had definitely happened here, but it didn't look like it related to Cicero Smith.

While the Sault police and the paramedics were sorting out the wounded from the corpses, he had looked for any kind of clues on the computer equipment that was there. It was a dead end. They'd been wiped clean. There was nothing to back up Smith's story and just as importantly no clues to the creators of the mayhem that they were cleaning up.

Hopefully later the two men that were still alive would be willing to shed some light on the mystery. At least at his point, no matter what they said, it wasn't going to help Cicero Smith. Murphy found the thought strangely comforting.

≈ 22 ≈

Excitement ran through the Long Island house as Jason and Bob returned. He came in and set up his laptop on the table and assumed his regular place. He began, "What we found was amazing. These crystals solve some of the greatest mysteries of the ages."

As the program took over, the crystal that had held the image of the pyramid came up. Everyone crowded in tighter for a view. Isabella was closest. At the bottom of the crystal was text. Part of it was in a language they had never seen before, but it was similar to the writing they had found that created the format codes. Below them was text in Egyptian and then Greek and Mayan. Isabella shook with excitement, she'd never dreamed they would have this kind of luck. The crystals came with their own Rosetta stone!

She had no trouble translating the Greek and Egyptian. The Mayan was a little more difficult. They both were saying the same things so it also held the unknown language did too. This particular crystal was explaining in detail the process for constructing a pyramidical structure. There were details on stone placement, angles of the cuts and how interior chambers and halls were placed. The crystal solved one of the great riddles of the ages, how the pyramids were built.

Another crystal held the instructions to create a colossi in statue. Starting from the feet and working to the head it led the reader step by step through the process. Another great mystery, the Colossus of Rhodes explained.

They went on, the Sphinx, the legendary statue of Zeus, the Lighthouse of Alexandria, Mausoleum of Mausolus, the lost Temple of Artemis, and several more. Their images were projected on the screen, most had never been seen before by modern eyes, only speculated on as to their appearance and existence, now a mystery no longer. The crystals were truly a find of the ages. No longer would they have to theorize and hypothesize on their creation. It was now before them, the genius of the ancient world was laid bare, exposed for mankind, magnificent and beautiful in vision, the intricacies of the great wonders of the ancient world were revealed!

And nothing more. There was no history of lost continents and races wiped from the earth. There were no clues to the origins of the strange language which graced the crystals as the primary language.

McKenzie spoke breaking the enchantment of discovery that had gripped everyone else. "You mean we went through all of this for a set of blueprints?"

Isabella turned and scowled at him. "These aren't just any set of blueprints. These are the greatest accomplishments of ancient man. These crystals prove they were shown how to do them. Some culture long ago came to them and instructed them in the art of creating these great megalithic structures. I'm guessing that the ones you found in Bimini were either Mayan structures or even something pertaining to the giant heads of the Olmec or both. Think of what we could have learned from those."

McKenzie wandered away and poured himself another scotch. "Blueprints," he muttered.

* * *

Cicero Smith sat across from Murphy. He had been explaining to Smith how he had come across the scene of the fight at the warehouse, but there was no sign of any Lazarus Fane. "Your story didn't pan out Smith. There won't be any deals for you." Murphy was enjoying this. He really wanted Smith to fry. There was something about him that didn't elicit sympathy.

"It was her," he spouted through his gritted teeth. "It was that bitch. She did this. She's the one you should be looking for."

"Now what are you ranting about?"

"It's that Dr. Isabella Carter, the Archaeology professor from NYU or U of M or whatever university she's working for. She's the one that attacked the warehouse. You can bet that everything that went down there was because of her."

"Let's see if I got this straight. You expect me to believe that mess back at the warehouse was caused by a woman archaeology teacher from NYU?" Murphy couldn't stop himself, he laughed. He laughed hard.

"Smith, I'm almost gonna miss you around here. You can be real entertaining. But here's the deal," Murphy leaned over into Cicero's face and with a dead serious tone he said, "If you think that telling me crap like this is going to get you into psych, you've got another thing coming. I'm going to make sure you burn. Got it?"

Murphy turned and walked away still chuckling to himself. "Archaeology teacher, hahaha."

* * *

Isabella was staring out of the tall window of the Long Island house. Going back home to Michigan had got her thinking. She still had a home there, it was currently unoccupied.

McKenzie was lying back on the couch giving his knee some comfort. He had a drink of scotch. "I guess I'm going to have to start looking for another diving job. By the time I get anywhere, my knee should be just fine. A couple more scotches and it won't matter anyway."

Jason was making himself a drink as well, a martini, very dirty. "I don't know what I'm going to do. I can live off from what I have saved for a while, but I'll get restless. With the boss dead, I'm sure the company will fold and I'm through." He took a sip of his drink. "Perfect."

Isabella held onto her vodka and cranberry, seeming not to hear, her mind was on something distant. They had taken the students back to NYU now that the danger was gone. It was just the three of them now.

Jason walked over and plopped down next to McKenzie. "Well Mac, you can stay here as long as you like. I've kind of gotten used to that overcooked cuisine you call food."

"Hey, if you wanted gourmet you should have hired a chef. But thanks for the offer. I appreciate it."

The two of them looked at Isabella who was still staring out the window. "Earth, calling Dr. Carter. Do you read me?" called Mac through cupped hands.

She chuckled. "Yea, I read you. I was just thinking about something."

"Well, that's quite obvious, what?" asked Jason.

"Home, the Soo."

"Huh?" both of them responded.

"The U.P., where we just were. I was invited to Isle Royale in Lake Superior by the National Park Service to investigate an ancient culture there that mined copper. I was thinking if we used LIDAR on the entire island. It might show us some secrets. It seemed to me somebody ought to go look, maybe three somebodys. You in?"

* * *

Eldon James Fane sat sipping an old fashioned. The cool beverage felt good in the Nassau warmth. Yes, everything had gone as he had planned. Ever since he had sent the crystal he got from McKenzie to Lazarus his plan had gone like clockwork. Meeting McKenzie had been chance, but sometimes fate simply worked that way. It had been easy to make it look like the crystal had come from one of Lazarus' lackeys. There had never been any doubt that his brother would contact Dr. Carter to analyze the crystals. It was a match made in hell that could only erupt in a war, one that he had put all of his money on Carter winning. Their hatred for each other wouldn't let it end any other way, other than in the death of his brother.

Eldon had done his part, keeping Lazarus off balance, giving Carter the chance to make the moves she needed to get herself in the position to bring down Lazarus. The shooting in Egypt had been to push Carter into thinking she was in an increasingly desperate situation. He'd made sure there would be an address left behind so she had a trail to follow.

When he had brought Jason into play, it was the boost she had needed. He'd almost convinced himself that he was trying to save the world, instead of his real intent. He knew Jason was riddled with ethics and would side with Carter even though it would cause a conflict over his loyalty to Eldon. Smashing the crystals had insured she'd never give them up therefore forcing her to take Lazarus out.

He had been grateful for the timing of the assassination attempt by Cicero though he had actually expected it sooner. The New York Messenger Service had never had his address, so he knew Cicero's deception for what it was. He'd put on one of those light Kevlar vests under his suit two days earlier waiting for someone to make the attempt. The blood pack had been easy to arrange. Cicero had been in such a hurry to get in and get out, he'd never looked very closely and Eldon had counted on that. It was a stroke of luck that a maintenance man was in his office at the same time when the grenade went off. He provided the body the police wheeled out. They never give out names of victims right away and since he was in pieces, identification was lengthy. Eldon had enough time that he leaped behind the reception desk in the hall. He'd left the building, mingling with the other evacuees.

Yes his plan had been brilliant, it had been perfect, now Lazarus was dead, he'd seen it on a miniature closed circuit video he'd had installed in his brother's building just before he'd blown up his office, forcing him to the warehouse. Eldon had been able to watch everything. Now Lazarus' empire was his. He was the sole heir and lawyers had been working to gain control of it since the boat blew up. They had found close to two billion in assets. It was a nice chunk of change. One that he was willing to wait for as the lawyers did their work. With no Lazarus, it was only a matter of time.

The old fashioned was cool and sweet as he sipped it. One of the hotel porters walked up. "Call for you sir," and set a phone down next to him. Eldon was puzzled. No one knew he was here. Hell, no one knew he was alive. He picked it up, there was a voice on the other end. "Hello brother…"

About the Author

Mikel B. Classen has been writing and photographing northern Michigan in newspapers and magazines for forty years, creating feature articles about the life and culture of Michigan's north country. A journalist, historian, photographer and author with a fascination of the world around him, he enjoys researching and writing about lost stories from the past. He is founder of the U.P. Reader and is a member of the Board of Directors for the Upper Peninsula Publishers and Authors Association. In 2020, Mikel won the Historical Society of Michigan's, George Follo Award for Upper Peninsula History.

Classen makes his home in the oldest city in Michigan, historic Sault Ste. Marie. He is also a collector of out-of-print history books, and historical photographs and prints of Upper Michigan. At Northern Michigan University, he studied English, history, journalism and photography.

His books, Au Sable Point Lighthouse, Beacon on Lake Superior's Shipwreck Coast; was published in 2014 and Teddy Roosevelt and the Marquette Libel Trial; was published in 2015 by the History Press. He's written a book of fiction called Lake Superior Tales, which won the 2020 U.P. Notable Book Award. Points North is a non- fiction travel book published in 2019 which has received the Historical Society of Michigan's, "Outstanding Michigan History Publication," along with a 2021 U.P. Notable Book Award. Since then, he has released, True Tales, the Forgotten History of Michigan's Upper Peninsula; and Faces, Places, & Days Gone By, a Pictorial History of Michigan's Upper Peninsula. Mikel is co-author of the Yooper Ale Trails along with Jon C. Stott all published by Modern History Press.

To learn more about Mikel B. Classen and to see more of his work, go to his website at www.mikelbclassen.com.

Join us for epic adventures in the U.P. on land and lakes!

Pirates, thieves, shipwrecks, sexy women, lost gold, and adventures on the Lake Superior frontier await you! In this book, you'll sail on a ship full of gold, outwit deadly shapeshifters, battle frontier outlaws and even meet the mysterious agent that Andrew Jackson called "the meanest man" he ever knew. Packed with action, adventure, humor, and suspense, this book has something for every reader. Journey to the wilds of the Lake Superior shoreline  through ten stories that span the 19th century through present day including "The Wreck of the Marie Jenny," "The Bigg Man," "Wolf Killer," and "Bullets Shine Silver in the Moonlight."

Mikel B. Classen is a longtime resident of Sault Sainte Marie in Michigan's Upper Peninsula. His intimacy of the region, the history and its culture gives this book a feel of authenticity that is rarely seen. As a writer, journalist, columnist, photographer, and editor with more than 30 years experience, his breadth of knowledge is unparalleled.

"It's clear that Mikel B. Classen knows and loves the Lake Superior area of Michigan and brings it to life in a delightful way. If you want frequent laughs, unusual characters who jump off the page, and the fruit of a highly creative mind, you've got to read this little book."
-- Bob Rich, author, *Looking Through Water*

From Modern History Press
Learn more at www.MikelBClassen.com

This book has been a labor of love that spans many years. The love is for Michigan's Upper Peninsula (U.P.), its places and people. I've spent many years exploring the wilderness of the U.P., and one thing has become apparent. No matter what part you find yourself in, fascinating sights are around every corner. There are parks, wilderness areas, and museums. There are ghost towns and places named after legends. There are trails to be walked and waterways to be paddled. In the U.P., life is meant to be lived to the fullest.

In this book, I've listed 40 destinations from every corner of the U.P. that have places of interest. Some reflect rich history, while others highlight natural wonders that abound across the peninsula. So many sights exist, in fact, that after a lifetime of exploration, I'm still discovering new and fascinating places that I've never seen or heard of. So, join in the adventures. The Upper Peninsula is an open book--the one that's in your hand.

"Without a doubt, Mikel B. Classen's book, *Points North*, needs to be in every library, gift shop and quality bookstore throughout the country--particularly those located in Michigan's Lower Peninsula. Not only does Classen bring alive the 'Hidden Campgrounds, Natural Wonders and Waterways of the Upper Peninsula' through his polished words, his masterful use of color photography make this book absolutely beautiful. *Points North* will long stand as a tremendous tribute to one of the most remarkable parts of our country."

--Michael Carrier, author *Murder on Sugar Island*

Learn more at www.PointsNorthBooks.com
From Modern History Press

Enjoy a Visual Trip to See How People Lived and Worked in the U.P. in Centuries Past!

Classen's pictorial history is the next best thing to a time machine, as we get a front-row seat in the worlds of shipping and shipwrecks, iron and copper mining, timber cutting, hunting and fishing and the everyday lives of ordinary folks of Michigan's Upper Peninsula across more than 100 years. *Faces, Places, and Days Gone By* peers into our past through the lenses of those that lived and explored it. See what they saw as time passed and how the U.P. evolved into the wonderous place we know today.

From the author's unique collection, witness newly restored images from long lost stereoviews, cabinet cards, postcards and lithograph engravings. From the Soo to Ironwood, from Copper Harbor to Mackinaw Island--you'll never see the U.P. in quite the same way!

"With his book *Faces, Places, and Days Gone By*, historian Mikel B. Classen has achieved a work of monumental importance. Drawing from his collection of archival photographs, Classen takes readers on a journey in time that gives rare insight into a vanished world." -- Sue Harrison, international bestselling author of *The Midwife's Touch*

"Mikel Classen's new book, *Faces, Places, and Days Gone By*, belongs in every library in Michigan. And when I say every library, I'm talking about every public, high school and college storehouse of knowledge." -- Michael Carrier, MA, New York University, author of the award-winning *Jack Handler* U.P. mystery series

Learn more at www.MikelBClassen.com
From Modern History Press

www.ingramcontent.com/pod-product-compliance
Lightning Source LLC
Chambersburg PA
CBHW050357030726
47503CB00006B/1904